PRAISE FOR *LETTERS IN TIME*

"*Letters in Time* is like a wonderful meal with a delicious balance of engaging characters (both sweet and bitter), a fascinating peek at history, a captivating community, and a slow-burning romance for dessert."

—Donna K. Weaver,
USA TODAY Bestselling Author

"Once more, one of my favorite authors, Susan Reiss, has crafted a story that keeps the reader guessing. *Letters in Time* reflects the author's creativity and ability to write 'outside the box.' She writes about enduring love. She delves into old mysteries that affect the present. Can't wait to read the next."

—Amazon Review

"Susan Reiss captures the magic, mystery and charm of that quintessential Eastern Shore town – St. Michaels. Secrets lay hidden for generations among the stunningly beautiful estates along the Miles River. Can't wait for her next book."

—Kathy Harig, Proprietor,
Mystery Loves Company Bookstore

"Delightfully different! This book was different than the mysteries I tend to usually read. It very cleverly blends a current day story with a historical paranormal twist that was quite touching."

—Amazon Review

PRAISE FOR DIARIES IN TIME

"This book gets into your heart and captures your soul. I couldn't wait to read the next page, yet I didn't want the book to end. A stunning and outstanding novel that will move you as few others have. Very Highly Recommended." - Amazon Reader Review

"A delightful saga that is so believable!" - Goodreads Review

"A wonderful tale of life filled with struggles, tragedy, love, memories and everything in between. The author does a great job at conveying it in both books I've read. Emma, both of them, are strong women. Both struggling to lead their lives their own way in their own lives. There is no sex, smut, or anything to ruin a delightful tale. - Amazon Reader Review

"The characters, plot, and storyline were again well written and fully developed. *Diaries in Time* adds a Who Done It aspect as well. I recommend this novel to all who read historical fiction.
  - Amazon Reader Review

"Each story grabs you by the heartstrings and doesn't let go - it is so intriguing, it kept me turning the pages to the end." - Amazon Reader Review

"A nice mix of modern and historical mysteries." - Goodreads Review

"Readers will encounter twin sisters, legends of buried treasure, mourning jewelry, christening gowns, old diaries, silk fabrics, bridal gowns, red-bottom shoes, loves lost, bullets dodged, wedding ceremonies, and spouses gained. This was another engaging novel by a lovely author I've come to admire!" - Goodreads Review

"I really enjoyed this and the book before it as well. Weaving the history along with the present gave added depth to the story." - Goodreads Review

"The details are intricately interwoven to provide the reader with a gripping story full of surprising twists and turns as the modern Emma searches for the truth behind the conflicting tales she finds. Both excellent character development and beautifully presented descriptive prose describing the area keep the reader captivated." - Amazon Reader Review

PRAISE FOR ST. MICHAELS SILVER MYSTERIES

MESSAGES IN TIME

SUSAN REISS

Ink & Imagination Press

INK & IMAGINATION PRESS
an imprint of Blue Lily Publishers

Copyright © 2022 by Susan Reiss
All rights reserved.

ISBN: 978-1-949876-64-2

Cover Design by Rachael Ritchey, RR Publishing

Website: www.SusanReiss.com
Instagram: AuthorSusanReiss
Twitter: @SusanReiss
Bookbub: Susan Reiss
Goodreads.com: Susan Reiss
Facebook: Susan Reiss

For all my Beta readers,
Advance readers…
and readers just like you!

CHAPTER ONE

"Every moment of light and dark is a miracle."
—Walt Whitman

It was early when I pulled open my bedroom curtains to find a spectacular Eastern Shore morning, filled with sun and birdsong. When I'd lived in Philadelphia, I'd peek out from my high-rise condo to see the brick and glass building across the street; masses of cars, cabs, and busses jockeying for position far below; staffers squeezing into the morning coffee lines so they could get to their cubicles first, hoping to impress the boss.

I'd only been an observer, not part of that corporate world. My job had required me to be ready in my kindergarten classroom to greet my gaggle of students when they tumbled through the door. My clothes, hair, and attitude had to survive a day of little hands smeared with jelly, paint, or blood and tears from a playground mishap. They'd loved touching my long blonde braid, found it comforting like a favorite bear. It was a way of life I cherished, but reality had other plans for me.

Now, living on the Maryland Eastern Shore, a gentle breeze of fresh air caressed my face with the warmth of spring. A whiff of pine floated through the window from the lofty evergreens. Brilliant sunshine sparkled on the ripples of the creek flowing by the Cottage. This was Chesapeake Bay country with nature on the doorstep, inspiring views around most corners, and a slower pace to enjoy it all.

Was this the place I belonged, the place I would rebuild my life? I shrugged off the question and gave the world a big smile. *Yes, I'm in the right place, for now.*

There might have been other places I could have gone to heal from the injuries suffered in a near-fatal car accident but being here, at Uncle Jack's Cottage, was the perfect place for me. The only downside was my favorite uncle had passed away quietly while I was in the hospital. His greatest gift had been leaving me this wonderful place filled with memories and love.

Eager to enjoy the day, I dressed quickly in jeans, a shirt, and grabbed a sweater in case the sun ducked behind some clouds. I wanted to skip down the steps to the kitchen but caught myself before I did something stupid. My injured leg was much better. The nightmare of surgeries, crutches, a walker, and a cane were all in the past. But there was no reason to risk another injury.

I took the steps slowly which allowed me time to remember my kindergarten classroom filled with active, loving children. That time was coming again, I promised myself. But right now, it was time to scoot into the kitchen to make coffee. Armed with a steaming mug and a chocolate chip cookie, I headed out to the stone patio overlooking the creek and the majestic Lone Oak on the far shore, ...and froze in my tracks.

A man in a brown suit sat slumped over the patio table.

I should have rushed back inside, grabbed my phone, and called the police. There was no reason for anyone to be on my patio. Not here, miles away from anywhere. It was not TJ, the farmer who lived up the drive at Waterwood House. He had helped me with so many things since I'd moved to the Cottage: driving me to appointments and the library, helping me understand the ways of the Shore, and, above all, being a good friend. He would never be caught in a brown suit. That giddy thought born from nerves led me to do something foolish. I yelled at the stranger.

"Are you hurt? No? Then go away!" I tried to sound menacing, but it was hard to do before I'd had my first cup of coffee. "HEY! You need to get out of here."

No response.

A mourning dove cooed *Who, who*. Good question. Who was this man?

"HEY!" I yelled loud enough to wake the dead.

Still nothing.

I marched over to the chair. "I'm talking to you." I poked him hard in the shoulder. "Wake up!"

In slow motion, he sagged out of the chair and crumpled to the stone patio. I reached out in time to keep his head from smacking the hard surface. Was he asleep? Was he dead? I was a terrible person because I didn't really care. I just wanted him gone.

Wait! Did he groan? This was no time to be selfish. I rushed into the kitchen and dialed 911.

CHAPTER TWO

EMTs can administer CPR, glucose, and oxygen. Paramedics can insert IV lines, administer drugs, and apply pacemakers because of their higher level of education.

The dispatcher alerted emergency services then asked if I could render assistance. I almost told him I knew what to do with a young child, but this was an adult and a stranger. He assured me help would arrive soon. In minutes, I could hear the sirens in the distance. The land was flat, and sound travelled well over water. The lights and sirens had alerted TJ and he was banging on my door in moments.

I called out, "I'm on the patio." The sirens were getting closer.

He rounded the corner in a rush. "Emma! Are you okay?" He'd left his house so fast, he'd forgotten his baseball cap that normally covered his light brown hair. His rugged face usually had dimples, but he wasn't smiling now. There were only creases of worry on his forehead and around his hazel eyes.

After I assured him I was fine, he looked at the body crumpled on the stones. "Who is he?"

"I don't know." The wailing sirens cut off. "Help is here. Maybe they can find out."

TJ followed me around to the driveway to meet the ambulance. After leading the responders to the patio, we were directed to go inside the Cottage and wait.

The Cottage had experienced several unhappy situations since I'd arrived, so I was glad the emergency services people were in charge. Nervous, needing something to do, TJ and I brewed fresh coffee. It was good to have TJ with me. His presence was comforting.

"Emma," he said gently. "You should have called me right away."

"I didn't want to bother you. You're busy. This doesn't have anything to do with me." It was easier to think about my friend than the stranger on the patio and what was happening outside.

"You know I'm here for you," he said.

I nodded. TJ had a way about him, calm and confident. It wasn't arrogance. Far from it. He didn't need to impress anyone. He knew who he was, a college-educated farmer, proud of what he was doing. He was happy working the land, facing the challenges nature threw at him, learning the complexities of technical innovations, and doing the flat-out hard work.

I envied his understanding of himself and his patience with the world around him. Maybe someday I would figure out where I fit in, then I could walk a path with assurance, rather than feeling so uncertain about what I should do and where I belonged.

I leaned my forehead against his chin. "I'm sorry if I scared you." Quickly, I recounted how I'd found the man in the brown suit on my patio and called 911. I left out the part where I'd confronted the stranger. It was a stupid move and would have upset TJ even more. I didn't want to face any suggestions I move back to Philadelphia or find a roommate.

Fortunately, a uniformed police officer interrupted us when he knocked on the open kitchen door. "Ms. Chase?"

"Come in, officer." I told him. "What can I do to help?"

He moved carefully through the century-old doorway almost too narrow for all the equipment hanging from his waist and flak jacket. Part of me appreciated his care of the painted woodwork, but a knot of fear was tightening my insides.

I had to know. "Is he dead?"

The young, lanky officer shook his head in quick jerks. "Truth be told, you might have saved his life. The paramedics think he is dehydrated and suspect something else is going on."

TJ and I exchanged a quick look of relief. I sank into a chair as the knot inside me slowly untied itself. I needed to savor the knowledge the man would be all right and I was safe.

"How do you explain a sick stranger collapsed on Emma's patio," TJ snapped.

I was taken aback at TJ's harshness. Then I figured the stress of the last several months had affected him, too. I stayed quiet to hear the officer's reasoning.

"I don't have an explanation at this point, but I will," he announced. "My name is Officer Wilson, and you are...?"

TJ stood and held out his hand. "I'm Thomas Jefferson Wood, but people call me TJ." He added he was my friend, neighbor, and owner of the surrounding acreage.

"Well, sir, it is unnerving to find a body on the patio early in the morning, especially way out here. They're going to transport the man up the road to the hospital in Easton as soon as they have him stabilized. The old guy was lucky he collapsed here where you could find him." Officer Wilson pulled a wallet out of his pocket." I found his identification."

He showed us the man's driver's license. "His name is Phillip Kincaid from Philadelphia." The officer turned to me. "Do you know the man?"

I took a closer look. "No, I've never seen him before." I turned to TJ. "Have you?"

"No, I have no idea who he is," he said, which was saying something since he knew just about everybody in the area. "I don't understand. The Cottage is off the beaten track. How did the man get here?"

"Can't answer that yet," Wilson said. "We'll canvass the area. His car is probably broken down somewhere, on a shoulder or in the weeds." He turned back to me. "Aren't you from Philadelphia? Sure you don't know him?"

"No," I said to the officer. "I lived in Philadelphia for years, but I don't know him." The officer continued to gaze at me, silently. "It's a big city!" The statement sounded defensive, even to my ears. His suspicious attitude was upsetting me.

Officer Wilson continued to watch me for a long moment then he took something out of the wallet. "It says here he is a university professor." He turned the ID card around to show us. "Are you sure it doesn't ring a bell?"

I was so distracted by his arrogant and suspicious tone, I forgot to mention my Uncle Jack had been a professor at the same university. I guess I never truly appreciated the way Homicide Detective Craig Mason spoke to TJ and me. He was an old friend of TJ's and I'd gotten to know him as he investigated some sad situations recently. Thankfully, nobody died today, and he wasn't needed here.

It occurred to me if I was more cooperative, this officer would leave sooner. "No, I don't recognize his picture or his name. I am familiar with the university." The officer stood straighter, eager to hear more. "It's where my uncle used to teach."

Wilson jumped on the new lead. "Good, may I speak with

him?" His eyes flicked between the doorways to the hall and dining room, expecting to see Uncle Jack walk in.

"I'm afraid it's not possible."

The officer's eyes took on a glint of suspicion as they focused on me.

"Sadly," I continued. "He passed away."

The officer's shoulders sagged. "Well, I'll have to wait for the doctors to allow me to interview the professor. Thank you for your time, folks. We'll be out of here shortly."

Without any hesitation, he made his way carefully outside again.

TJ and I exchanged silent looks. We made fresh cups of coffee and sipped the hot brew while standing at the door, watching the paramedics work until they bundled the man into the ambulance and roared away followed by the police car.

CHAPTER THREE

"Some people are so much sunshine
to the square inch." –*Walt Whitman*

As the emergency services people left the Cottage and Waterwood property, TJ and I both sighed with relief. We were glad to close the book on this event. I yearned for the calm and stillness of the land surrounding the Cottage. Only, after the uproar this morning, I wanted... no, needed to find some answers."I don't understand." I said, my voice just above a whisper. "I don't understand how the man ended up on my patio. And I'd like to know why. The only connection I can see is through Uncle Jack, but he hasn't taught there for several years. How could such an old connection bring a stranger to my patio. I—"

A growl of car tires on my gravel driveway drew our attention to the window. My brain echoed with the thought of *Now what?* My early spring morning filled with sun, beauty, and delight had become a center of chaos.

A bright red Porsche Cayenne sat at the bottom of my front steps. "Maureen," I breathed. "I forgot she was coming over this morning."

TJ was already on his way to the front door when a mad flurry of knocking sounded through the Cottage. He opened the door and wasn't given a moment to say hello. Maureen blew past him madly calling out my name.

"Emma? EMMA! Where are you?" She was frantic.

Before I could respond, she circled back to TJ. "Is she alright? I saw the ambulance. Is she hurt? The drug dealer didn't come back and—"

TJ grabbed her flailing arms. "Maureen, calm down. Emma is fine."

It took her a moment for the words to register, but when they did, she leaned into him with a hushed *Thank goodness*. Then she straightened up and cocked her eyebrow. "If she's alright and you're here, who was in the ambulance?"

"We're not exactly sure." TJ brightened when he saw me walk out of the kitchen. "But I'll let Emma explain."

"Emma! Where is she?" Maureen said with a rush of breath.

TJ smiled. "Take a look behind you."

She turned with a jerk and rushed at me. Over her shoulder, I could see TJ barely able to control a laugh as the large woman engulfed me in a breath-defying hug.

"I'll leave you ladies to it," and he was out the door.

"Maureen, Maureen." I pleaded. "Please. I'm okay."

Finally, she released me, and I drew in a deep breath.

"You're sure you're alright," she said, as she inspected me from head to toe, looking for some kind of injury or disfigurement.

"I'm fine." I said as I pulled her into the kitchen. "Coffee?" It seemed to be my solution for everything today.

"After such a fright, I could use a drink." She laughed out loud and gave me another hug, gentler this time.

The surprise must have shown on my face. "It's barely ten o'clock in the morning." Did this sophisticated woman who'd retired from a fabulously successful advertising career in New York have a problem?

"Oh Emma, sometimes you are so easy to tease. Do you really think I would risk a charge of Driving Under the Influence and have them take my lovely chariot away from me? If so, you don't know me very well. If we were in The City where I could walk or hail a cab, I would have a single malt scotch right now! But we're not."

"Then coffee it is. And speaking of New York, what is with the new haircut? I don't believe any of your old friends would recognize you!" It was true, she did look different. Those long, luxuriant silver locks were gone. Now, she had a short, pixie style. Fun. Sassy. Definitely not an *old-lady-style*.

"Do you like it?" For a brief moment, this confident woman was a little uncertain.

"Like it?" I scrunched up my face, inspecting her new look. "Like it? I LOVE IT!" And we filled my kitchen with peals of laughter. It was such a relief to share something other than illness and upset.

It was time to sit down and catch our breath. Thankfully, my little coffee machine would brew separate cups of coffee for us. I couldn't handle the dark roast Maureen preferred. My nerves would be jangling for days. With mugs in hand, she suggested we sit on the patio. I hesitated. It wasn't a crime scene. It was only a place where a man, a stranger, had picked to take a nap. Instead, we decided to sit inside where we had spent hours over the past several months talking about writing. We had met at a meeting of local writers. TJ had wangled an invitation for me from a friend in the group. I still cringed when I thought about that night. What a disaster it had been and how I had vowed never to go again. But Maureen saw something in me and conspired with TJ to get me to attend the next month's meeting. I was glad they did.

Over the winter months, we spent many pleasant hours in front of the fire, discussing elements of the writing craft.

Maureen introduced me to the writing prompt, a question or statement designed to challenge someone to write a well-crafted paragraph. It was hard in the beginning. I was ready to give up. Maureen was not.

I grew to trust her. I continued to write based on prompts and I had to admit, it was becoming fun. I was no longer afraid of Maureen's critiques. They were never *criticisms*. While the creative director for a major New York ad agency, she had learned how to nurture and develop creative talent.

But, on this day, she wanted to talk about the collapsed body I'd found on the patio. After I filled her in, she sat back in her chair, looked around at the pine trees, the Lone Oak, the open sky, and frowned.

"I don't know, Emma. You're way out here in the middle of nowhere. Was the man looking for you? How did he find you here, all alone."

"I'm not alone. TJ is right up the drive," I countered.

"Yes, he is," she agreed, "when he's not working his own fields or helping other farmers miles away."

I felt my resolve wavering. "Nobody knows I'm here."

Maureen lowered her chin and shot me a disbelieving glare from under her well-shaped eyebrows. No words were needed.

"Okay, there was that one time when..." I began, though she was still glaring at me. "Okay, a couple of times, but they were unusual situations. I think—"

"I think..." Maureen's words overrode my own. "You need one of these." She reached into her designer purse and pulled out a pistol. "It is small, compact, and can get the job done, whether it's frightening someone or worse. And it is rather pretty." She held it so we could both admire it as sunlight glinted off the pearl handle.

She must have read my mind. She pulled the pistol away from me. "I'd let you hold it, but it would be a mistake. You are not trained to handle a gun, right?" I shook my head and she put the gun back in her bag. "That's how accidents happen."

"You mean it's ..." My voice shook a little. Everything was suddenly very real.

"Yes, it's loaded. We do not want any mishaps. I think you should take some classes, then we can talk."

I revealed to her I had once asked TJ to loan me a gun for protection. "He flatly refused. Said I could get someone killed."

She nodded. "He was right. Not everybody can pull the trigger, even when there is a threat. You have to know what you're doing before you touch a gun." She sipped her coffee. "Don't get me wrong. I'm not in favor of automatic weapons and such. They are fine for the military, but I don't need a weapon like that. Most civilians don't, but we won't discuss it now."

"I find it amazing you can carry a pistol in your purse." It seemed a little surreal to me, a reaction I didn't expect. "I thought..."

"The U.S. Supreme Court struck down the need for concealed carry permits so I'm legal." She leaned toward me and extended her index finger to make her point. "The most important thing is training before you touch a gun. It looks so easy on TV or in movies. It's not. Think about it and the training, too." She flopped back in her chair with a smile. "But I'm a stickler for getting the right training."

"Message received," I said, thankful to have such a caring friend.

Maureen finished her coffee and set her empty mug down. "Good."

My cell phone rang. "Excuse me, with everything that happened this morning, I'd better answer it."

Maureen nodded and took our mugs into the kitchen. It wasn't long before I joined her there. "That was the police officer."

13

"Everything okay?" she asked.

"Yes, but peculiar. The man I found on my patio this morning has been admitted to the hospital for observation. Evidently, he is diabetic and had an episode, or whatever you call it."

Maureen nodded. "No wonder he passed out, but it leaves open the big question—why did he come to the Cottage?"

"We may know soon. The man is awake and stable, but he refuses to talk to the police." I tapped my lips with my finger, thinking. "He says he will only talk to me, explain to me why he was here." I frowned.

"What's wrong?"

"It doesn't feel right. I don't know this person," I said with hesitation.

"Then you must go to the hospital," Maureen said with delight. "We need answers." She paused when I didn't join in her enthusiasm. "What's wrong, Emma? You do want to know why he was here, don't you?"

"Yes, I do," I answered slowly. "I just wish the world would leave me alone for at least a little while.

"Sadly, that's not the way it works, my friend," she responded. "At least you have been offered an opportunity to find out why. You're lucky." She headed for the kitchen door. "I'll get my purse and get out of your way." She paused when I didn't react. "Are you afraid?"

I tilted my head to the side. "Maybe a little."

"Do you want me to go with you?"

I took a step toward her. "I don't want to impose on your time. I—"

"Nonsense!" she declared in her big voice she saved for special moments. "I love a good mystery. Besides, you need a ride, correct?"

I gasped and closed my eyes. I had done it again. I was so used to being independent, I'd forgotten once again how I still refused to drive, a lingering side effect of the accident. "You're right, I need a ride."

"Then I shall be your chauffeur. Get your things. You need to take advantage of this opportunity before the man changes his mind."

"But what will you do while I—"

"Errands. There is always something I need. You'll text me when you're finished. I shall swoop in and pick you up." She had a stern look on her face as she put her hands on her hips. "But you must pay the price for this service. You must tell me *everything*. We can talk over lunch, my treat. Come on. Oh, this will be fun," she murmured as she headed to the door.

"I need a minute to change."

She looked me up and down, at my sweat pants and sweatshirt. "Better take two!"

Soon, we were climbing into her Porsche and heading up Route 33 to Easton. I was impressed how calm I felt as Maureen happily shifted through the gears with confidence. Before she bought the car, she went to the Porsche Driving School in Atlanta where she worked with a personal driving coach. On the day a semi crunched my car, I'd had no time to consider, debate, or look for an alternative. There were only moments to act and survive. Since then, I had slid behind the wheel of a vehicle only once. To save my own life. Riding in a car or even a truck still terrified me, now knowing what could happen when things went wrong on the road. Maybe I should go to a driving school to rebuild my confidence.

I put the idea on hold as Maureen turned into the hospital parking lot and I caught a glimpse of Officer Wilson pacing by the door.

CHAPTER FOUR

"We read and write poetry because we are members of the
human race. And the human race is filled
with passion." – *Walt Whitman*

The officer led me to the elevator and, as we rode up, I
asked if there was anything I should know?

"The professor is waiting for you. His name is Dr. Phillip
Kincaid. It would probably be good for you to use his name. It
might help keep him in the present moment."

That made sense. "Anything else?"

Wilson shrugged. "Keep him talking. I need to know why
he trespassed on your property. I tried to find out, but he will
only talk to you."

I followed him down the hall until we reached the door to
the professor's room. "One more thing," the officer said
softly. "He agreed to allow me to stay in the room while he
talked to you. If you feel uncomfortable at any time, just give
me a sign and we'll leave. No harm done. Don't worry if you

can't get him to talk. I'll get the information I need another way."

What was he going to do? Torture the poor man? I was tempted to tell him to wait in the hall, but it was time to get answers, not cause more problems. The tension in my shoulders and neck was easing. I was ready to meet my intruder.

I stepped into the room, which was typical of a hospital, painted a pale pink. It was probably meant to give the patient a healthier glow by reflection. It didn't do much for the man lying in the white sheets and blanket in the regulation hospital bed. A machine was monitoring his vital signs. Two lines carried the contents of IV bags into his arm. He was about average size except for his round belly and a fat face with heavy jowls that hung below his chin. A light film of sweat shone on his forehead and his bald pate was fringed with thin gray hair. Even on a normal day, the professor must not look healthy. Today, he looked terrible. I knew diabetes could devastate a person. It was vital for the patient to take care of himself. In this case, it seemed the disease was winning.

As I was about to suggest to Officer Wilson, we come back another time, the patient stirred. It took him several moments to focus on me standing at the foot of his bed. It felt too intimate to stand near the head of his bed, next to him. Too close. After all, he was a stranger.

He spoke. "Are you…" His voice was raspy as if he hadn't spoken for a long time. He swallowed and began again, stronger now. "Are you Emma, Jack's Emma?"

I nodded.

"Wait," he said, getting a little agitated. "My glasses. I need my glasses."

The officer rushed to the side table and handed them to him. "Here you are, sir."

He fumbled then set them on his nose. "That's better.

Now, I can see you." He squinted. "I think I can see a little bit of Jack in you, around the eyes."

"You knew my Uncle Jack?" I asked, forgetting my hesitancy and my commitment to listen.

"Knew him. Admired him. Respected him..." He let out a deep sigh. "And envied him."

"Envied him? Why?" I asked.

The officer gave me a puzzled look. This line of questioning wasn't what he wanted. I ignored him. This man had known my uncle, the man who was the stability, the rock of my life. He knew him as a professional, an academician, a part of Uncle Jack I'd barely experienced. I wanted to know.

The professor continued. "I envied his passion. The passion he had for his subject: the American Civil War." The man dropped his eyes to the blanket stretched over his body, as his face reddened. Not from the disease, from embarrassment.

As I took a step closer, Wilson whispered, "Ask him why he was at your place." The words sounded like a hiss. I wasn't going to rush this poor man and I wasn't going to be bullied by this officer. Sweetly, I responded. "You can wait outside if you want." He got my message and took a step back. I turned my attention to Dr. Kincaid, Uncle Jack's colleague.

It was a serious admission—envy of a colleague—for someone to make at the university level. I wanted to acknowledge it with whatever grace I could muster. "You are right. He was passionate about the Civil War and was always hungry to know more, not about the munitions and troop movements. He wanted to know more about the nuances of the war and people's reactions to it."

The professor chuckled. "You knew Jack." Then added quietly, "He was a good man."

I found myself staring at the professor's face without wrinkles and heavy fat and realized with a start, I knew him. "Wait! A long time ago, a man came to the Cottage during my summer visit. He spent a long time talking with Uncle Jack, monopolizing his time and attention." I burst out, surprised. "That was you!"

A big smile lit up the man's face. "You remember? I must have made an impression on you."

I rubbed my forehead and avoided his eyes.

The professor must have realized I didn't remember anything else about him and said, "I'm not surprised. You didn't like me very much. Probably wanted me gone, out of the Cottage and Uncle Jack's life. You moped around and finally went outside to play." He glanced out the window of his room, remembering. "I'm afraid we talked most of the afternoon and Jack invited me to stay for dinner when I didn't have trouble driving at night." He chuckled. "We went outside and called and called for you. I was getting worried and felt guilty. But Jack knew you so well. He knew where you were and told me to follow him. We went down a path, I think, and came to this secluded cove surrounded by crape myrtles in full pink bloom. It was a heavenly spot. You were sitting in an old rowboat partially pulled up on land, totally engrossed in a book."

I couldn't stay mad at this man. Uncle Jack had brought him to my special place, special to this day. "He always knew where to find me. If I wasn't there, he knew to worry." Tears threatened to spill from my eyes. "It was a great loss to me when he passed away," I said, hoping my voice wouldn't crack. It was still hard for me to talk about the man who had been so important in my life, a man who was now absent.

It was time to learn about the professor's present-day actions, but I wanted to use a gentle approach. "You do know Uncle Jack passed away." A grief-filled jolt hit me as I released how much time had passed. "It's been almost two years."

"Yes, I was sad when I heard the news." Tears glistened in his eyes. "It is hard to lose a friend."

"Why did you come to the Cottage when you knew he wouldn't be there?"

Wilson, who was sitting in the corner, straightened up as if someone had pulled on his puppet strings. This was the answer he needed, the one to determine if a crime beyond trespassing had been committed. The patient's gaze fell on the blanket again and he let out a deep sigh. I waited politely for an explanation, but all I got was silence.

"Professor," I said, with some steel in my voice. I wanted the truth and was on the alert for a lie. "Why were you at the Cottage?"

"I'm so embarrassed."

"Don't be," I said, hoping to coax out more information. "Please tell me."

"I made the trip down here to the Shore to see if Jack had left an important piece of his research at the Cottage. I went through his office at the university, even helped pack it up. You got the boxes, right?"

"Yes, they are stored in the garage." I remembered the building tucked in the woods where Uncle Jack had stored an antique plantation desk. It had introduced me to Daniel, a man from another age, and changed my life. Could another mystery be sitting under the same roof?

"Good, but there was nothing there except class notes, his musings about teaching and all. What I wanted to find wasn't in his office." With this revelation, the man sagged into himself with only the pillows holding him in place. "I'm sorry I passed out on your patio. This disease... life is getting harder every day. They had to take some of my toes... it makes it hard to walk. Guess I just got too tired."

"It's okay. Would you tell me what you hoped to find at the Cottage?"

With another sigh, he said, "I guess there's no reason to keep it a secret any longer. As you know, Jack's passion was the Civil War, especially how it played out on the Maryland

Eastern Shore. It was a place of conflict unique to this region."

The officer piped up. "Maryland stayed in the Union. Even I know that."

I suspected the idea of a mystery and the Civil War had fired up his imagination and he forgot he was supposed to be investigating a possible charge of trespassing. But the outburst must have appealed to the professor's nature. He pushed himself up on the pillows and brushed back his hair with his hands to better address his audience, though it was only the two of us.

"You're right, Maryland stayed in the Union, but just barely. There were many Southern sympathizers throughout the state, but they were concentrated on the land east of the Bay. There, plantations flourished, and landowners benefitted from the free labor of slaves. But keeping Maryland in the Union was absolutely necessary to the country's survival."

The officer put his elbows on his knees and leaned forward. "I don't understand,"

A trace of a smile brushed the professor's lips. He was in his element now. "Visualize the nation's capital, Washington City as it was known then. It was built on land originally donated by Virginia and Maryland. Virginia seceded from the Union. If Maryland followed Virginia's lead, the Confederacy would completely surround the capital. In no time, the city would have been crushed, and the Union would have lost its leadership. No, Lincoln had to use whatever means necessary to stop the state from seceding."

"I've learned how tensions here led to some ugly situations. There was widespread support for the South, but pockets of Union feeling and abolitionist attitudes like St. Michaels, made life difficult for some people." I cleared my throat. "I appreciate the history lesson, but it doesn't explain why you were at the Cottage."

"Jack was always curious about this situation of split

loyalties pitting friend against friend, even brother against brother. It was a small microcosm of what was happening throughout the country and easier to study."

"Is that why he bought the property originally?" I'd always wondered why he chose a second home here and not on the New Jersey Shore which was closer to Philadelphia and a more logical place to be.

"Yes, it is. Plus, it is a beautiful place, close to nature, the water, and my dear friend certainly loved his steamed crabs," he said with another chuckle.

The memory of our crab feasts made me smile, too. When I was old enough to speak my mind, I insisted I pick my own steamed crab. It wasn't as easy as it sounded and a lot of work for little fingers. But Uncle Jack was always patient. It took forever for me to dig out those succulent morsels. I remember one time Uncle Jack put a half peanut butter and jelly sandwich by my place so I could keep up my strength as I tackled the crab. As I got older and with his guidance, it wasn't long before I was whipping through our catch. Beginning when I was a little girl, I would spend some and then almost all of my summer vacations with Uncle Jack at the Cottage. It was a gathering place for other family members, too. Looking back on it, the word *idyllic* comes to mind.

But it didn't explain what brought this man to my patio.

CHAPTER FIVE

"Poetry, beauty, romance, love,
these are what we stay alive for." --*Walt Whitman*

The man glanced at my face and must have seen the determination there. "Alright, it's time for me to confess. But one more piece of historical information first. The Union had an established network of spies to provide intelligence to the United States. Remember, it was young, but still a nation of the world. When the Southern states seceded, the Union forces were better equipped to follow troop movements, supply trains, and so on. It was vital information the Union could use to cripple and ultimately defeat the enemy. The South had a strong military tradition and some well-trained leaders, but it didn't have an established intelligence apparatus. It needed spies with credible information and secure routes to relay messages south. It fascinated Jack." The professor took in a deep breath. "Near the time of his retirement, Jack told me he had found a lead to what might be a Confederate spy, unknown to historians. He believed the spy had a connection to the Maryland Eastern Shore, right in his backyard. He was going to spend his free time following the trail. The last time we spoke, he said he'd found something."

"What was it?" the officer blurted out.

"I have no idea, son. He was never specific. I don't think he expected the stroke to take his life before he made his discovery."

The officer sat back in his chair, disappointed. Then raised his head and wanted to know why this *find* was so important.

"When you're on the police force, you're judged by your discipline, skills, and how many cases you close, right?" The officer nodded. "In academia, especially on the university level, we are judged by what we discover, the connection of facts we make, the books and articles we write. It's called *Publish or Perish*. Being a good teacher isn't enough. We have to do research, meaningful research, too."

I cocked my head to the side. "I thought it was true in the STEM disciplines: Science, Technology, Engineering, and Math."

"You're right and now there is STEAM, which adds the Arts to the list. But the concept of research and writing for publication applies to all professors across the board. If Jack had found his unknown spy, he could have authored articles, a book, and done speaking engagements about this piece of history. He could have talked about the person, who was probably a man since it was a long time before Mata Hari appeared on the scene. He could have disclosed the method of encryption used and ways to pass the information."

The officer interrupted. "Is it really important now? After all, the war was fought more than a hundred years ago."

Quickly, the professor corrected him. "More than 150 years ago. And yes, it's important. We are fascinated with secrets. Think of the CIA, the Central Intelligence Agency, and the NSA, the National Security Administration."

"Yes, but—" the officer interjected.

"Yes, I know. They are geared for the secrets and techniques of today but located right outside the gates to the NSA is a small building called the National Cryptologic Museum. It is just on the other side of the Bay, close to Fort Meade. They have the enigma machines the Nazis used to almost win World War II. They have a great exhibit about the Battle of Midway, and so much more. They have the background on the Union spies. They would have loved to know about Jack's unknown spy to add to their historical collection."

I took a few steps around the bed, considering what he'd said. Every once in a while, I'd come across an article about almost ruthless competition in academia. I'd never thought of Uncle Jack—mild-mannered, inquisitive—in that context, until now. "So, you're saying you want to find this special something you think Uncle Jack discovered and to bring it to light to enhance his reputation. Do I have it right?"

When the professor couldn't meet my eyes, alarm bells started ringing in my mind. "Am I correct?" I asked again.

He gave a half nod. "You are correct… in part."

"Which part would that be?" I demanded, ready to protect Uncle Jack.

The professor looked up at the ceiling as if asking for divine guidance. There being none, he continued. "The first part. Yes, I want to find out what he discovered."

"And?" I encouraged him to finish, before I pounced.

"And I want to develop it, put it in perspective so the information can take its rightful place in the historical annals…"

Disappointed in my uncle's colleague. "…to your credit." I completed his statement for him.

He peeked up from under his bushy gray eyebrows and exhaled. Exhausted and exposed. "Yes." Then he added, "And Jack."

I'd heard enough. I turned to Wilson. "I think we're done here. Do you have everything you need?" He nodded. "Then I'll say—"

"Wait!" The professor cried. "I must apologize. I did not mean to upset you. I asked around and checked real estate listings to find out if the Cottage had changed hands. There was no record." He shrugged. "I assumed the property was still in probate or something and was vacant. I apologize again."

I looked at him for several moments, taking a final assessment of the man who thought of my uncle as a friend. Somehow, I doubted Uncle Jack truly valued him as a colleague, let alone a valued friend. Then I said, "I hope you did your academic research with more care than you did about Uncle Jack's affairs and the Cottage. I hope you feel better soon." I turned to leave, but his next words made me pause.

"And therein lies the problem. My students were more important to me than the research. I have always put my time and effort into the students, reading and commenting on their papers and their thought processes. But that doesn't count for much among some academicians. They want research and publications. I did what I could and barely made tenure. I invested in my students. But now, my situation has changed. I find I'm thinking now about my legacy and the outlook is rather glum. I fear I'm running out of time. I have diabetes. It is ruining my body bit by bit. Though I'm still young enough to make a mark, I don't think the disease will allow me the time to accomplish what I hope…" His mouth tightened. "I needed a shortcut."

He reached his hand out to me. "Now you know why I came to your Cottage. I didn't expect to feel so weak. I couldn't make it back to my car. It must still be there, parked down the road?"

I glanced back at the officer who was making a note. "We'll check the area."

The professor sighed. "I remembered the patio where we had spent many hours debating historical points, trying to make sense out of the actions of men. They were magical times I will always treasure."

"And you felt comfortable coming to what you thought was an unoccupied house? Were you going to break in? With no idea what you wanted to find?"

He nodded. "I was trying to save myself. I was selfish. I apologize."

I stood there with my hand on the door handle trying to process his confession. It sounded sincere... and desperate. It was obvious the man was ill. If I hadn't found him, the paramedic said he might have died right there on my patio. Obviously, he wasn't very good at taking care of himself, but his comments about his students touched me.

"Miss Emma, are you ready to go?" Wilson asked.

I turned and marched back to the bed. I stood right by the pillows so he could see me clearly. "I'm sorry, but I must say, you are a pathetic human being."

He lowered his head. "I know."

"And it's obvious you're not taking care of yourself."

He repeated, "I know."

"But if you were a friend and colleague of Uncle Jack's as you claim..."

He raised his face, his eyes filled with hurt and a bit of pleading.

I closed my eyes, hoping I was making the right decision. "If you are well enough tomorrow, come to the Cottage and we will look for this elusive discovery together. I make no promises. I doubt we'll find anything, but we can look."

His face brightened like the sun. He was about to say something but stopped when I raised my hand.

"I do this only on one condition."

"Anything."

"I'm not sure how this works, but Uncle Jack gets primary credit on the publications. If not—"

"I agree, wholeheartedly." He flashed a wide smile. It must have encouraged his students when they did good work. "And officer, if I tell you where I left my car, maybe you could arrange..."

Officer Wilson scowled, but he responded. "We'll get it to you."

The professor beamed with satisfaction. "That's wonderful. They're releasing me this afternoon. I'll take care of myself, get a good night's rest, and be at the Cottage tomorrow morning at 10 o'clock, if it works for you. I will have a chance to see someone before I meet you and return to school." He shifted his head and stared off at nothing. "Yes, it is time to go back to campus even though I have failed."

I put out a hand and touched his arm. "You have not failed, at least, not yet. We may still find Uncle Jack's find. Come tomorrow morning at ten."

"Thank you, Emma."

"And, professor, come by the front door this time."

"Yes, ma'am," he agreed happily.

It was late evening when I finally reached TJ and told him what I'd learned at the hospital. I told him the professor was coming back to the Cottage the next morning *by the front door.* He didn't laugh, which was odd.

"I can't be there, Emma." He sounded so apologetic, like he was letting me down.

"TJ, it's fine. I can do this. It might be fun working with the professor to find Uncle Jack's great discovery."

TJ agreed, but he didn't convince me. Then he said he had in incoming call.

I had the feeling something was wrong.

CHAPTER SIX

"The future is no more uncertain than the present."
                                                    —Walt Whitman

The next morning, I opened my bedroom curtains to see what kind of day nature had concocted for us mere humans. Another wonderful creation for a spring morning: bright sunshine and more. I had to admit I didn't have the patience to take in all the nuances of the day's weather. I was distracted by the idea of the professor's visit. He was due to arrive at ten. I glanced at the clock and saw I still had time for breakfast and some preparation. How was I going to help him locate some new discovery he believed Uncle Jack had made before his death? It was supposed to reveal a secret history of the Civil War?

The idea would have sounded fanciful if I hadn't done it before.

Oh, not in the scholarly way the professor needed. But the information and story I had uncovered with TJ's help had certainly satisfied our curiosity and added to his family's history. The methods and research subjects we'd used would never be accepted by the world in general. So, we kept our association with Emma and Daniel of the nineteenth century to ourselves.

Downstairs, I stepped into the room Uncle Jack had used as his den. There were a few bookcases there. I hadn't had time or reason to go through the books. Maybe there was something of use there? Uncle Jack didn't have a secret cache or safe where he might have stashed some documents or artifact, at least none I knew about. Maybe the professor would have some ideas, I thought as I headed to the kitchen for my first cup of coffee.

I stood at the kitchen window taking the glorious first sip of the day and realized I might be prowling through my uncle's things most of the day. I didn't want to miss this early spring morning weather. I laughed to myself, remembering the fright I'd had just twenty-four hours earlier when I'd found the professor hunched over my patio table. Imagine my surprise seeing the man in the same place again.

Instead of fear, this time I sighed, feeling a little exasperated and manipulated. "Really, professor. You can't keep popping up on my patio like this. Our arrangement was you would come at ten o'clock and at the *front door,* not my patio."

When there was no reply, I took a step forward. "Professor?" I thought he must have passed out again from the exertion of walking around the Cottage to get to the patio. Diabetes was a cruel disease. It seemed to be taking a serious toll on his body. He might have been right when he said he was running out of time.

Still no response. I put my mug down on the table. "Professor!"

I put my hand on his shoulder and gave him a little shake. "PROFESSOR! Really, you—"

His body sagged forward. His forehead fell against the

metal patio table. I winced. I didn't mean to hurt him. A trickle of blood pooled at the wound and dripped through the openings of the table meant to drain away rainwater. Not blood.

Yesterday, I thought the man sitting on my patio was dead. I was wrong.

Today, he must have fallen asleep again.

But something was different. He hadn't reacted when he hit his head. His skin was pasty. Something was seriously wrong.

I reached out to touch his neck, afraid of what I would or would not find. But I pulled my hand back, unable to touch him. *Don't be such a wimp!* I ordered myself. I closed my eyes and reached out again. My fingertips brushed his cold skin, searching for the throb of a heartbeat. I pulled my hand away. I couldn't find a pulse because there wasn't one.

He needed CPR. I leaned him back in the chair so I could...

Horror filled me. I snatched my hand away.

Nothing could help him. This wasn't a natural death.

Blood, glistening in the morning light, had soaked his shirt red.

Someone had stuck a knife in his chest.

It was murder.

My legs felt rubbery. I wanted to close my eyes, block out this sight of horror. I took a step away and staggered. I grabbed on to the table. I couldn't fall.

What if—

My eyes searched the shrubs. What if killer was still here? I turned and lifted my head to scan the woods, thick and close to the Cottage. The sun's rays penetrated the branches and pine needles here and there, creating pools of light a killer could avoid. The breeze made the shadows dance...or was it a person moving around. Or waiting... for me.

I had to get to safety. I had to get inside the Cottage. I had to walk. I took two quick breaths. Better. Holding on to the table and then a chair, I moved to the open space between me and the kitchen door. The world started spinning again. If I let go of the chair, I could fall. Hit my head on the stones. I couldn't stay here. Not safe!

Breathe. Again. Yes, that helped. My pulse, banging in my ears, slowed a little. I pulled my body up to stand tall and let go of the chair. The world reeled. I grabbed it again.

I didn't want to move, not ever again. But a voice inside wouldn't shut up.

GET INSIDE! CALL 911!

CHAPTER SEVEN

"If any thing is sacred, the human body is sacred."
—*Walt Whitman*

I focused on the kitchen door and safety within. Inside, the phone would bring help.

Breathe! Now!

I pushed forward across the stone patio to the stone steps, staggered inside, and slammed the door shut. Leaning against it, gasping for air, I felt safe. But outside...

I set the deadbolt TJ had installed and forced my wobbly legs toward a window. Outside, there was only a breeze off the water swaying the pine boughs and the sun lighting up the deadly scene on the patio.

My hand shook as I grabbed the landline phone. My fingers trembling so badly, I kept hitting the wrong buttons. 9-1-1. It should have been easy. Finally, I hit the right buttons and call connected. I almost passed out in relief.

The dispatcher answered and when I began my report, he

stopped me. "Wait, you called yesterday morning. I was the one who got your call. Is this a prank?"

"No, it's not!" Frustration and shock boiled over. I pulled the phone away from my ear yelled, "THE MAN IS DEAD! Send help."

I forced myself to take a deep breath. Hysterics weren't going to help. "I'm sorry. There is a dead man on my patio. Yes, it's the same man who was here yesterday, but—" There was no way I could explain. Why didn't he understand? "SEND HELP!" I yelled and threw the phone across the room. It hit a cabinet and clattered to the floor.

My whole body was shaking... in fear, in anger. It didn't matter. I needed TJ.

But the phone lay on the floor. Should I just run up to Waterwood House? Stop! Breathe! Holding on to the counter so I didn't pitch over into a heap, I picked up the phone, touched the on button, and heard a beautiful sound. A dial tone. At least it didn't break. I let my body drop into one of the chairs and braced my elbows on the table to help stop my hands from shaking so much then hit the speed-dial number to contact TJ.

When he answered, these words gushed out of me, "TJ, come now. Please."

My legs were like jelly as I made my way down the hall. I ran my hand along the wall for support while TJ jiggled the doorknob and hammered with the knocker. "I'm coming!"

When I finally got the door open, he burst in, grabbed my shoulders, and demanded to know what was wrong. Even Ghost, his white Labrador retriever, was upset as he stood at my feet panting, his eyes wide and round.

"Are you alright?" TJ needed to know.

I took his hand and led him to the kitchen door, opened it, and pointed outside. I squeezed my eyes shut. There was no need for me to look again. The scene was imprinted on the inside of my eyelids. When I heard TJ gasp, I knew he had seen the professor's body.

"Is he... what is in his chest? Is he...?" He lurched forward, but I pulled his arm so he wouldn't go outside.

My voice croaked when I finally spoke. "He's dead. I called the police."

Disbelief drove his voice high up the scale. "There's a knife in his chest."

I nodded.

TJ took a step back into the kitchen, put his hands on my shoulders, and moved his face close to mine. He spoke softly and slowly. "Emma, did you..."

I raised my eyes to his, fear, hurt, anger, all swirling around inside. TJ thought I'd killed him.

"Emma, did he attack you? Did you...?"

I could only shake my head. My knees were weak. It was hard to breathe.

He tightened his grip on my shoulders and steered me back to the kitchen chair. I felt better after taking some deep breaths and sipping some water. Better now, especially with TJ by my side. I was ready to deal with the police who were calling out from my open front door.

"We're back here, in the kitchen," TJ shouted back.

Heavy, booted footsteps came closer and Officer Wilson stood tall in the doorway, his face creased with concern. He had come to the Cottage the day before. He had sat in the hospital room, listening to the professor's explanation and confession. He would understand. The painful knots in my neck and shoulders began to unwind.

"Miss Chase?"

I looked up at him and felt burning hot tears make tracks down my face and drip into my lap. "Officer, I—"

But the officer was looking straight at TJ, suspicious. His eyes narrowed. His body tensed.

"Don't..." I held up my hands to ward off a disaster. "He's mine."

"Officer, I'm TJ Wood. We met..."

As TJ explained, the officer relaxed a little and moved his hand down to his side.

The ambulance siren cut through the quiet as it approached and shut off abruptly. It had arrived.

"Ms. Chase, you reported a— "

I interrupted him. I didn't want to hear the word we were all thinking: murder. "I tried to find a pulse."

"You touched him." It was more of a declaration than a question.

I nodded.

"Anything else? I need to know," he insisted.

I shook my head, only because I couldn't think. Couldn't remember.

The paramedics stormed into the room, poised to act, hunting for the victim.

"He's out there on the patio," TJ said, pointing out the kitchen door.

The officer directed the team then turned to TJ. "Get her out of the way, in a different room, but don't leave," he ordered.

Holding on to me with his arm around my shoulders, TJ led me through the whirl of people and equipment to the living room. I plopped down on the sofa, wanting desperately to lie down and sleep so I could wake up from this nightmare. Wake up to the quiet of my Shore spring morning.

TJ stayed with me but paced around the room. His constant movement kept me awake and connected to what was happening outside. Seeing the scowl on his face, I wondered if he was thinking what I was thinking: What had happened outside my window while I was asleep?

I did not want to think about it so, I focused on him as he turned to sneak a glance out the window, trying to figure out what was happening outside with the police and emergency services. But he was distracted, constantly consulting his watch. He stopped pacing by a window for a long moment, then took off his cap, smoothed down his hair, and reset it on his head. It was a nervous habit I'd seen him do many times.

Finally, he sat down next to me and asked, "Are you okay?" His eyes were kind, and his voice was soft, but his left foot was tapping the rug.

"I'm rattled, but I'm fine. Really," I said, hoping I sounded convincing. When I saw his foot go still, I braced myself.

"Emma, I can stay if you need me." He looked at his watch and scowled. "But I have an appointment in twenty minutes."

I jumped up. "Then you need to go." I tried to sound brave but didn't feel it inside. I patted his arm. "You should go."

"The farm where I'm meeting my client is less than thirty minutes away. If you call, I can—"

"That's ridiculous. You have things to do. I'm fine here. I'm safe. The emergency guys are taking care of the professor."

Officer Wilson stepped into the room.

I went on. "And the police are here to keep me safe. I know this officer. So, you see, I'm fine." I gave TJ a little push. "Go to your appointment."

TJ flicked a quick look at Wilson. It didn't register with me that the officer wouldn't meet TJ's eyes. If it had, I would never have let TJ leave me alone.

CHAPTER EIGHT

"These are the days that must happen to you."
— *Walt Whitman*

After TJ drove away and we were alone, Officer Wilson came and stood close to me, too close.

"You can sit down," he said.

As I sat down on the sofa, a little chill crept over my skin. The man remained standing, towering over me, so when I looked up, my neck felt a little awkward.

"I need you to tell me exactly what happened this morning, specifically what you did?" It was more of a proclamation than a question.

"Me? But I—"

"When you came downstairs this morning, it must have been frightening, upsetting ..." He cocked his head and shrugged one shoulder. "maybe even maddening to see the professor on your patio again. It was an intrusion."

I sat quietly, listening to the officer give this dramatic oration, thoroughly confused. Several other times, I had listened to another member of law enforcement, Homicide Detective Craig Mason talk about other crime scenes and scenarios, but never with such extraordinary description of emotions. What was Wilson doing?

The cop continued. "Obviously, you value your privacy." He swung his hand around the room, but I soon realized he meant the place where the Cottage was situated. "You're living out here, miles away from town. Out in the middle of nowhere." He dropped his hand at his side. "I can understand how you must have felt. Imposed upon. Maybe even violated. After all, this is your space."

I couldn't let this go on any longer. "Officer, I—"

But he didn't lose a beat. "You're a human being and human beings have a natural reaction when they feel cornered."

"Officer, I can—"

"I can understand why you probably reacted the way you did. It was totally natural." He said, nodding lightly.

Frustrated, I stood up. "Just a minute. I—"

"Sit down," Wilson ordered.

Worry grew inside me. Where was he going with all this? Was he making a case...

His voice got louder. His eyes flashed. He was ready for his big finish. "You were tired of this man's intrusion into your home. Yesterday, when you talked to him at the hospital, you were kind and patient. I was there. I saw how you acted. And I remember how you directed him to come to your front door this morning. Not the patio. Once, you could understand, when he was sick, but again?" The officer rested his hands on his heavy equipment-ladened belt. "You had to teach him a lesson."

This young man, this rookie, was full of himself. He was making a case to an invisible jury that I was the murderer. I jumped up. "Now, wait just a minute," I shot back at him.

"Please sit down," he said almost sweetly. A friendly

39

smile slowly spread over his face. "It's okay. You can tell me. When you saw him again today, you went into the kitchen, pulled a knife from the drawer or the knife block on the counter, went outside and plunged it into his chest. Right?"

"WHAT?" I screamed. "NO WAY! HE—"

"You were right!" He yelled at me. "You told the dispatcher the man was dead. Because you killed him," Wilson declared as judge and jury

I felt like he had slapped me. In the silence, I struggled to find words. "I-I-I..." I tried again. This time, my voice was going right up the scale, driven by terror. "I didn't kill him."

Fear tightened my chest so my lungs could barely move air. It hurt, but I had to speak, defend myself. "I didn't kill anybody." I barely squeezed the words out.

"You did it!" He fired back.

"No!" I was desperate to make this man understand. My hands were moving around, trying to find something to hold on to. I took a deep breath and forced them in my lap. "Office, I didn't hurt anyone. You met me yesterday. You saw us at the hospital. We were good." A wave of emotion threatened to swamp me. "I didn't do this."

Officer Wilson straightened his shoulders. "As you say, Miss Emma. But under the circumstances, I need to read you your rights and—" He reached for the handcuffs on his belt.

"WHAT?" Shocked, I jumped to my feet. "NO!"

"Now, ma'am..." Wilson reached for my arm.

I jerked away like it was deadly reptile. "Get away from me."

He stepped closer and grabbed my arm. "Now, ma'am, I need you to cooperate."

"I don't need to do anything," I screamed. "You need to get away from me. I know someone who—"

"Sure. Yes, ma'am." He groaned as if it was another boring day at the office.

I felt the hard steel of a handcuff encircle my wrist then

the click sounding like the end of the world. My world. As he turned me around, I couldn't breathe. I couldn't make my lungs work. They were frozen in my chest.

"Stop," I gasped. "Please stop. I can't breathe."

"You're alright. I just need your other wrist..." he reached for it and clamped the other handcuff on me.

My arms were pulled behind me. It hurt. My shoulders strained against this unnatural position. Somehow, my lungs started working again. The oxygen to my brain made me realize how embarrassed I felt. How degrading this was. With a couple of clicks, I'd lost my freedom.

My brain registered the cop's voice behind me, right by my right ear. Feeling the little puffs of air from his words sent terror through me. "...to remain silent. Anything you say can and will be used—"

"STOP!" A man's voice boomed from the hall.

The whole Cottage seemed to shake with the force of his voice. Blood drained from the officer's face, so it matched the poor professor's dead pallor.

I turned to see my savior and was grateful to find see a face I knew. Detective Craig Mason. Thank goodness. He knew me. When I'd been sucked into the middle of other situations, he'd been there to protect me and nail the killer. Killer. The word made me shiver as if an arctic wind had blown in. Someone had murdered the professor right outside my window. Right there on my patio.

Officer Wilson stopped his movements, the detective continued in a calmer, quieter tone. "Yes, you can stop now! It won't be necessary,"

Wilson found his voice. "But detective, the facts—"

"The facts," the detective repeated, "as we know them so far, could lead in all kinds of directions. Unless you have compelling evidence like Miss Emma's fingerprints on the knife, I think we can rely on her not to leave town as we pursue this investigation. Do you agree, son?"

I thought the young officer was going to sink into the floor from embarrassment. He couldn't form the words of agreement so, he just nodded.

"Then I think you can remove the cuffs from Ms. Chase's wrist."

Wilson fumbled the keys out of his pocket and released me.

"Now, I think you should oversee the crime scene activities outside."

"Yes, sir," and Wilson almost ran from the room.

As the detective sank into an arm chair by the fireplace, he held out his hand toward the sofa. "You can sit down if you like."

I followed his instruction and noticed the hearth needed cleaning, ashes from the last fire of the winter season lay there in a heap. Like the body outside. A life now ended.

"...Emma?" Craig waited. "Emma!"

Craig's voice penetrated my thoughts. "Yes? Yes. I'm sorry. What did you say?"

A small smile touched his lips. "Nothing. Just trying to get your attention." He leaned back in the chair. "Lousy way to start the day."

I didn't know if he was asking me or making a statement. I simply nodded. I was glad we could sit silently for a few minutes so I could settle myself.

"Okay." Craig sounded exhausted. He had no real enthusiasm for the case in front of him, but, with a sigh, he started doing his job. "Emma, I'm sorry, but I need you to go back to the beginning and tell me everything you know."

I began the story with as much detail as I could.

"I will want to talk to you again later, but before I look at the crime scene, I have one question for you."

I raised my head, listening to Craig's every word, but when I heard his question, my head sagged. "Do you have any idea what Jack discovered?"

I slowly shook my head.

"No idea at all?" He had trouble accepting the fact I had no idea. "It must be something impressive and important to warrant the taking of a human life."

I shook my head slowly. "I have no earthly idea."

"Alright then. While I'm gathering the facts I need, I'd like you to look around the Cottage, maybe through anything he might have left," Craig said. "What the professor was trying to find might be sitting out in plain sight."

I sighed. "It would really help if I knew what I was looking for. It could be anything, some kind of paper, a letter maybe."

"It could be a Civil War artifact," Craig suggested, "like a gun or bayonet."

"True but isn't it a stretch to connect it to spies, the kind of connection he believed existed," I said with little hope.

The detective frowned as his eyes fell on a small bronze bust sitting on the mantel. "It could be a bust." He frowned as he picked it and read the plaque on it. "Though I don't think it would have any connection with Mozart." Disappointed, he replaced the bust in frustration.

"Uncle Jack loved Mozart." I stared out the window and a thought began to form. "You may be on to something."

"A bust of the spy here at the Cottage?" Craig didn't succeed in hiding a chuckle. "Maybe there are secret papers stuffed up inside."

My brain was clearing. "Let's think this through. Uncle Jack bought the Cottage years ago. Why?" I asked.

"Because he wanted an escape?" Craig suggested with a shrug. "It's a fairly easy drive, easier than using all those interstates along with everybody else trying to get to the beaches."

"New Jersey was the more logical choice." I got up and started to pace. "He came here, to the Maryland Eastern Shore. See if you can follow my logic: Uncle Jack was a university history professor and a historian with a fine reputation. He specialized in the Civil War. Not in its armaments and ammunition. Not in battle strategy unless you followed his writings about *what might have happened if ...* if one side knew about the troop complement of the other. But he wasn't really interested in military aspects. I realized I'd never seen a gun or dagger or bayonet among his things. The idea of winning a peace by fighting a war that pitched brother against brother, friend against friend as the Civil War had, sickened him. He preferred to talk about the effects the war had on the population, people who weren't involved in the fighting. People who were trying to live their lives."

I walked over to a framed map of the state. "I remember he liked to point out the Eastern Shore started as part of the Catholic colony that later became the state of Maryland, people here had vastly different sympathies by the 1800s than their counterparts in the central and western parts of the state. People here wanted to maintain their way of life based on their plantations and slave labor. Sure, there were pockets of resistance, but for the most part, the majority of the landholders wanted to join the South in cessation."

"I didn't know." Craig went back and stood at the mantel again. "I must have missed history class."

I pointed to the map. "The Mason-Dixon Line theoretically cut the area into North and South. As you can see, Talbot County is well South of it. This is where those disagreements and differences played out among normal people during a war." I put my hands on my hips in frustration. "These things have been here since I was a little girl. They aren't *the find* I'm looking for."

Craig took a deep breath and straightened his jacket. "See if you can find something to qualify as his big discovery. I have to look at the crime scene and try to figure out what happened here. Emma, look around and let me know if you find anything."

44

I stood in the middle of my living room, alone, thinking about my past months here. I'd learned about the residents of Waterwood and the Cottage, uncovered some of their hopes and dreams and secrets, but I'd had letters and diaries to guide me. For this quest, I had nothing.

"Uncle Jack, if you can offer some guidance, I'd really appreciate it." I spoke those words to the empty room... and received nothing in response. This time, it was up to me.

CHAPTER NINE

"Not I, nor anyone else can travel that road for you.
You must travel by yourself."
  —*Walt Whitman*

I t was hours before the police and the crime scene team
left. They said I could stay in the Cottage... as long as I
stayed *in the Cottage*. The patio was cordoned off by tape, but
it wasn't necessary. I was the only civilian around and the last
thing I wanted to do was go and sit on my patio. It had been
one of my favorite places, but now, I wasn't sure if I'd ever go
out there again.

I kept seeing the professor slumped back in the chair, a
knife sticking out of his chest. The poor man. Had someone
planned to kill him on my patio or was it just a place of
convenience? I'd have to ask Craig.

My phone kept lighting up with calls from people I knew
in the area as news of the murder spread. Maureen was the
first to call. TJ called, too. They both wanted to come over,
especially after I told them I had almost been arrested. With a

laugh, I tried to show I was fine. A good night's sleep would help me keep my mind focused on the present, instead of snapping back to those images from the morning.

Before I headed upstairs to bed, I went around the Cottage checking the door and window locks I'd asked TJ to install only months ago. Then I made the rounds again, just to be sure. The Cottage was buttoned up tight, safe from the big, bad world outside. I wished I could do the same for my mind.

When I finally made my way up the stairs, I was dragging. The shock of the discovery, the adrenaline rush when the emergency people arrived, the alarm and outrage at being read my rights and handcuffed in my own living room... all of it had sucked the energy out of my body. As I climbed into bed, I was sure I would fall asleep as soon as my head touched the pillow. How wrong I was.

I was haunted by sensations: the cold, clammy feel of the professor's skin when I felt for a pulse; the blinding blue and red lights of the emergency vehicles; the cold stab of fear warning of someone lurking in the woods. Then my logical mind went to work. Why was the professor attacked here? Did he know someone was following him? Why didn't he bang on my front door?

Lying there in the dark, the only conclusion I could reach was Uncle Jack's mysterious find was at the heart of it all. He liked to collect things, unusual things. Things with some kind of special significance. The plantation desk now safely ensconced in the cabin down the path was proof. Tomorrow, I'd have to walk around the Cottage, room by room, to see if something stood out. It could be anything: a uniform or gun, maybe a daguerreotype or ambrotype if I remembered the technical terms used for photographs more than a century ago. Maybe a picture revealed something important in the background?

I fluffed my pillow yet again to get comfortable, but all I did was irritate my wrist where the police officer had snapped the handcuff. I could still sense its cold metal against my warm skin. It reminded me how demeaning it was. Of course, I knew that I had done nothing wrong. I had not taken a life. But if this officer jumped to the conclusion I was a killer, things could change quickly.

I shivered and pulled the light comforter close around my neck and the *what ifs* came fast and furiously. What if the knife was from my kitchen and my fingerprints were on it? What if Officer Wilson arrested me? Would he put me in his police car with one hand on my head so I wouldn't hit it? Where would he take me? Would it smell? Would there be violent people there? I'd seen TV shows. I— It was too awful to think about.

I burrowed down for comfort. What if I was wrongly accused and convicted? What could I do to protect myself?

I stroked the silky surface of the pillowcase. Soft, soothing things had always surrounded me, even in the hospital, but right now, I did not feel comforted. I pulled the sheet and comforter over my head and teardrops threatened to leak through my lashes.

It helped to remember Detective Craig Mason was in charge. He trusted I had done nothing wrong. But what if the evidence forced him to change his mind? TJ would help as much as he could. My sister would wail.

No, I couldn't rely on other people to protect me. I had to advocate for myself. Protect myself. I had to make sure things didn't get out of hand. My last thought before I finally fell asleep was, *I had to take care of myself.*

CHAPTER TEN

Spring is the time to plant corn, soybeans,
and sunflowers. – *A Farmer's Wife*

The next morning, the sun sent bright rays through my
bedroom window, the one where I had forgotten to pull
the curtains closed. When I couldn't hide from the light any
longer, I peeled the covers back and slid my feet to the floor.
Finally in a standing position, I swayed a little, feeling drunk
from worry and lack of sleep.

I was awake enough to realize I had a decision to make. I
could close the curtains and dive back into bed or I could get
the day started. There really wasn't any debate. I knew I
wouldn't get a good night's sleep until this whole situation
was resolved and the police had the killer in custody—the real
killer, not the one they suspected. Me.

Carefully putting one foot in front of the other, I headed to
the shower. The hot water did its magic. I put on dark rose
fleece pants and a matching top. I combed my wet hair into a
bun on the top of my head. I noticed it took me a little longer

than normal to do these things. My movements and decisions were deliberate. The joy of greeting the morning just two days earlier was missing. I refused to go to my window and look out at the weather and landscape. I had to get to work, do what had to be done to make sure I was safe.

Somehow, I choked down a slice of toast and lingered over my coffee while sitting at the kitchen table. Normally, I'd sit outside to ponder things, but it wasn't an option now. The crime scene tape strung around the patio flapped in the wind, ordering me to stay away. Resolving to deal with the professor's murder and searching for a valuable Civil War find was easier done in the dark of night. When the new day had dawned, I knew what I wanted to do: find this Civil War-related object and discover the killer so the police would leave me alone. What was so important it was worth killing someone? It was time for action. But I had no clue to how to accomplish those goals. Now what?

Finding Uncle Jack's discovery sounded like a simple place to start. I made a fresh cup of coffee and set out to search each room of the Cottage to see if he had stashed *it* —whatever *it* was—someplace here.

The obvious place to look was the den. Yes, he'd lived here at the Cottage alone, but the den was his sanctuary. When I was younger, I always had this nagging feeling I should have an invitation before I could walk into his room. He'd always been a gracious, welcoming host to his family and friends and shared all the other rooms with them, but the den was distinctly his own place.

As I stood in the middle of the den and looked around, I realized I had already made a number of changes. This is the room where I had the plantation desk placed after it was discovered in the garage. I had added some of my favorite books to Uncle Jack's collection on the shelves. A small table from my condo was nestled in the corner to hold my printer. And, most important of all, I had replaced his outdated TV. I looked around and smiled. I thought he would have approved. This was one place in the Cottage where I felt closest to him.

There was no time for nostalgia or sadness. Back to work.

Uncle Jack was always fascinated by history, especially the American Civil War. Over the years, he'd collected memorabilia of that time. Uniform insignias, daguerreotypes and ambrotypes, and maps. They'd all been carefully preserved under glass, in frames, or tucked inside glass cabinets so they could be appreciated. They had been on display in his den since I was a little girl. I checked each one to see if he'd made any new additions, just to be sure. No, everything looked the same. Time to keep looking.

I went from room to room, carefully looking at each space with an eye for a Civil War artifact. Nothing jumped out at me. With a groan, I started opening closet doors and rooting around for something that might have been stashed in the back, on top of a shelf, down in a corner. Was it sitting in something like a box to protect it? Every box I did find held old clothes, linens, old bills... in other words, nothing stood out as being stored with care.

A knock at the door saved me from despair.

"Emma! It's me," the familiar voice called out. TJ had great timing.

We sat down in the kitchen with steaming mugs of coffee, Ghost, his white Labrador retriever, making himself comfortable under the table.

I waved away TJ's apology for leaving me yesterday. "Don't be silly. You had things to do. Spring is your busy season, right?"

He nodded. "One of them."

"Anyway, I think the officer was waiting for you to leave before trying to arrest me. He probably knew you would cause a ruckus."

TJ put his mug down on the table. "And he would have been right! I can't believe—"

I patted his arm. "It's okay, TJ. Craig came along at the right time and put a stop to it." I had to chuckle. "You should have seen the look on the officer's face. He was scared witless."

"I'm glad you can find the humor in it." His right eye narrowed. "Emma, it's not a laughing matter. That officer was serious."

"Dead serious." What was wrong with me? This was no time for funny quips. "I'm sorry. You're right. Things could have gotten complicated and emotional. You're right, plus the fact Craig hasn't found the killer yet kept me awake most the night."

TJ smiled. "Probably just your way of easing off the stress. I'll say it again. I'm sorry I left you, but I hope you know I'm always as close as your phone." He patted his pocket. "Mine is here all the time. If something happens, if you need my help, call me."

I nodded, touched by his sincerity. I wouldn't try to speak because I didn't trust my voice would sound normal and not betray the emotion I felt pent up inside.

He downed the last of his coffee and dramatically placed the mug back on the table. "That was good, but this working man has to get back at it. What are you doing today..."

"Since I'm not behind bars?"

TJ screwed up his face in mild disapproval.

"Okay, okay, enough with the jokes. I'm on a quest to find Uncle Jack's mysterious find, what the professor thought was here in the Cottage."

"Any luck?"

"No, nothing. "Do you think..." I hesitated, always nervous about asking for access to TJ's house, the main house of what was once the sprawling Waterwood Plantation.

"You want to look around Waterwood House? After the excellent sleuthing you did with Emma's diaries, I can hardly say no. You might even find something valuable and important." He dropped his eyes. "Though I doubt it. Jack didn't leave anything there, but go on, you might find something to inspire you."

"I just want to poke around the attic a little bit," I explained.

"Okay, but I won't be able to join you on the hunt." He got up and headed for the door, Ghost on his heels. "I have impatient clients who always want to be next in line, equipment needing tweaks and repairs, and, of course, my own field to prepare and plant."

He stopped in the doorway and turned his deep blue eyes toward me. "Emma, I mean it. If you need help, you call me. Period. Done."

He called out his final good-bye as he opened, but I didn't hear my front door close. I followed him. "TJ? Is something wrong?"

He stood there with his lower lip stuck out. "I was just thinking about one of the last times Jack was up at the house. We talked about a lot of things, but he asked me if I knew anything about..." TJ looked up at the ceiling and closed one eye. "What did he say?" Then he lowered his chin and shook his head. "Thought I had something for you but can't remember. Sorry. I guess I have too much on my mind." His lips tensed. "I hope you find something up at the house. Gotta run." And he closed the door.

For a moment, I thought TJ had a lead, but no. He was right. He had a lot on his mind with spring planting and all. Now, a murder and a mysterious find. I felt guilty adding to TJ's stress. It was time for me to follow my instincts and see if I find some inspiration at Waterwood House.

CHAPTER ELEVEN

"Be curious, not judgmental."
—*Walt Whitman*

Out in the fresh air, I wanted to skip up the tree-lined drive to Waterwood House. I passed tall pines, old maples and sturdy oaks standing guard. The color of the evergreens looked refreshed from winter's onslaught. The trees with bare branches were beginning to show off their spring growth about to burst forth into tender green leaves. This was perhaps my favorite time of year here on the Shore. The landscape lay full of promise, the air getting noisy with birdsong and the open fields looking damp and fertile as they awaited preparation and seed at the hand of farmers like TJ. He worked so hard to help grow the things we needed and create a better way of life for other people, people like me. The promise of sweet corn in the coming months teased my tastebuds and made me smile.

It was a miracle Uncle Jack's lawyer had hired TJ as a handyman to take care of the Cottage when I'd first come to the Eastern Shore to heal. He was to take care of chores like changing light bulbs, raking leaves, making needed repairs. But TJ had taken the lawyer's last comment to heart: Do whatever you can to make her life easier. And he had. It was mind-spinning how fast he responded to my calls and texts. He'd coaxed me to keep my physical therapy appointments, though he was dealing with a most reluctant patient. And he did it all at the expense of his schedule.

I remembered when I had first told him about my correspondence with Daniel, a former resident of Waterwood. TJ had tamped down his shock and yes, fear at the fact I was exchanging letters with ghosts. Then, he had actively encouraged my research to uncover their trials and secrets. I guess I hadn't truly appreciated it those past months, especially now that he wasn't with me as often.

Now, Emma, I lectured myself, *the man has work to do. He has a life of his own. You can't expect him to constantly give up things for you.*

I deserved those harsh words, but he had shown such a giving spirit along with the one thing I probably valued most of all from a man in my life: honesty. When I married my high school sweetheart, I thought it was for life. I hadn't expected him to lie and chase after anything in a dress or scrubs when he went to work as a doctor. His deception had hurt me deeply, to the point I believed I could never trust a man again.

With TJ, it felt like I was seeing the true person, not what he wanted me to see. His honesty was helping me lower my own walls I had built to protect myself. Could TJ be—

I told myself I was being ridiculous. I'd known the man only months, not even a full year. True, we had been through some extreme and unusual experiences together, but still, knowing someone for a period of time was important.

I had known the man I married for years... and look how it worked out!

I had to stop talking to myself. There were more pressing

questions to work out. It was time to stop looking back and to stop wondering about a feeling that might never blossom into something.

Right in front of me was the possibility a treasure or at least a clue was waiting for me at Waterwood House, a place I love to visit. The heart of Waterwood Plantation, it dated back to the early 19th century. Of course, I wouldn't get the full impact of its architecture since I was approaching by land. Its front door faced the water to welcome guests to the grand home who usually arrived by boat. It was faster and more comfortable than navigating the rutted roadways. Still, seeing the large and well-balanced dimension of the house from the back still made my breath catch. I found the key under a flower pot and opened the kitchen door. Yes, it was a cliché, putting a key there, but it was better than leaving the house unlocked the way TJ used to do.

In the foyer, the loud bongs of the grandfather clock greeted me as it struck the hour. Its deep melodic voice reverberating through the house transported me to another time when such reminders of the time were a normal part of life. The clock itself, remarkable in its simplicity, had been made specifically for Waterwood House. The beauty of the mahogany clock case showed in the rich patina of the wood. Two slender finials at the top reached a good eight feet above the floor. The hand painted clock face featured Roman numerals so the delicate hour, and minute, and second hands of intricate black steel could mark time for the family living here. Time of happiness and pain. Time of loneliness and hope. Its voice only silenced when death came to the house.

I turned away, not wanting to think about the professor's lifeless body and looked to a painting by the front door. It was a portrait of the former mistress of this house, a woman with whom I shared a first name, Emma.

The lady had been born and raised here in the mid-1800s. After her marriage, her husband had moved in. When her father died, the last male in the family, Emma's husband became the lord of the manor and showed his true nature, a cad of the first rank. I'd gotten a sense of his personality from the letters written to me by Daniel, son of the Waterwood plantation manager and Emma's childhood friend. Later, Emma's words written in her diaries had reinforced those nasty impressions. In her own hand, Emma had written of terrible things committed by her husband, Joshua Collins, including an unspeakable offense against his wife.

I shook off those memories. This was not the time to think of them. "I'm sorry, Emma," I whispered. "I will deal with the situation, I promise. Right now, I have to try to protect Uncle Jack's reputation and save myself from being falsely accused of murder again." I gazed at the painting for a moment. I felt sure the woman with flawless pale skin, eyes the color of the deep blue waters of the Chesapeake on a sunny day, and the soft mouth touched with a soft smile would understand.

I headed to the elegant staircase with its broad wooden banister smoothed over the years by the hands of many people long gone. I felt them looking out at me from the portraits lining the walls as I climbed the wide steps. There were men in their finest garb popular in their time. They all shared a stern expression as if the responsibility of Waterwood lay heavy on their shoulders. I wondered what they would think of seeing their descendant TJ, smiling, celebrating the life he was making here.

Paintings of their wives, daughters, or gatherings of the whole family together also hung on these walls. When I'd first found Emma's diaries, TJ had brought down a painting he had found in an upstairs bedroom. It showed a proud and pompous man, a worn and miserable-looking Emma, and their children who were oblivious to the unhappiness around them. The painting showed more than the people who inhabited the house. Various areas of the Waterwood plantation were represented in the background to show the extent of their holdings and source of their wealth and social standing. TJ had returned that painting to obscurity in favor of the lovely portrait of his elegant ancestor now hanging by the front door.

I continued my climb up the stairs to an array of rooms and the door to the enormous attic where I'd found so many of Emma's secrets. Maybe I would find something to help me on my search today. At the top level, I headed down the hallway to the simple-looking door leading to the attic. Over the winter months, TJ and I had worked a little to reduce the dust and appearance of spiderwebs in the high corners of the rafters until the unheated area became too much of a challenge. I was never one who enjoyed wintry weather. I was delighted to find we had made some progress. When I entered the attic and moved toward the back, my movements didn't raise a cloud of dust. When I got to the tall bookcase standing against what appeared to be a brick wall, I stopped. This was the entrance to Emma secret room where she'd kept her personal treasures and mementos of her hopes and dreams. No, I wouldn't find anything helpful there. Uncle Jack wouldn't have known about Emma's room. It was only recently I'd learned about its existence from a letter that appeared on the plantation desk.

The rest of the attic seemed to stretch on for miles, filled with the stored valuables and castoffs belonging to family members who had occupied this house for more than two hundred years. The Civil War was fought during only a sliver of that time. I wished TJ and I had tried to organize some of the things by time period. It would have been so helpful now. But really, how could I be sure if the rocking chair by the armoire dated back to the 1860s? What about the clothes surrounded by mothballs in the armoire? No, we'd need an expert.

Then I saw a special piece once treasured by someone living in the Victorian Era and would be a valued *find* for anyone today. A large ornate bird cage hung from a support.

The gold color of the metal bars and the filigree gave it a formal air. Though it looked delicate, it would have provided a fine and substantial home for a brightly colored bird favored during that period. Or it might have been home to a small flock of canaries meant to entertain the family and guests with their song. Now, its ornate door hung open, its occupants long flown away. I started to reach for the cage, but quickly drew my hand back. Yes, it was lovely and shouldn't be locked away in this dusty attic, but this wasn't my house. I'd mention it to TJ, but I was on a mission and had to stay focused.

There were a couple of portraits stacked against a wall. Surely, they were people who didn't have an important connection to Waterwood. Family portraits were hanging on the walls of the main staircase. Even so, I made a mental note to ask TJ, just in case.

As I wandered around this wild assortment of treasures, giveaways, and junk, my mind was filled with possibilities of things that might qualify as a Civil War artifact, but it would take a long time to investigate and research. I took a few photos with my phone of things. Then I remembered he'd never come up to the attic. The steps would have been too much for him. Still, Waterwood might hold a clue to send me in the right direction. I put the phone back in my pocket and concentrated on what was in front of me.

I spotted several trunks pushed together by a wall. Two were piled on top of one another. They didn't have the rich patina of trunk I'd found in Emma's secret room. These bore the scars—heavy nicks, scratches, and dents—of extensive travel. I wiped away the dirt and dust above the lock on the top trunk. There, initials carved into the wood: **JTC**. The trunks belonged to Emma's husband, Joshua Thomas Collins. I felt resentment on Emma's behalf begin to bubble up inside me. I'd found evidence he had roamed far and wide, to parts of the United States and over to England and Europe. There was a mention here and there in local Baltimore, Philadelphia, and New York newspapers of Mr. Joshua Collins, Talbot County, attending a major social event or visiting a notable family member or pillar of the community. It appeared he had no qualms leaving Emma behind to run the Waterwood Plantation and maintain the family.

I hoped this man no connection to Uncle Jack's valuable find.

CHAPTER TWELVE

"Keep your face always toward the sunshine
and shadows will fall behind you."
        –Walt Whitman

I walked to another area of the attic and put my hands on
my hips in awe at how much *stuff* a family could collect
over more than 150 years. I had first come here filled with
excitement and curiosity, but now overwhelmed by the sheer
volume of things, and I hadn't really started looking in
earnest.

I began with an armoire crammed with clothing. Was I
looking for a Civil War uniform? Then I realized a uniform,
sword and scabbard, or spurs wasn't the type of thing Uncle
Jack liked to collect. If he'd found those type of items, he
would turn them over to a museum or institution. Then I
considered a trunk. Surely, TJ would have mentioned if he had
carried such a bulky thing down the stairs for him.

I was looking at a conglomeration of things that would
thrill many historians, but I was beginning to think Uncle

Jack's big find wasn't here. The value of this place was only to inspire me.

A crack of lightning jolted me out of my musings. It heralded springtime storm crossing the Chesapeake Bay to the Eastern Shore. Weather systems traveling from the west often collided with systems from the south saturated with humid air and rain. The area might be caressed with a gentle rain or whipped into a frenzy by a severe thunderstorm. It was hard to know what to expect. The weather apps were not always right. I was grateful for the warning. If I didn't want to spend the afternoon at Waterwood House to avoid getting wet, I had to get back to the Cottage.

By the time I got to the door, rain was already coming down in sheets. I listened for several minutes. No more thunder. One of the first things TJ taught me about weather from a farmer's point of view was *If you hear thunder, take cover.* Lightning could strike as far away as ten miles from the center of a storm. We saw the result of such a strike last fall. A bolt of lightning had set a farmer's field on fire. And it wasn't even raining where we were. Lightning was something I didn't want to mess with.

I waited a little longer at the front door just to be sure. No rumbles. No cracks. Yes, I thought it would be safe to scoot back to the Cottage, but now I had to deal with a steady downpour. I would be drenched as soon as I stepped outside, but I didn't want to wait for the storm to pass. It could be hours. I just needed an umbrella. I went to the kitchen door and looked around. Nothing. TJ must keep one in his truck if he uses one at all. Then I remembered something in the foyer.

There, in the corner, stood an antique wood stand primarily designed to hold walking sticks or canes. There was an individual spot for up to ten of them so they couldn't rub up against each other and mar the finish or do any damage. Nine of the slots were filled with unique and unusual canes, but right now, I needed to grab the big, black umbrella with a plain wood handle.

I ventured out the kitchen door, faced wind-whipped raindrops, and set off down the driveway leading home. As I zigzagged my way around the puddles formed by the downpour, I had to chuckle. Imagine finding an umbrella stored in an antique walking stick holder. A purist would have been appalled. I was thrilled. Thanks to the size of the umbrella, I stayed mostly dry. My feet and calves took the brunt of the wetness. I hoped my sneakers would dry out someday.

A roaring came from the middle of a nearby cornfield. I wasn't the only one caught by the sudden storm. TJ was maneuvering his tractor out of a muddy spot. One winter night as we had sat in front of a roaring fire, TJ had expounded on the challenge of gauging the right amount of moisture in a field in the spring. If there wasn't enough, the seeds would have difficulty pushing up through the hard, dry soil to the sunlight and die. If there was too much water in the field, the seeds could rot. The farmer had to read the weather patterns. If a heavy downpour like this one fell on a field recently planted, some or all the seeds might wash away, and the farmer would have to start again. He had chosen a stressful profession. I was glad he was calm enough to notice me and wave.

With the Cottage in sight, a deep-throated rumble of thunder sent a vibration through the air and land. It must have affected the clouds because the heavens opened, and sheets of rain obscured everything around me. I sprinted to the door, unlocked it, and threw myself inside. Every part of me was dripping. Raindrops plopped off my nose to my clothes or down to the floor. Water was streaming off the umbrella. I wasn't sure what to do with it. Even if I dashed to the kitchen or bathroom on this level, I would leave a stream of water I would need to mop up. I was looking around for another possibility when I noticed a small umbrella stand tucked in a corner near the door. Funny how I'd never truly noticed it until I needed it. The stand, made of hammered copper, had a little tray at the bottom to catch any leftover raindrops. Perfect.

As I placed TJ's umbrella among the few already in the stand, I noticed something that, according to a purist, didn't belong there. Wasn't it odd I'd found an umbrella among the canes at Waterwood House and now, at the Cottage, I'd found a cane in the umbrella stand?

I pulled it out of its hiding place and felt a surge of excitement. It wasn't a heft cane with a curved handle meant to help support an elderly, unsteady person. It wasn't exactly delicate, more substantial. And definitely antique because of the glowing golden patina suggested it was made of walnut. Such luster only came with care and age. The handle was unique, a knob of such size must have been designed for a man's hand. A delicate lady of the 19th or early 20th century would have had trouble holding on to it.

At first, I thought the top of the knob might be a deep blue enamel, but on closer examination, it appeared to be made of a stone known as lapis lazuli. Its intense blue color reminded me of the azure waters around the Greek islands. In the center of the blue disk was a small white five-pointed star. The star motif was repeated around the knob in silver.

Where did you come from? And why were you hidden among polyester umbrellas? Why did Uncle Jack keep a fancy cane in his umbrella stand? What happened in the last months of his life?

So many curious questions. If I had been here then, I'd *know* the story of this cane. Instead, I was laid up in the hospital and a rehab facility recovering from the aftermath of the accident. I shook my head to get rid of the guilty thought that I wasn't here when he needed me. If only...

A sharp knock on the door right next to me made me jump. I opened the door.

"OH! Were you waiting for me?"

I couldn't respond. I felt like TJ had caught me in the moment I felt guilty for not being with my Uncle Jack in his final days.

"Emma? May I come in?" he asked. "It's pretty wet out here." He shook the rain off his rain gear and set it just outside the door to drip.

The entry way to the Cottage was so small, we had to do a little dance so we could both stand on the little rug put there to catch rain and mud. I could smell the fresh scent of earth and rain on him. Would I notice such a thing on someone who was just a friend?

I focused on what he was saying. "This storm sure blew up quick. I got back early from my appointment and thought I'd do a little work on my front field but couldn't do much once the rain started. I saw you from the tractor and thought I'd drop by. How did you make out at the main house?"

I looked around. "Where's Ghost?" The dog was never far away from him.

"I left him in the truck. He is curled in a nest of towels so he's happy and drying out."

"Oh, before I forget." I reached into the stand and held out the wet umbrella. "This is yours. I borrowed it for my walk home in the storm."

He held his hands up, declining to take the wet rain gear. "Thank you, but I think I'll pick it up after it dries. I'm sure there are a ton in that stand by the door."

I shook my head. "No, this was the only one. Every other spot was taken by a cane."

"Maybe I'll take it when I leave. Now, tell me what you found in the attic."

"Once again, I was impressed and overwhelmed by everything in your attic, but it's not what I found in your attic.

It's what happened when I got home. I didn't want to carry the dripping umbrella through the house, so I stuck it here in the umbrella stand."

"O-kay," he said slowly, not understanding the importance, yet

I could barely suppress the smile spreading on my face. "The surprise is what I found among the umbrellas in the stand right here."

CHAPTER THIRTEEN

"When the materials are ready,
the architects shall appear."
– *Walt Whitman*

I lifted the walnut cane and held it out in both hands to show TJ. "This is what I found."

"Wow, it's beautiful. May I?" He took it from my hands and ran his fingers lightly of the smooth shaft. Its rich finish showed off the dimension of the wood grain. "I don't remember ever seeing one like this. It didn't come from Waterwood. I can't believe you found it. It might have stayed hidden there for a long time." He inspected the knob then frowned a little. "What is this?" "He pointed to something below the base of the knob. "Is it damaged?"

I looked but couldn't tell. "I'll be right back." I rushed to the den and came back a moment later holding up Uncle Jack's old magnifying glass and peered closer. "It looks like a small carving...initials maybe?" I rubbed the area with my thumb to remove some of the dirt that had accumulated over the years and looked again. "I think it says, *JTC*."

"JTC?"

"Yes," I said. "Aren't those the initials of Emma's husband, Joshua Timothy Collins?"

"He's my relative and I had no idea." TJ drew his eyebrows together a little. "How did you find out?"

I smiled a little and gave him a light punch on his arm. "If you spent more time in your attic, you'd be amazed what you'd learn about your family."

He gave a little sigh. "You're right. I guess I'm just more rooted in the present than the past." Now, it was his turn to smile. "That's why I keep you around."

"Very funny." I looked at the initials again. "Yes, those initials match the trunk I found in your attic. It saw some heavy use. Nobody took loving care of his trunks the same way they did of this walking stick. He must have oiled it all the time to keep it in such good condition." Then a thought sent a flush of heat to my face. "TJ, Joshua didn't take care of his cane. He had slaves do it."

He reached out and rubbed my arm. "I know, Emma. It was wrong, yes. It should never have happened, but it did. It was another time."

He was about to hand me the cane when his eyes grew wide. "Wait! Is this…? Could this be…"

"…Uncle Jack's mysterious find? I'm not sure but it might be. Think about it, if you want to hide something valuable, something important, where is the best place to put it?"

TJ shrugged and looked around as if he'd see the answer.

"You hide it in plain sight."

"Like an umbrella stand?" TJ caught on at once. "With a bunch of modern umbrellas. Brilliant!"

"Right! He was organized. He wouldn't have randomly left an antique walking stick buried in a bunch of umbrellas." With a note of triumph, I said, "I'm not sure, but it may be

Uncle Jack's mysterious find." I folded my arms. "But what makes it so special?"

We stood there quietly, gazing at the cane. Neither one of us had an answer. After a few minutes, I looked at TJ, his wrinkled forehead suggested the same question had crossed his mind, too.

"What does Joshua's cane have to do with...? What is the significance?" The questions were coming fast. "Why is it so important somebody would kill to find it?"

"He must have found the carved initials the way we did. The connection to your family must have captured his interest."

TJ rubbed his chin. "I'm not so sure it's the whole story. Remember, you said the professor thought it was a *major* find leading to more research, publication of articles, even a book. I think you're just starting your quest." He checked his watch and peered out the window. "It looks like the rain has let up. Won't be able to get into the fields now. Too wet. But while the land is draining, I can keep a couple of appointments. Good luck with everything." He gestured at the cane then he looked me straight in the eye, his face showed no emotion. "Emma, promise me you'll be careful."

"Of course."

"Promise me." He almost sounded like a stern father.

"I promise."

Then in a light, airy way, he said, "Let me know what you find." He opened the door and headed into the muggy air. Calling over his shoulder, he suggested, "Maybe you should ask your correspondent down in the cabin about it. See what she knows?" Then he stopped and turned toward me. "Emma, maybe that's not such a good idea."

I waved good-bye with a laugh. "Don't worry, TJ. Everything will be fine." I closed the door to prevent any more conversation on the topic. I hadn't thought about writing a letter, but now I realized it was a great idea.

When I first moved to the Cottage, I'd moved Uncle Jack's plantation desk from the garage to the den. The next morning, I'd found a letter on the desk addressed to Emma and signed, Your Loving Servant, Daniel. After several exchanges of letters that did not require stamps or the services of the post office, I learned Daniel was a young man who lived in the mid-19th century who was searching for his love also named Emma.

It had been upsetting when it first became clear I was corresponding with a ghost. When I'd finally told TJ what was happening, he almost came unglued. He'd been so opposed to what I was doing. It was bad enough I had a ghostly correspondent. The bigger problem was Daniel hadn't realized he was dead. TJ was deeply concerned what the ghost might do when he understood the situation. It's what made TJ's casual suggestion so radical. To think it was only a few short months ago, TJ had flipped when he learned I had left another letter on the same desk addressed to Daniel's long-lost love, Emma, with whom I shared a first name. It was almost comical he would now suggest I send her another letter about this cane. Still, I thought it was a terrific idea. It was time to get to work.

First, I grabbed my phone and took some pictures of the cane. It would be better to work from them than leave Uncle Jack's great find out in the open. He had stashed it away for a reason. Now, someone interested in it had lost his life. There was more danger here than anyone would have expected.

I returned the antique cane to its hiding place in the umbrella stand and headed into the den where I had set up a small computer desk. It wasn't as comfortable or inspiring as the big plantation desk, but it would be fine until I found something I liked better.

I opened my computer, began my search to learn about antique canes. The number of sites and blogs just on the first page was dazzling. One fact popped out. A piece like the one hiding in the umbrella stand was called a walking stick. I was surprised to learn it was considered a fashion accessory as well as a defensive weapon! Often, a sword would be concealed inside. Looking at everything, I realized the research on this one simple item, including sorting through the examples, was going to take a long time. Suddenly, the knocking registered someone was at my front door.

CHAPTER FOURTEEN

"Either define the moment
or the moment will define you."
—*Walt Whitman*

My visitor was impatient. I called out I was coming, but the knocking became even more insistent. It must be TJ in a hurry. But what I saw framed in the doorway turned my body into a statue. Words of welcome froze on my tongue. Fear spread through me. The uniformed police officer named Wilson, with all his tools to enforce the law hanging from his belt, was standing on my front step. I could still feel the sensation on my wrist when he had snapped his handcuffs closed. His slow smile was not in greeting, but satisfaction. He must have seen or at least sensed the fear he'd triggered.

"Hello again, Ms. Chase. May I come in?" he said as he stepped across my threshold.

Before, he was impatient, all macho with me. Now, he was polite, almost pleasant. What was going on? My eyes searched the area outside, hoping to see Craig, the homicide detective I knew and trusted, the man who had saved me from being arrested by this man. But we were alone. And it made me nervous.

Reluctantly and oh so slowly, I closed the door and turned to this officer of the law. "Of course, what can I do for you?"

"Is there someplace we can sit and talk, maybe in the living room?" The room where he had read me my rights.

"Of course," I held out my arm to indicate the direction, like an 18th century English hostess featured on Masterpiece Theater. The thought meant I had to fight hard to tamp down a nervous giggle.

He walked into the room as if he owned the place and sat down on the sofa, my usual domain. I had no choice but to take a chair.

"Have you come," I started to say, but had to stop. My voice was squeezing out the words in a squeak. I cleared my throat and began again. "Are you here..." Yes, that sounded better. "to tell me you found the killer?" Mentally, I crossed my fingers.

He looked down and slowly shook his head. "No, ma'am. We're good, but not magicians. It's barely been a day since we, you found the body." Without another word, he raised his hand holding a plastic evidence bag with a bright colored stripe. It swung slowly, back and forth from his thumb and forefinger.

My eyes followed the movement of the bag, weighed down by the object inside. "Is it ..."

"...the knife used to kill the professor? Yes." He pulled it back so I couldn't touch it.

I felt a shudder crawl up my back and down my arms. "Did it tell you anything?" I focused on trying to control my body and voice but failing to hide how much this officer scared me.

Yes, he was a police officer just sitting there holding up an evidence bag. He wasn't arresting me. He wasn't reading me my rights. He wasn't taking me into custody. Maybe it was his imposing posture, his dark blue uniform, the bullet-proof jacket—a constant reminder violence could happen at any moment. Maybe it was the way he narrowed one eye, his left one, when he looked at me, as if he could see straight into my soul. Suddenly, I wanted to run away, screaming. But I forced my body to sit still in the chair as I waited for his.

"Yes, in fact, it did. We found fingerprints on the handle."

"Really?" I asked. "Did it tell you who killed him?"

His lips spread into a slow, unnerving smile again. "First, we know the victim didn't die immediately. His prints show he tried to pull out the knife but failed."

A shudder ran through me. Wilson noticed and his half-smile made it clear he was enjoying my distress. He continued as if we were talking about the weather. "Those weren't the only prints we found. Others were smudged which tells us the killer wasn't very smart. The killer didn't wear gloves and didn't wipe the handle afterwards." He gave me the slow smile again as he asked, "Do you consider yourself an intelligent person, Emma Chase?" He held out the bag with knife again and let it swing free.

I couldn't think of a response. I just sat there watching the bag swing back and forth.

"Nothing to say?" He stood. "Well, facts don't lie. We found two clear prints. I have to ask you to come with me to the St. Michaels police station."

I put my hands in my lap and held them tightly, hoping he hadn't seen them start to shake. I lowered my eyes to mask my reaction to what I feared was coming next.

"The prints belong to you. You are now a person of interest. If I had my way, I'd be reading you your rights."

"Do I need an attorney?"

He raised his eyebrows. "Do you?" He waited for an answer, but when he didn't get one, he went on. "I think I got it right the first time, but the powers above my pay grade want to move slowly. It seems you have some influential friends." He folded the bag around the knife and put it away. Ever the gentleman, which added to my fear, he said, "Shall we go?"

I resolved to use the time it took to get to the police station to calmly make a plan of action. At least we'd be around people instead of an open area with only newly planted cornfields, geese, and 100-foot pine trees as witnesses. I followed him outside where he opened the back door of his dark blue police car. "I'm afraid you have to sit back here. My computer and law enforcement gear don't give you enough room to sit in the front." He chuckled, but in a mean way. "I don't normally carry visitors."

"Okay," I mumbled. Once I was inside, I understood why an officer always put a hand on a suspect's head. It would have been easy to knock myself out. The roof over the back compartment was lower than a regular car. The smell of a cleaning solution hung in the air, almost making me gag. A metal grill separated me from the officer, probably for his protection from a violent criminal, which I was not. After what felt like a longer than normal trip to St. Michaels, the officer walked me to the back door of a nicely renovated old house converted to a police station and into an interrogation room with a desk in the center.

"Sit down," he instructed and motioned to the chair on the far side of the desk away from the door. Then he left, closing the door firmly behind him.

Leaving a suspect alone must have been one of their interrogation tactics. There was nothing for me to do except think about what I might have done and to look around the no-frills room. High on the wall near the ceiling, a small camera with a bright red light watched me.

No, I told myself, *it was trained on the chair I'm sitting in.*

Its red light was on which meant they were recording what I did. How creepy. I was suddenly aware of my body.

Don't move, I thought. *Don't look nervous.* WHY NOT? I wanted to shout. *I haven't done anything wrong.*

Then I felt it. An itch on my forehead near my hairline. My immediate reaction was to lift my hand and scratch it, but would they see it as a nervous reaction, a sign of guilt? I forced my hands to stay in my lap until I couldn't stand it any longer. I scratched the itch as he walked back in the room and put a file and the evidence bag on the top of the desk between us.

"Okay," he said as he made himself comfortable in the only other chair in the tiny room. "Let's see if we can uncover the truth here." He tapped the knife. "Emma, did you kill Dr. Kincaid?"

I was so startled by his blatant question, I stammered. "N-n-no. NO!" I repeated more forcefully. "I did not kill that man or do anything else to him. I only offered to help him find this special thing he said Uncle Jack had. I—" I was yammering. I was breaking the first rule when accused of something by the police. Be clear and succinct in my answers. No yammering. I closed my mouth and sat still.

The officer's mouth twitched as if stifling a laugh. Serious again, he asked, "Then how do you explain why we found your fingerprints on the murder weapon?"

"I don't know." Yes, that was better.

"Do you recognize the knife? And let me warn you, we're getting a warrant to search your house, especially the kitchen. It will not go well for you if you deny knowing this knife and we find more knives like this one in your house."

"May I look at it?"

He held up the evidence bag.

Leaning forward, it was a little hard to see through the plastic, but it was obvious they hadn't cleaned the blade. Dried crimson streaks of blood were on the blade. The professor's blood. With a little shiver, I forced my eyes to inspect the rest of the knife, hoping it was nothing like the knives Uncle Jack had accumulated in his kitchen drawers. This wasn't a knife used to set a table for dinner. It was hefty, too hefty even for a steak dinner. It wasn't a chef's knife, a thinner boning knife, or one used to chop vegetables. But it looked familiar somehow. The handle was wood and looked a little dried out as if from constant use. I looked at the blade again, trying to ignore the blood. It was substantial, bigger than a regular steak knife.

Steak knife! Yes, that's why it looked familiar. It was the kind of knife a restaurant might use when serving a steak or roast beef. Just what I'd had for dinner when TJ and I had gone to Oxford about a week ago when the temperature plummeted again to shake the winter doldrums. TJ had been anxious for spring to arrive and so was I.

I sat back. "Yes, I know this knife. I used it—or at least one like it—at dinner recently." I madly searched my mind, trying to remember the day and the name of the restaurant. "It was Tuesday I think, last week. TJ and I had dinner in Oxford. I don't remember the name of the restaurant, but it's a favorite of TJ's. He can tell you… and confirm the day."

Finally, I had found a way to checkmate the officer. TJ would corroborate my story. I flopped back in the chair and let my arms dangle at my sides. I was so ready to go back to the Cottage.

But the officer wasn't done. He took me through a list of tedious questions: Was I right or left-handed? Did I steal the knife from the restaurant? When they tested the blade, what would they find?

Traces of roast beef from my dinner, I wanted to scream, but I tried to answer each question calmly.

Finally, the door swung open, bumping into the officer's chair. "Okay, I think we have what we need for now, officer," announced the homicide detective. Craig. My friend.

I wanted to jump up and throw my arms around him. Saved!

But I waited until they conferred, the officer retrieved the knife from the table, and went away.

"You know we're just doing our job, Emma," Detective Mason said as he entered the room. "The officer will confirm what you said with TJ and the restaurant."

I focused on his face, hoping to find some comfort there, but his strong jaw was tight. Lines spread across his forehead and around his eyes—lines not from age, but from what he had seen, stories he had heard, probably in this very room. He was doing his job now.

I couldn't contain the question thrumming through my mind. "Why, how would a knife I used at a dinner out end up ..." I swallowed. The words *in the professor's chest* stuck in my throat.

He shrugged. "It's simple. Either you killed the man..."

I cringed in horror and pushed my chair back, wanting to escape.

"Or..." he continued. "Somebody is framing you for the murder."

I gasped. Neither was a good thing. "But who... why?" I was stammering again but felt safe raising these questions with Craig.

"I don't have the answers yet. We still have a lot of work to do. He turned toward the door. "Thank you for coming in and—"

"Don't I get a ride home?"

He paused. "Oh, right. You aren't driving yet."

"Maybe not ever," I added, feeling sheepish.

"I guess I can get—"

I swallowed the scream, *No, not that officer.* "If *you* drive me back to the Cottage, I'll show you something you might find interesting." Thankfully, he took the bait, and soon, we were headed down Route 33.

Craig left me alone with my thoughts. At first, it was a good thing, then reality started to creep in. I'd just been questioned about a knife with my fingerprints on it. A law enforcement officer had come to the Cottage, my home, and escorted me to the police station.

I squeezed my hands together. Nerves. A delayed reaction to what had happened. My breath was coming in short gasps. I had to calm down so Craig wouldn't notice. I didn't want him to get the idea I had something to hide. I turned to my passenger window and forced myself to take a deep breath. Then another. I had answered their questions about the knife, marked with dried blood. The knife used to murder Dr. Kincaid. The knife had my fingerprints on it. I shook my head a little. It was all a delayed reaction to what happened... and what could have happened.

I forced my hands to open and saw traces of the black ink left there when Craig wanted to confirm my fingerprints matched those on the knife handle. They did. It would have been easy for them to arrest me or at least hold me as a person of interest. TJ would have helped, I think, probably. My sister would have had hysterical fits. Craig would try to help, but he had a job to do. There was only one person I could count on. One person who could protect me. Me.

I was the only person in the unique position to draw conclusions from what Dr. Kincaid had said and what Uncle Jack had hidden at the Cottage. My hands relaxed and I breathed deeply at last as Craig turned on the driveway to the Cottage and what I believed to be Uncle Jack's Civil War find. I knew what to do to save myself and accepted the challenge.

CHAPTER FIFTEEN

"If you've done it, it ain't bragging."
— *Walt Whitman*

At the Cottage, the detective's muscular body and tall stature almost filled my little entryway. "So, where is this mysterious find?" He said as he looked toward the living room, down the hallway, up the stairway, not sure where to go.

"Right here." I reached into the umbrella stand and drew out the walking stick. Holding it across both hands, I held it up.

His face scrunched up in disbelief. "A cane?"

"Actually, I think the proper term is walking stick, I suspect there is something worth killing for, though I have no idea what, yet." I explained how I'd found it to the umbrella stand, an unlikely place for Uncle Jack to keep an antique.

He listened politely then said, "Are you forgetting your uncle kept a valuable antique desk in his garage in the woods?"

His comment unnerved me. Did he know the truth about the plantation desk? He and TJ were friends. Had TJ told him... No, he would never reveal that secret. I made a little joke about Uncle Jack being a little eccentric at times and the folly of a man buying furniture that was too big for a small cottage. I steered the conversation back to the walking stick. "Thank goodness, we just had a heavy rain, and I needed an umbrella, or I might never have found it." I held out the antique for him to inspect.

"I did a search on Google," I continued. "about canes and walking sticks to find out more, but there was too information to wade through. I need an expert in Civil War memorabilia." I sighed. "I haven't had time to start the search since..." I gave him a wry smile, trying to inject a little humor in this situation. "I am a Person of Interest."

Craig closed his eyes. "Now, Emma. You know we have to investigate all possibilities. Your index fingerprint was clearly on the handle and there were more smudge prints and partials belonging to you."

"But how? I've never been arrested," I said.

"You were a teacher, right? The school system did a background check and..."

"...you have my prints. Got it."

Craig looked at the walking stick then glanced up at the ceiling as if looking for inspiration. After a moment, he said, "I just might know someone and he's right here on the Shore." He handed me back the antique. "I need to check something."

He went to his unmarked car. After a few minutes, he came back inside, all smiles. "I think we got lucky. I called a guy who helped us arrest a ring of thieves breaking into big houses and selling the antiques at his auction house right under his nose. His cousin who works with him is a Civil War buff. Want to take a ride? He's eager to see the piece."

"Yes! Maybe we can clear up this mess and get back to normal," I said.

"Normal!" The detective laughed. "Like catching a killer?"

I rolled my eyes. "You know what I mean. Let me get something to wrap around the walking stick so it doesn't get dinged. If it is the real thing, it must be valuable."

Soon, we were whizzing up the road to Easton, the county seat, and onto the main highway to the mid-Atlantic beaches. The auction house we wanted was along the way. When we pulled in, it seemed a little odd to find an expert in history here. The place looked more like a country auction with a tractor and some other farm equipment by the entrance. The main building was well-kept and freshly painted. I would have guessed they had more early American living room furniture upholstered in orange and green than antiques, especially those with historic significance. When I walked inside, I saw in a flash, I was wrong.

The past met present in a huge room. There were substantial armoires, oil paintings with heavy frames, and a dining room set made up of a table for twelve, matching chairs, and the china cabinet/breakfront. The set would be too long and tall for most modern homes today. And there was so much more. It would have been fun to explore.

Stacked metal folding chairs for the bidders stood along a wall until they were needed. Modern technology had entered the antique auction house. An impressive television monitor hung above the auctioneer's raised podium at the far end of the room. There must be a camera tucked away until the auction when it would focus on some small detail or give the bidders one more close look. Country music was playing through the sound system. It seemed a little out of place but whatever kept people working was the right thing to do.

I was about to wander into the hodgepodge of things on the floor when a booming voice stopped me.

"Detective! Welcome!" A man walked toward us with his arms open wide as if he was about to deliver a big hug. This approaching Big-Personality was rather short in stature, but his curving handlebar moustache was another reason why he stood out. He dressed the part of auctioneer, business-like, but casual: blue jeans with a knife-edge crease and a polo shirt with stitching over the left pocket—*Blue Crab Auction Center* and *Billy Bob, Auctioneer*. The man was the auction house, and the auction house was him. I ordered myself to keep a bland expression even though a bubble of laughter threatened to pop out. *Billy Bob*. Really? I was sure this trip was a fool's errand. We needed to find someone who was truly knowledgeable and reliable.

Billy Bob made his way around the forest of antique furniture in the center of the cavernous room. "Detective, it's good to see you again. Forgive me, but I hope you're not here on official business." The man's laugh echoed off the walls.

I could imagine Billy Bob put on quite a show when he was working an auction. A good auctioneer handled his audience of buyers with care. It took a friendly personality, knowledgeable tidbits about the auction lots, a rapid delivery to get people caught up in the bidding, and true showmanship to get the prices he wanted. A little Southern twang didn't hurt, especially in an auction house away from the carpeted auction rooms of New York filled with serious collectors—I mean, antique snobs—in the big cities. People who went to auctions in the country were on the lookout for a deal or a real find. The twang, as many politicians knew, seemed to inspire trust.

Craig shook the man's beefy hand. "It's good to see you again, Billy Bob. But I'm afraid I'm here on a case."

"Not theft again, I hope." His blue eyes focused on the detective's face. All light congeniality was gone.

"No, not this time," Craig assured him. "I'm after a little information."

The bright smile was back. "Good to hear. Thieving is bad

for business and can drag a man's reputation through the mud real fast."

Craig introduced me and explained I had inherited something from my uncle.

"Good to meet you, ma'am. Name's Billy Roberts," he said as he extended his hand. "But everybody calls me Billy Bob. If it's information you want, you've come to the right place," he said with a laugh.

"The item may play a part in a case I'm working on," Craig added.

Billy Bob's smile faded. "If it's your case, it's serious. Somebody died. Hope it wasn't somebody I know?"

Craig' eyebrows shot up. "You may know him. Dr. Phillip Kincaid from Philadelphia. Ring a bell?"

"A kind of non-descript older gentleman. A history professor from a school on the other side of the Bay. Around Philadelphia, I think. Is he...?"

"Yes, I'm sorry," Craig said quietly. After waiting a moment out of respect, he asked, "What can you tell me about him?"

The big man crossed his arms and looked away at nothing. "Well, I wouldn't say he was a regular. I think he lives...lived in Philadelphia somewhere which makes it a long drive for him to come to an auction. He used to come more often. He knew one of my regulars. They would come together."

Craig and I exchanged a glance. We both had the same thought: Uncle Jack.

The big man leaned back a little and chuckled. "We called them The Professors," he said with a smooth Southern accent. "They taught somewhere on the other side," he said, dismissing the Western Shore of the Chesapeake Bay and the rest of civilization.

I had to hide my smile. Spoken as a true Eastern Shore native, he'd be happy if *those people* from the other side stayed over there, unless they had money to spend at his auction house. Then they could cross the Bay Bridge, buy, and go home.

"The professors were always interested in historical things, especially from the Civil War. They hit it off with my cousin Wendell." Billy Bob rolled his eyes. "He's nutty about the Civil War, too. When those three got to talkin', there ain't no way you could get a word in edgewise." Billy Bob reached out and touched Craig's arm and whispered, the Southern twang gone. "He was a nice man, the professor. You're not here because he went peacefully. I know you are homicide. How did he die?"

Craig drew in a breath.

That was all Billy Bob needed to hear. "You catch the guy who did him in?"

Craig gave him a quick nod. "I'll give it my best shot. You mentioned your cousin on the phone. Is he still here? We drove down to see him. I've got something to show him."

"Yes…" Something or someone had snagged Billy Bob's interest. He looked over my shoulder and called out, "No, Lil' Pete, wait. I'm coming." He swung his attention back to us. "I'm sorry, I have to go. Wendell is in the office." He waved his hand in the general direction of the raised platform for the auctioneer. "He's waitin' for you."

Craig began to thank the man.

"Yes. Yes." His eyes strayed back to whatever was behind me. "Glad I could help." He patted my arm and murmured "Nice to meet you," and he rushed off.

I turned to see who or what was more important than talking to the police.

Billy Bob hurried over to a man who would have stood out almost anywhere, but especially in a sea of jeans and T-shirts. His gray slacks and starched Wedgewood blue dress shirt, open at the neck, with the sleeves rolled up just above the wrist, screamed *custom tailoring*. It was casual elegance at a high price. I now understood why Billy Bob had sprinted across the auction area, leaving the police behind. Money talks, and, I guessed, money beckoned.

"Do you know the man over there?" I asked, barely moving my lips as I glanced around at the men in the middle of the floor, organizing the antique pieces and photographing the lots.

Craig shook his head. "No. Don't know if I need to. We'll see." He walked to meet Cousin Wendell.

CHAPTER SIXTEEN

PROVENANCE is a record of ownership of a work of art or an antique used to help establish its authenticity or quality.

–Dictionary Definition

We followed the sound of raised voices beyond the auctioneer's platform where a woman and a man stood in the middle of a sleek office equipped for the 21st century. There were computers, printers, monitors for security cameras keeping track of things, and phones. Lots of phones. Billy Bob's auction wasn't a hick operation. His customer base must reach out to the Western Shore and beyond.

"Are these the folks you're waiting on?" asked the woman who was short and round in the middle, probably from a little too much fried chicken so popular on the Eastern Shore and a few too many donuts, a staple at auctions like this one. "We can finish up later."

He nodded. "I think so." Wendell didn't look like he was born into the same family as Billy Bob. He was wispy thin as a stalk of corn that would bend in a breeze. He reached out his skinny hand and unusually long fingers to Craig. "Wendell Roberts, sir, and you are…?"

"Detective Craig Mason." Craig carefully clasped the offered hand, careful not to crush it. "And this is Emma Chase."

Wendell's eyes fell on the wrapped bundle in my hands. It was more intriguing than I was.

"Thank you for making time for us," Craig concluded.

"Nice to meet you both." He gestured toward an open door. "Why don't y'all come into my office."

As we sat down, I scanned his inner sanctum. The desk was neat and organized with papers tucked into labelled file folders. The phone on his desk had a bank of buttons for incoming lines. Reference books from *Miller's Guide to Antiques* to *Antique Guns* crammed his bookcase. From what I could see, more than three shelves had books and catalogues dealing with the Civil War. I could see why this man and Uncle Jack had a lot to discuss.

Wendell sat down carefully in his chair as if apologizing for putting his weight there. He gently leaned back and folded his hands on his skinny chest. "So, you're Jack's niece."

I put the package on my lap, out of his line of sight. He shifted his attention to me and focused his gaze. Was this the way he inspected an antique item?

"Jack was always talking about you. He was proud of you. It's a shame he is gone. At least it was quick. Good for him."

"Not so good for me. I didn't get a chance to say good-bye." I dropped my eyes, a little embarrassed about the quickness of my remark and the hitch in my voice.

"Don't worry," he said. "He knew how you felt about him. No question. None." He turned his attention back to Craig. "What can I do for you? Happy to help if I can."

Craig told him about the investigation, without going into details. "Wendell, you know people who bid on things from the Civil War."

I'd seen Craig handle other investigations and had to look away. I had an inkling he was preparing to drop his favorite question like a bomb into the interview.

With a look of innocence, Craig asked, "Wendell, do you know who killed Professor Kincaid?"

Wendell's eyes grew wide. "Killed him? Dr. Kincaid? He's dead?"

Craig paused to allow the man to recover from the shock then explained what had happened and why we were in his office. "Let me ask you again," he repeated gently. "Do you know who killed Dr. Kincaid?"

Wendell's eyes grew wide and his mouth fell open a little. It took a few moments for him to find his voice. "Detective, I have no earthly idea. You're right, I know... knew both Jack Finlay and Dr. Kincaid through the auction. I can assure you, I don't know any murderers."

Without missing a beat, showing no disappointment or apology, Craig continued. "What can you tell me about the two men?"

"Let me see." His eyes fell to the papers on his desk as if looking for the answer there. After a few moments, he looked up and addressed the detective. "Everybody liked them, both of them. Even people who lost to them in the bidding. Jack was firm, resolute in his bidding. Never looked at anyone other than the auctioneer when a lot was on the block. Dr. Kincaid was the opposite. He wasn't an aggressive bidder. The professors, as we referred to them, came to the auctions together many times and chatted with people over coffee and doughnuts."

"So, you don't know of anyone who was offended by Dr. Kincaid or felt cheated by him?"

"Absolutely not."

"I see," Craig said, suggesting the interview was over. But it wasn't. "We brought something with us and would like to know what you can tell us about it."

"I'd be happy to help." Wendell made a space in the center of his desk. "Put it right up here."

With a nod from Craig, I put my package down and pulled back the large towel to reveal the walking stick. Craig started to explain, but Wendell held up his hand for him to stop. His eyes were glued to the rich wood fashioned into this piece so long ago.

"Yes, I remember this. Jack showed it to me. Said he picked it up in a barn sale somewhere." He scratched his cheek, thinking. "When he came, it wasn't too long before he died. I offered to buy it off him right then and there, but Jack said it wasn't for sale."

"Why did you want it?" I asked.

The look he gave me suggested I had asked a stupid question, but his words were polite. "Look at it. It's a beautiful piece."

"Is it special?" Craig asked. "Other than its good condition and all."

Wendell looked at Craig for several moments. I suddenly realized what they meant when people said his face was like an open book. I wasn't sure... was there a little tic of the man's left eye? Did his mouth twitch as if he was trying to suppress an unpleasant laugh at Craig's expense? Maybe I got the impression something more was going on here by the way he raised his chin. Was he gauging the depth of the detective's ignorance? From the subtle changes in his expression, I decided it was the latter.

This skinny man held his emotions below the surface, but he had trouble hiding those feelings. For some reason, they marched across his lean face for all to see. With a start, I realized I'd better tune into what the man was saying. I only hoped I hadn't missed anything important.

"...agree. As you say, it is in perfect condition," Wendell's eyes followed his hand as he lightly ran his fingertips over the smooth shaft of the cane. "considering its age."

"Which would be…?" Craig asked.

"Oh, I'd say 160 years, give or take two or three years," Wendell responded.

I jumped into the conversation. "You can date it so specifically? To within a couple of years? Amazing."

The Civil War expert shook his head. "No, dear lady, it's not guesswork or a parlor trick. I'm certain."

I was a bit offended by what he said. I wasn't a *dear lady* or a *little lady* but buried the feeling.

Wendell responded with a little sigh. "It's really quite simple…" he paused for effect. "if you know what you're looking at."

"Which is…?" Craig said, a little impatience leaking into his attitude.

"First, the wood is Black Beech. Its patina is consistent with age, as I've said. The silverwork around the handle or knob is quite fine. I believed the disk is made of lapis lazuli. It was probably used here because of its intense blue color. It is a semi-precious mineral many people believe has protection and healing properties." He tapped the blue top and continued. "Notice, there is a small silver star embedded in the lapis. The five-pointed star motif is carried through in the silver design around the handle. I believe it is significant."

"Which is…" Craig said to encourage him to continue.

I thought I caught a little sigh escape the lips of the reference expert. I glanced at Craig, hoping he'd missed it.

"Are you familiar with the Bonnie Blue Flag?" Wendell asked us.

Craig and I both shook our heads.

"Well then, allow me to educate you. After Fort Sumter fell to the Confederates at the beginning of the Civil War, the victors needed a flag to fly over their newly acquired landmark."

"Wouldn't they have used the Confederate Flag?" I asked.

"I suppose they would have if it had been in existence.

Remember, the bombardment and surrender of the Fort marked the formal beginning of the war. The only flag they had available was known as the Bonnie Blue. It was an uncomplicated design, a medium blue background with a single white five-pointed star in the center."

I sat up straight. "Like the design on the handle?"

"You are correct. This design and the age of the item suggests a Confederate gentleman owned it or someone who had sympathy for the Southern cause."

Craig rubbed his chin. "Is it historically significant?"

"A piece in this fine condition with a clear connection to the confederacy may be of interest to a museum or a collector." Wendell tented his fingers and silently watched Craig stand.

"Well, I want to thank you for your time and the information. Emma?"

"Don't you want to know the value if it was sold at auction, the right auction?" Wendell said quietly.

Craig paused and waited for him to share the information.

"I would probably estimate its value to be between $3,000 and $5,000."

Craig's eyebrows shot up in surprise. Then he turned to me. "Sounds like you hit the jackpot, Emma."

The money would look good in my bank account, but I didn't think it was a reason to commit murder.

As I stood up to leave, I said, "Thank you for the information."

When Wendell spoke again, we stopped in the doorway. "Did you open it?"

"Open what?" asked Craig.

"The walking stick, of course."

CHAPTER SEVENTEEN

SECRET: something private, not meant to be known or seen.
–*Dictionary Definition*

Craig and I walked back into the office and resumed our seats. Wendell's mouth curved into what seemed a triumphant smile. "Yes, if I'm not mistaken, we should find a secret compartment here." He looked at me and asked, "May I?"

I nodded. He reached for the cane, one hand on the knob handle and the other on the straight stick about halfway down and turned. Nothing happened Wendell did not appear concerned as he repositioned his hands and turned with a little more force. At first, nothing happened and then with a little jolt, the handle began to turn and free itself from the rest of the cane. The smell of alcohol suddenly drifted into the room.

"I often find a flask hidden inside a gentleman cane. They drank a lot back then. It's a curiosity, but not that unusual." He picked up the two pieces and screwed them back together.

"I'd be interested to know where Jack got his piece. It is a fine example of the period."

"I wish I could tell you," I said, not really sure if I would. "I'm afraid the information died with him."

"What a shame. Where there is something like this, there might be other things of interest." He held out the cane to me and I sensed some reluctance. "Would you be interested in selling? I may have someone who might be interested in a private sale."

For a brief moment, the money was tempting. "No, I don't think so. It has sentimental value. I'm sure you can understand."

As Craig and I stood, he added, "And I believe it is part of an ongoing murder investigation."

The comment made Wendell wince. "Of course. But if you change your mind about selling..." He handed me his business card. "This is my number."

I took it and thanked him.

"One more thing you should know," and he looked straight at me. "Referring to this piece as a cane is correct, of course, but it is more appropriate to call it a gentleman's walking stick."

I stifled the laugh that threatened to burst forth. Here we were standing in the bare bones but efficient office in a simple building on the Lower Shore. This was not exactly the center of cosmopolitan living and Wendell was acting like we were in an auction house in New York. Billy Bob could turn on the simple Southern charm when he wanted, but this man had knocked the rough edges off and took pride in his polish but kept it under wraps for the most part. There was something off about this man, but I couldn't figure out what it was. I'd have to ask Craig what he thought when we were safely back in his car.

But I didn't have long to wait. Craig must have sensed something, too.

As he reached out to shake the man's hand and thank him, he asked, "Did the professor contact you at all recently?"

Wendell stood, smoothed down the front of his dress shirt, and raised his head slowly, intentionally, to look Craig straight in the eye. I thought there was a flash of defiance there.

Finally, after a silent moment, Wendell sighed. "Yes, he called me." Then he clamped his mouth shut.

Had Craig caught Wendell in a lie or was he hiding something? Was there something going on here that was not above board?

Craig must have been thinking the same thing because the detective closed his eyes slowly then opened them again. "And why didn't you tell me? You know I'm a homicide detective. Your cousin told you. You know I'm here as part of investigation. And you withheld this information? Why?"

Wendell drew in a short breath through his nose. "You didn't ask."

"Okay, I'm asking now." When Wendell didn't respond, Craig added, "We can discuss things here or at the station in Easton." Craig shrugged. "Your choice."

Wendell hesitated then gestured to our chairs again. While we sat down again, the expert struggled to find a comfortable position, crossing then uncrossing his legs. Control of the conversation had shifted to Craig. Wendell squeezed his lips together. I wondered if he was trying to decide exactly what to tell the police and what he could withhold rather than blurting out the truth. I tried not to fidget in my chair since it was clear Craig was prepared to wait him out.

Finally, Wendell uncrossed his legs again, put his elbows on his desk, and leaned toward us. "Phillip, Dr. Kincaid did call me about a week or so ago. I'd have to check my notes if it's important."

Craig's impatience bubbled over. "Okay, Wendell, do you want me to pull the truth out of you, syllable by syllable? I

can do it. And if I do, I promise, it won't be pleasant for you."
Craig stood up. "And we'll—"

"No! I'll tell you." He cleared his throat. "Sorry, this is painful. Phillip was a friend, a good friend. He told me over dinner once he was sick and his condition was getting worse. He was concerned about his reputation and the legacy he would leave behind and..." Wendell took a deep breath. "And he was running out of time." He glanced down for a moment then met my gaze. "He told me your Uncle Jack had found an historical piece, an important piece, to confirm a suspicion he had long held."

"What was it? Was it this cane, this walking stick? How do the two fit together?" My questions came out in a flood.

Craig reached out and touched my hand. His message was clear: Let him tell the story in his own way for now.

Wendell continued. "The important thing is I don't know! One thing was clear. *If,* and I do mean *if* Jack found something historically important, it would have something to do with the Civil War. It was his area of study, his expertise, his passion. Was it this piece you've brought me?" I gestured to the cane now wrapped again in the towel to protect it. "I don't know. If I had to make a guess..." He paused.

Craig waggled his head a little, clearly getting tired of the man's game. "Please do. Make a guess."

"Then I would have to say the historical mystery is there, in your hands. An antique gentleman's walking stick." He leaned back in his chair as if exhausted by his revelation. "What it might be is beyond me."

I almost blurted out a clue I had discovered—the connection to Waterwood House and TJ's ancestor—but quickly clamped my mouth shut. There was something about this man I didn't trust. I didn't want to give him any information to move him ahead of Craig's investigation."

"Is there anything else you want to tell me?" Craig asked.

"Was the phone call the only conversation you had with him before his death?"

"No," Wendell folded his fingers together and inspected his nails. "He came here a day or two later. He wanted to talk to me in person he said." Wendell raised one shoulder and shook his head a little. "I don't know. Maybe he wanted to see the whites of my eyes when we talked about this mysterious piece. Maybe he thought I was lying? Maybe he thought I knew more than I did... than I do."

"And do you know more?" Craig sneaked the question into his silent pause.

"No, I didn't then," Wendell admitted as he looked down at his hands folded on his desk. "He brought someone with him."

I perked up. There was someone else, someone new who had been lurking in the shadows. Was this the someone who had followed us when TJ and I went out for dinner? Was it the person who had grabbed the steak knife I had used and later plunged it into the professor's chest? Was this person who had diabolically planned to frame me for the man's murder?

Craig and I both spoke at once. "Who was it?"

"Her name is Dr. Elizabeth Abbott," he said.

"Local?" Craig wanted to know.

Wendell nodded. "Phillip said she bought and sold antiques and knew something about things from the Civil War period. After we talked about war pieces, she said she was looking for some specific floral prints that are not easy to find. I don't normally see those things here."

Craig and I stood. "Anything else, Wendell?"

"She left her name with me," he said quietly.

"What?" The word exploded from Craig, then continued the duel with Wendell, a duel he was determined to win. "She? I want her name," he roared.

I thought Craig was going to go right over the top of the desk. Wendell must have thought the same thing, too. He stood up so quickly his chair slammed into the wall. Then he took a step away from Craig. "Yes, yes, I'm sorry. She gave me her name and telephone number." Wendell's voice was tight with fear. "S-s-she wanted me to let her know in case any floral prints came through our auction." With fake enthusiasm and a wooden smile, he added, "We offer quite an eclectic collection." Craig wasn't buying his conciliatory attitude. Wendell had pushed him too far.

Craig held out his beefy hand and snapped his fingers. "Now!"

"Yes, sir!" Wendell responded, opened the top drawer of his desk, and after a moment of shuffling through things, he pulled out a business card. He began to copy the information on a separate piece of paper.

Craig snapped his fingers again. "I'll take the card."

Wendell put it in his hand at once.

Then Craig said with reassurance, "Don't worry, I'll return it..." Then he added with a snarl only I could hear when we'd left the office, "When I think of it."

CHAPTER EIGHTEEN

"From this hour, freedom!
Going where I like, my own master."
—*Walt Whitman*

I n the main auction room, Craig didn't slow down to say good-bye to Billy Bob. He only had eyes for the front door, but I slowed my pace to wave a good-bye and to watch the man who had drawn Billy Bob away earlier. They were still talking. The scene drew my attention because everyone seemed to be buzzing around the man.

Nothing really stood out about him. He was short, maybe not as short as my 5'7" but close. His white hair had receded so far back there was only fringe, as they called it, over his ears. His mouth was drawn into one of the broadest, happiest smiles I had ever seen, but was it an honest expression? From behind his thin rimless glasses, sapphire blue eyes reached out like lasers and wouldn't allow you to look away. An energy radiated from him that captured everyone's attention and drew them to him. Magnetism and money. What a combination.

Watching carefully, I noticed the man looked away while Billy Bob was talking about something. He had glanced over to a slight man wearing dark slacks and a clean white T-shirt standing by a far wall. The epitome of non-descript, except he was one of the most handsome, most dangerous-looking men I had ever seen. He was a Greek god come to earth. His wavy jet-black hair was tousled with one curl hanging down over his right eye. The carefully trimmed beard and mustache I'd heard called designer stubble added to his devastating looks. He pretended to examine a lot for an upcoming sale, but it was a ruse. His piercing black eyes barely left the man who had drawn everyone's attention.

"Emma? Come on." Craig waved at me to follow him outside.

I could barely drag my eyes away from the young man who belonged on the cover of a romance novel. As I turned toward the door, I noticed Wendell scurry out of his office and across the room to join the group and whisper something to Mr. Casual Elegance.

"EMMA!"

Craig was impatient, but I was torn. There was something happening inside the auction house, something important. I could feel it.

But I had no choice when I heard him honk the horn. As I sprinted over to Craig's car and opened the door, someone call my name. Wendell waving his arm madly over his head.

"Go on," Craig sighed. "See what he wants. It might be important but hurry."

I put the walking stick and its protective wrapping in the car and met Wendell in the middle of the drive. "Yes? Did you forget something?"

"Actually, I have something for you," he said brightly.

I glanced over Wendell's shoulder and saw Mr. Casual Elegance walking toward us. The other people including Billy Bob followed close on his heel.

"Emma," Wendell began. "I'd like you to meet—"

Mr. Casual Elegance ignored Wendell. "Stanley Archibald Holt. Please call me Stanley."

I was a little surprised by his formal manners, but I could go with it. I took his hand and shook it. "Hello, I'm Emma Chase."

With the formalities over, he jumped right in. "I understand you are Jack's niece."

I nodded.

"And you knew Professor Kincaid?"

"Not well. I met him briefly the day before he died," I explained.

The man looked down and gently shook his carefully arranged silver waves. "Yes, a terrible business. A tragedy. I understand he fell victim to violence."

"Yes, in fact, the homicide detective investigating the case is in the car. I can introduce—"

Stanley held up his perfectly manicured hand to interrupt. "Not necessary. I am glad someone is on the case." He shook his head slowly again. "It is a great loss. People thought well of him."

I was having a little trouble imagining Stanley, this attractive, obviously monied individual, having anything in common with the professor who was a bit frumpy and unwell. "How did you know the professor, if you don't mind me asking?"

"Not at all," he said with a smile. "I met him here." He gestured behind him to the auction center's building. "In fact, it was your Uncle Jack who introduced us."

He must have seen the confusion on my face so, he continued. "We all seem to take an interest in this auction for different reasons, different interests. It's not the first-time friendships have been born over auction lots and certain items. The professor was highly knowledgeable," he then added, "As was your Uncle Jack, of course."

"What certain items?" I was confused.

"Why, things pertaining to the War Between the States, of course."

"Excuse me," Craig called out from the car. "Emma, we need to go."

I had more questions, but I couldn't keep Craig waiting any longer. "I'm sorry, Mr.—"

He held up his index finger as a signal for me to heed what he was about to say. "Stanley, call me Stanley."

"All right, Stanley. I'm afraid I have to go. It was nice meeting—"

"I know you're doing important work." He reached into a pocket in his sports jacket, pulled out what looked like a business card, and handed it to me. "Give me a call sometime soon. We should talk, dear Emma, Jack's niece." He stepped back to give Craig's car plenty of room to maneuver. "Call me."

"I will," I murmured and got into Craig's car. Stanley made me feel a little uncomfortable, but he was another connection to Uncle Jack, another one I didn't know about until today.

We drove away and headed up Route 50. "Fill me in," Craig said.

I told him what little had transpired with Stanley Archibald Holt. "He said he knew both Uncle Jack and Professor Kincaid." I looked down at the elegant cream-colored stock paper with raised black lettering. "I have his card."

"Good. Who is he?" asked Craig.

"I'm not sure."

"You have his business card, and you don't know?" Craig shook his head in disbelief.

"No, I'm afraid it isn't a business card. It is more of a calling card. Name and a cell number."

"No company name? No title? No email address?" He

drove, keeping an eye on the highway while trying to catch a glimpse of the card.

"No," I shrugged. "It looks like a fancy calling card."

"I've seen them before," Craig said. "They are given out by high-net-worth individuals who have a property here and they aren't given out to just anyone. We'll check him out. Right now, I want to know about the professor's associate who came with him to see Wendell. She might have key information about Jack's walking stick. She may be able to explain why he thought it was so important."

This investigation was taking off and raising more questions than it gave us answers.

He added with conviction, "I want to call her and if she answers, I want to meet her, okay?"

I nodded and he took the next side road and stopped so he could make the call and take notes, if needed. In about a minute, we were back on the Route 50 again.

"We're all set. She'll see us now," Craig confirmed.

"Us? Now?" I was excited to be included.

"Yes, unless you want to go home and—" he offered with no enthusiasm.

"No, I'd love to go. I have so many questions and she might be able to clear this up. As special as it seems to me, I can't believe a hidden compartment for a flask is unusual or special." I settled back with a smile of satisfaction. "I'm glad we have Uncle Jack's find with us."

At least I thought it was. I looked over my shoulder at the bundle on the seat. The walking stick seemed like such a small thing, too insignificant to justify murder. We had an opportunity to put it to the test. "I can't wait to see her face when we unwrap it," I said, hoping he would agree. I glanced at Craig and, even in profile, saw he was frowning. "That is, if you think it's the right time to reveal the secret.".

"Let's play it by ear." Within minutes, he made a turn off the main highway, the next step in e a treasure hunt.

CHAPTER NINETEEN

"Standing at ease in nature,
master of all or mistress of all.
—Walt Whitman

W e drove up to a small house with what reminded me of an English garden. The front yard was neat, its beds clearly defined by small shrubs. When I opened the car door, the distinctive scent of boxwoods engulfed me. The dark earth looked rich and ready for spring planting and summer flowers. Clearly, an avid gardener, retired from a real-life job, lived here. It was the only way I could imagine all this work was done or perhaps she was spending a fortune on a landscaping service.

A brick walkway laid out in a herringbone pattern led to the front door painted periwinkle. The gentle shade of blue blended with her garden setting of calm beauty. Such a thoughtful garden element suggested the owner was attentive to even the smallest details. The door opened and my first impression was confirmed. Waiting for us was a petite woman with long silver hair framing a face with radiant skin. This woman must have been moisturizing religiously since her early twenties. Now, comfortably past retirement age, her life experiences had left a trail of soft lines and wrinkles. Her mouth turned down at the corners. Maybe life hadn't given her many reasons to smile.

Craig stepped forward, holding up his ID and badge. "Hello, Elizabeth Abbott? Detective Mason, Homicide."

Her hand flew to the flowered silk scarf knotted at her throat. "Oh, has someone I know been murdered.?"

"Yes, ma'am, I believe so. May we come in?" He said as he continued to the door and stepped through it.

It was fascinating to watch Craig work, like the way he approached this woman. He continued his walking pace. He didn't slow down to give her a chance to deny him access or to shut the door in his face. Somehow, his approach didn't come across as pushy or threatening.

"Yes, of course. Please come in," she said as she opened the door wide and stepped back.

I almost shook my head in awe. It worked every time.

Craig introduced me as his associate on the case. "Thank you for seeing us on such short notice, Ms. Abbott."

Her response was "You may call me Doctor."

My eyebrows shot up in surprise. While she led us down the hall, I was impressed that Craig showed no reaction to her response. His control must come from years of training and practice though we did exchange a silent question: What kind of a person is this?

As she led us down the hall to her living room, I noticed her emerald-green outfit: a well-cut tunic over a sedate pair of slacks with a scarf many colors wrapped around her neck. The way everything draped and flowed around her petite body suggested all was made of fine silk. No jeans, oversized sweater, or fleece for this woman.

Her living room was filled with light from the large

windows overlooking another garden. "This garden must be breathtaking in the spring and summer," I said in true admiration.

Her face glowed in response to the compliment. "You are too kind," she said politely, though it was obvious she loved what she assumed was adoration. "You should have come two weeks ago to appreciate the garden in its winter costume. It was time to take out the winter cabbage and prune back the deep green leaves of the pink Lenten roses. I had the crepe myrtle trimmed back so they will produce more of their showy floral clusters this season. I have all the colors: white, pink, rose, purple and burgundy." She smoothed her scarf. "It is hard to believe those stark wooden stalks produce such lush displays of leaves and color. So many plants thrive here on the Shore. I could have gardens with many varieties of plants which is one reason I moved here."

She invited us to sit down but didn't offer any refreshment. I felt like we hadn't passed the test yet to earn her time and attention.

Craig began, "I'm sorry to bring sad news, Doctor Abbott—"

She interrupted, "Just Doctor is fine."

As before, Craig covered his reaction. This time, I was pleased I could control mine though I was baffled by her insistence we call her doctor. After all, if someone is willing to have a more relaxed conversation in her own home, she would usually suggest a first name. Not this woman. She wanted to maintain her honorific of *Doctor*.

Craig cleared his throat again. "You might be wondering what brought me to your door. I talked with Wendell Roberts at Blue Crab Auction Center. He gave me the number you left with him."

Her eyebrows came together in a menacing way. "He was to notify me if he had a particular item for sale." Her lips tightened. "Not give it out."

I listened as they talked, but let my eyes wander around the room. Craig had taught me there was a lot to learn about a person from the things they kept in their home. It was obvious her love of flowers and gardening dominated her life. Then I had an odd thought. She surrounded herself with beauty, but it was beauty she could control. Inside, she'd chosen sky blue for the walls, a brilliant rose red sofa, and an organized mass of snowball white, woodland green, and tulip yellow pillows. Outside, she had control of her surroundings, too. She had selected the plants and managed their arrangements in her garden landscape. If a flower didn't perform as expected or a weed dared to appear, she could rip it out. Everywhere inside and around her home, she announced, *I know what I like. I am strong. I am in control.*

An arrangement of framed flower seed packets dated 1929 hung near a collection of watercolors. She noticed my interest. "Those are original seed packs. I collect things from gardens of the past."

"And you have done it very well," I remarked.

She paused, giving me a curious look, as if she was reevaluating me. Did she think I wasn't being sincere? It felt odd.

"Come and look at these things," she said as she walked over to another bookcase, leaving Craig behind. "You might find these pieces interesting as well."

I smiled when I saw a grouping of ceramic rose bouquets like the ones in my grandmother's curio cabinet. On another shelf was a delicate brass bottle with a narrow spout. I reached out to touch it.

Her hand shot out, stopping just short of mine. "Don't! The piece dates back to the mid- 19th century. It's fragile."

"What is it? It looks like---"

"What it is..." She interrupted without a smile. "is a plant mister for indoor plants,"

I gestured at the other things on neighboring shelves. "Are all these pieces antique gardening implements?"

"Yes, by collecting these pieces, I combine my two passions... gardening and history."

I slid my eyes over to Craig when the Doctor wasn't looking. He gave me an almost imperceptible nod to continue. "So many of these things don't look familiar. I can't even begin to guess what it is." I pointed to what looked like a small king's crown attached to a handle. It reminded me of the torch held high by the Statue of Liberty minus the flame.

Finally, I'd earned a smile from the woman along with a compliment. "You have an eye for the unusual." She took it down from the shelf and held the brass crown straight up and down. This is French, early 19th century. It is an apple picking crown." She moved it straight up a little bit. "You raise it around an apple while it's still on the tree, rotate the crown a little so one of the sharp edges cuts the stem, then you lower the apple safely to the ground without climbing on a ladder. It came with a long wooden pole which didn't fit here in my living room."

"It looks a little wicked with its sharp points," I commented.

She drew closer and considered it. "Yes, I suppose it does. The teeth make it look like a crown, but it is meant to allow one to pick an apple without bruising it."

My eyes moved to a lower shelf in the adjacent bookcase. "These things go to the other extreme. They're so dainty. Are they used in bonsai?" I'd always been intrigued by the Japanese art of growing and training miniature trees, but never had the time or patience to try it.

She gave a small sniff. "I suppose it is a good guess, but those pieces are meant for other tasks."

Careful not to touch, fearful of her response, I pointed. "That one looks like a tiny version of fireplace bellows." It was a pleated leather small bag and what I guessed was a brass and copper decoration in the shape of a flower.

She considered it for a moment. "It is not something you want to squeeze. You would release anything left inside."

I gave her a quizzical look.

"Insecticide powder. Using this small applicator, the gardener could control where the powder went." She straightened her shoulders and raised her chin with pride. "This particular dusting bellows dates back to the mid-to-late 1700s and is said to have been used by the British royal family. Before the reign of Queen Victoria which is my particular area of interest."

I pointed to the one thing on display I recognized, a small pair of clippers. "And what about those?"

"Ah, those shears are a pride and joy for me. The hunt went on for a long time. They are lady's shears for clipping a plant with a leaf or tiny branch out of place. Or she could clip an especially lovely flower. The shears are sterling silver, and the leather case is original and absolutely required. You see, the lady would carry the small shears in her handbag. She couldn't have its sharp points of the shears tearing up the lining."

Craig cleared his throat, and she turned her attention back to him.

"Yes, I imagine antique gardening implements are of little interest to you, detective." She moved to a forest green chair by the red sofa. "Shall we continue?" She lifted her chin a little, irritated by his interruption.

"I get the impression you are not pleased he shared your personal information with strangers. I want you to know he did the right thing in giving me your number." Craig clarified, "This is police business. I believe you may have information to aid in this investigation. Now, Wendell said he met you when Dr. Kincaid went to speak with him about a particular object."

She nodded once. "Correct." It appeared she was not going to give up any information easily.

Craig leaned forward showing his determination. "Would you tell me what the professor was looking for and why he wanted you in the meeting with Mr. Roberts?"

"First, you must tell me why it is important." she asked. "It is the professor's personal business and I feel a little uncomfortable talking about him behind his back."

I realized this cool, no frigid, character didn't know what had happened to Dr. Kincaid. Would she melt when Craig informed her of his murder?

CHAPTER TWENTY

"Give me a garden of beautiful flowers
where I can walk undisturbed."
--*Walt Whitman*

D r. Abbott sat with her hands neatly folded in her lap. She stared at Craig and insisted on knowing why the police were asking about her business with Dr. Kincaid.

Craig didn't delay any longer. "Doctor, I am sorry to inform you… your friend, Dr. Kincaid is dead."

The shock and grief didn't come. She didn't even take a moment to absorb the news before she demanded, "How?"

She wasn't mincing words, and neither would Craig. "The professor was murdered."

"Who killed him?" she shot back.

I was surprised at how she was dealing with murder. I wasn't expecting a grand display of emotion, but most people would have shown at least some small sign of shock, surprise, or grief. Maybe a shaking hand or a damp eye.

Craig cleared his throat. Had she surprised him, too? "I'm sorry for the loss of your friend."

"Who..." she began, but her voice cracked, the first true sign of emotion. She began again. "Who did it?"

"It is still early in our investigation. I'm hoping you can help us."

She smoothed down the fabric of her tunic top. Was her wall of calm cracking? "I can't imagine how, but I will if I can, detective."

"I realize this is a difficult time for you—"

She interrupted him. "Not at all. Ask your questions so you can leave."

"Alright, I have reason to believe this item may be at the center of this murder case. It is vital for me to understand what it was and why it was so important. Therefore, I would appreciate it if you would tell me everything you know. Your information may help me catch the killer of your friend."

"Where should I begin?" she asked, a little contrite.

"Why don't you start by telling me how you knew the professor," Craig suggested.

I settled back in the plush sofa to listen. I wanted to give her the impression I was almost bored by what she had to say, but I was listening intently. This woman was not going to give up control or share things she knew easily. I wondered why.

She inhaled deeply and crossed her hands in her lap. Then, with a sigh, she began. "I've known the professor for years. We were both in academia with specialties in history. I was at a prestigious university in New Jersey, which one is not pertinent to this conversation. As you probably know, his focus was U.S. history, specifically the Civil War. My area of concentration was the Victorian Era. As you may imagine, it is helpful for a historian to see artifacts, furniture, and other items of interest associated with the period of interest. The Civil War offers an abundance of buttons, stirrups, armaments... that sort of thing. Not of any great interest to me. But the professor enjoyed talking with one of our colleagues, a fellow historian, who used to live in this area. Occasionally I would join them for dinner or a glass of wine to exchange ideas and impressions. From time to time, we would attend auctions in Philadelphia, Baltimore, and Washington, D. C. We went to New York City a time or two as well."

"May I know the name of this other historian?" Craig asked.

"I do not think it would do any harm since he has passed away. His name was Dr. Jack Finlay."

"He was my uncle." The words were out of my mouth before I realized it. My response got a frown from Craig which I ignored.

Dr. Abbott cocked her head to the side, with renewed interest. "Ah, the connection. It explains why *you* are here."

I had more than a connection. I had a claim to information she had about Uncle Jack and Dr. Kincaid. I met her pointed gaze that was evaluating me again across the antique coffee table between us. I spoke clearly so she would get my message. "Yes, I am here, as his niece, heir, and executor of his will."

The woman's eyebrows shot up in surprise, then relaxed. She settled back in her chair. She lifted her hands from her lap and rested them on the arms of the chair. "The professor was given to understand Dr. Finlay had found a particular article from the time period. He had no idea what it was. Do you know?" Her blue eyes, once dull with boredom, now sparkled with interest.

"I may." I said, succinctly. I would play her silly game but give only as much as she was willing to give in return. Craig flashed me a look that said, Behave.

"As a matter of fact," he said. "We may have identified something of interest."

Her fingers gripped the arms of the chair. "And it is?"

"Oh, would you like to see it?" Craig asked in a nonchalant way.

I thought she was going to jump right out of her chair, but she quickly controlled herself. "Yes, I think I might find it of interest."

He turned to me. "Emma, would you mind bringing it in from the car please?"

I was a little surprised he was going to show her, but Craig knew a lot more about interrogation than I did. He handed me the car's key fob and I hustled out of the room to retrieve it as fast as possible. I didn't want to miss a thing.

When I walked back into the room and she saw I carried a rolled-up towel, her nose scrunched up as if she smelled something distasteful. I assumed it was because a towel is a personal item and had no place in her living room. I didn't care. I took my place on the sofa and held the towel above the coffee table, trying to be polite. "May I?"

"If you must," she said as she rose. After she moved the vase of flowers and a decorating magazine out of the way, she stood over me, waiting for me to unwrap the article. I did so with great care. I could feel her growing anticipation electrify the air. I kept my movements slow and careful. At last, I pulled away the last corner of the towel to reveal the walking stick.

Her face screwed up in disappointment, or was it disgust? "That's it? A cane?" She looked from me to Craig and back to the object we suspected was so important a man had been killed.

"It is a gentleman's walking stick. They were popular in Victorian England, weren't they?" I asked.

"Of course. Ladies also used a variety of walking sticks associated with certain occasions, such as a promenade in the park. To be accurate, they did not *use* them and certainly not the way Americans do today, to keep themselves upright. Back then, a person *wore* a walking stick. The formal walking stick was fashioned of a fine wood with fine silver workmanship. It was probably reserved for more formal occasions unless its owner was wealthy. Then there was no concern about it being ostentatious. The gentlemen could use it anytime during the day or evening. Ladies selected walking sticks to match their ensemble and the occasion, however, only an older person or a royal personage would wear a walking stick at a formal event." She reached out, her hand hovering over Uncle Jack's walking stick and looked up at me, grudgingly asking for permission.

I nodded.

She picked it up and inspected it from one end to the other "Do you know where Dr. Finlay got it?"

"Do you have an idea?" Craig asked in response.

"I wish I did," Dr. Abbott said with the briefest of sighs. "He used to prowl the region for promising barn sales and auctions. He checked out online auctions as well. He loved the hunt."

I nodded my head in agreement. "Hunting for things associated with the Civil War was one of his favorite things."

"Without knowing where he got this, it will probably be impossible to know who owned the cane. It could have been anybody." She turned her head in my direction and those icy blue eyes bore into me. "Are you sure you have no idea where he found it?"

I cocked my head and frowned. "Why would I lie to you? I want to know as much about it – no, even more about it than you do. And I want to help the police find out to killed Professor Kincaid." My back straightened with indignation. "I—"

She waved a hand in the air as if batting away a fly. "Yes, yes." She sighed. "I guess this situation has upset me more than I realized. I should apologize."

Yes, you should, I thought. But she didn't, not really.

Instead, she turned her attention to the detective. "One

thing bothers me. Dr. Finlay liked to pick up things on these outings of his."

I was ready to be done with this woman, but there might still be something to learn from her. "He brought home interesting pieces and kept them around the house."

She smiled like the cat who ate the canary and didn't get caught. "See? There might be something of interest only an experienced eye would see."

It sounded like Uncle Jack wasn't the only one who loved the hunt. I had to be careful. The last thing I wanted her to learn about was the plantation desk Uncle Jack had tucked away in the garage along with its secret connection to Daniel.

"Have you considered this is not the piece Professor Kincaid was searching for? Look at it. It appears to be a simple cane." She turned to me. "You should leave this piece with me. I can research its—"

There was no way I was leaving Uncle Jack's walking stick with this woman. I had to refuse firmly and politely. "Thank you for your kind offer, but I cannot impose. Besides, it is important to my family, and I wouldn't want to put the responsibility for its safety on you."

"Then maybe you should invite me to this Cottage you inherited. I might be able to spot something more valuable, more important than this piece. I would—"

Craig jumped in quickly. "This piece is interesting on its own. It's hiding a secret. Do you know what it is?"

The woman shot a look of impatience at the detective, grabbed the handle and lower section of wood, and twisted. "A flask. Not unusual." She screwed the pieces back together. "It's such a shame to waste this secret space for wine or spirits. I suppose a man must have his restorative. Instead, he could have hidden a knife there, protection if he needed it. Those were dangerous times. Or maybe the owner was ordinary, not worthy of attention or a threat."

I wondered if this woman ever had a kind word for

anyone. She returned the walking stick to the coffee table, her interest exhausted.

Now, bored, she admitted, "It might be of interest to a beginning collector. It does not have the earth-shattering historical significance Professor Kincaid, or you, believe it has." She sat back in her chair, finished with the subject.

"That's it?" Craig asked.

She shrugged. "The key you're looking for isn't here." She ran her fingers lightly over the wood shaft of the walking stick. They stopped at the place where I'd found the carved initials. "This is curious. I need to get my magnifying glass." She jumped up. "I will not be a moment."

I grabbed the walking stick and began wrapping it in the towel again. "It's not necessary. I've looked. It's just a little damage. Nothing special." I hoped Craig could read my lips when I mouthed, Let's go!

He frowned a little in confusion but stood up. "Doctor, I'm afraid we must go. Thank you for your help."

She rushed back in the room waving a large Sherlock Holms-style magnifying glass. "I have it now. I..." Her words trailed off when she saw us heading toward the door with the rolled-up towel under my arm.

"Thank you," Craig said again. "I'll be in touch if I have more questions." And we sprinted to the car.

As we drove down the lane, Craig asked, "What was that all about?"

"I don't like her. Don't trust her. The way she was trying to wheedle her way into the Cottage was creepy. And the way she assumed we were withholding information from her..." I groaned.

"Well, you were not telling her everything. You didn't tell her about the initials."

"I did it on purpose. It's none of her business. I don't need her snooping around and I don't need her to tell me who owned this walking stick. I already know. She doesn't get to nose around in TJ's family history."

"No, you're going to do it. You will tell me what you find, right?"

I took in a little breath. I wasn't used to having someone looking over my shoulder, someone like a police detective. What if Craig questioned my methods, how I discovered certain things. I couldn't exactly say, *Oh, I write letters to ghosts, and they tell me things.*

"Yes, of course." I said, and silently added, I'll make the information so compelling, you'll forget to ask how I uncovered it.

CHAPTER TWENTY-ONE

A calling card is used when a person prefers to promote himself rather than a business.

Craig drove up to the front steps of the Cottage and stopped.

"Thank you for an amazing time." I reached for the door handle.

"About the card Stanley gave you," he said.

I reached into my pocket and held it up for him to see. "I have it right here."

"May I see it?" He took it and handled it by the edges only. "May I keep this?"

"What? Are you going to check him out and run his fingerprints?" I asked.

"Yes, I am," he said.

I looked at him in sad disbelief. "You don't trust anybody, do you?" Then realized with a spark of excitement, it was a good thing. He was still looking for other suspects, not just focusing on me.

"Sure, I do." He wiggled his eyebrows. "But not everybody is who they say they are."

Craig was right, though Stanley struck me as a man who was probably more than he appeared. "Can I take a picture of it, at least? I'm curious about him."

He held out the card and waited while I took a shot. What did we ever do before smart phones? I frowned when he slipped it into an evidence bag.

"I want to preserve the fingerprints, just in case. Come on, Emma, I'm working a murder case. I suspect everybody."

"Even me?" I felt the tingle of the handcuffs on my wrist and the icy fear run through me. "Wait, don't answer that." Quick to switch the conversation, I entered Stanley Archibald Holt into Google and got so many hits. "Let's see what Google says about the man. Wow, there are articles about him in the *Wall Street Journal, New York Times, Washington Post, and the Los Angeles Times*. He has a Wikipedia page." I scrolled through pictures, lots of pictures of him in a tuxedo at a dinner, a gala, a microphone. Always with some young woman or other with perfect hair, perfect makeup, perfect gown on his arm. "He gets around. Want to see?" I turned to Craig. "I think we have the real thing here. One very wealthy man who is enjoying his money."

"Thanks for his card. I'll get it back to you when I'm finished with it." He gestured toward the Cottage. "Now, off you go. I have work to do." As I got out of the car and was about to close the door, he added, "Thanks for your help, Emma."

I waved goodbye as he drove away, sprinted inside, and locked the door. I wanted to get to work, too. First, I had to clear a place on the dining room table, where I researched Emma's diaries and the things from her secret room at Waterwood House. I turned on the chandelier above the table, squinting at the sudden flood of light. It was too much for regular use, but perfect for inspecting an antique of interest. Maybe TJ could install a dimmer.

TJ.

My life seemed to revolve around this man. I felt safe and yes, happy here on the Eastern Shore. But it was more than the place. The man who lived up the drive at Waterwood House played a big part. I had to give him credit for getting me through physical therapy so I could walk like a normal person and rely on the leg the doctors had almost amputated. He was fun and caring and liked to celebrate life's little triumphs. The search and discovery of so many of his family's secrets had filled empty spaces in my life I barely knew were there. Life events, like the hurt and disappointment from the divorce, finding a new place to live while I healed, dealing with the devastating results of the accident, had created those empty places. It had taken TJ and Uncle Jack to help me fill them again.

Uncle Jack.

To ward off the tears threatening to come again, I unwrapped the walking stick he had found and slipped it under his old magnifying glass on a stand. I began my inspection by focusing on the rough spot where I'd found the initials of Emma's husband.

JTC - It was small and somewhat obscured by decades of dirt. I gently flicked some away with my fingernail. Now, it was clearer to see. Was it just luck the Doctor hadn't caught it while making her initial inspection? Or had she ignored it on purpose, planning to manipulate me so the walking stick would stay with her? Then she could do her research in private and keep the results to herself. But I already knew about those initials, who had owned the stick, and more. I wasn't about to share what I knew unless I absolutely had to, if ever.

This simple piece of fine wood with its ornate handle triggered so many questions. I was convinced it was a valued possession of Joshua Thomas Collins. How had it disappeared from Waterwood House and popped up in a barn sale or auction? I might never know. The important thing was it had come home and maybe there was something to discover about the time Joshua used it.

From what I'd read in Emma's diaries about her husband, I knew he was a scoundrel.

He was a thief, stealing Emma's newborn daughter and selling her to someone on the Western Shore. In Emma's diary entry, she asked again, what happened to my daughter?

I'd become so emotionally involved in her story. I felt a deep need to find the answer though it appeared to be an impossible task. Families spent years researching their ancestors and too often came up with more questions and few answers. At least they had names, places, dates. I had almost nothing. No baptismal records. TJ's family had no record of the child in their Bible, except she had died at birth. A lie. There was a stone marker for the baby in the family graveyard. Another lie.

I rested my chin on my hand and stared at the walking stick.

Joshua Thomas Collins. Scoundrel. Thief. And what?

CHAPTER TWENTY-TWO

Mined in Afghanistan, Russia, and Peru,
Lapis Lazuli was thought by the ancients
to inspire and reveal universal truths.

.

N ow, curiosity gave birth to another thought. This
walking stick might point to answers about Emma's
daughter.

A slow, deep breath steadied me so I wouldn't overlook
something in my excitement. My slow, careful inspection
began at the top of the stick. The wood around the Lapis
Lazuli and silver handle looked polished. I wondered if men
had always worn gloves when they *walked out* in the 1860s.
Emma had written in her diary about Joshua traveling to
places like Baltimore, Philadelphia, and New York. His gloves
of superior quality worked as a polish cloth for the gemstone
and silver filigree around it. The small white star, probably
another gemstone, was set in the blue stone. The silver work
around the knob featured the same five-point star repeated
again and again. I twisted the knob as the Doctor had done

and the stick separated to reveal the flask. I looked at it carefully, but there wasn't a clue hidden here.

With the knob screwed back in place, I began a careful examination down the shaft using the magnifying glass. About two-thirds of the way down the shaft, I found it.

At least, I found something. A narrow line ran around the diameter of the stick. Was it part of the wood grain? No, too regular. A repair? If so, it was the work of a true craftsman. Could it be... No, the Doctor had said it was a waste the secret compartment hid for a flask.

One compartment. Maybe she was wrong. Maybe *this* walking stick had two.

I grabbed the stick firmly and twisted. Nothing. There wasn't even a hint of movement. Before I would allow myself to be disappointed, I remembered the first compartment hadn't given up its secret easily.

I wiped my hands—my palms were a little damp from the excitement—and gripped the wood shaft again. With a prayer that it wouldn't break it, I twisted it hard.

The pieces shifted. Carefully, I unscrewed the stick until there were two pieces. Inside the lower section there was a second compartment.

It was narrow, allowing little room for anything to be hidden there. I turned the piece upside down hoping something would fall out. Nothing. I put it up to my eye, hoping to see something. Again, nothing. I stuck my finger inside the opening, room only for about half of my little finger. There was something there, I could feel it. I twisted the shaft and pulled my finger out slowly. Something appeared, tightly coiled on itself, barely poking out of the opening.

It needed help to escape its hiding place. My thumb and forefinger were too large and clumsy. This work required a delicate touch. Maybe Uncle Jack had stored some tools to deal with historical things. Looking in the bookcases and drawer in the table by his chair yielded nothing. I even checked an old cigar box on a bottom shelf. It held a roll of tape and a marker... and a pair of tweezers with flattened tips. Perfect.

Working under the magnifying glass on the stand, the cleaned tips grabbed onto the scroll wedged tightly inside. With a little more force, it moved out of its wooden hiding place and sprang open.

I put the scroll on a piece of muslin left over from working with the diaries. It lay curled up. This wasn't a job for bare hands, dirty or moist with natural oils. Where were those white cotton gloves Charles, the reference librarian, had given me when I was working with Emma's diaries? After checking the kitchen drawers, I walked back in the dining room, put my hands on my hips, and looked at everything there. Seeing a small drawer at the right end of the antique buffet, I reached and pulled it open. The gloves popped out from the tight spot I'd stuffed them.

Now, properly equipped, I spread the coiled piece of heavy paper flat. It took great care, because there were a bunch of little boxes cut out of the sheet. Careful not to tear it in any way, I analyzed the position of the boxes and found they were in no particular order or placement.

Why was this piece of paper with holes cut out of it carefully rolled up and placed in a secret compartment of a gentleman's cane? There wasn't a word or even a mark to help me identify what this was. Quickly, I took a picture in case Craig needed a record of what I'd found. I examined it again under the magnifying glass, moving it slowly and systematically from the top to the bottom. Just as I was sure this was a useless exercise, I saw a black dot, one black dot in the center along the bottom edge of the sheet. Even under the glass, it was only a dot made with an ink pen.

Great. What did it mean? I folded my arms, frustration growing. How could the elation of discovery descend into frustration so easily? Staring at the page, one thing about the placement of the boxes made sense, maybe. They were all configured horizontally, not vertically. They weren't uniform but cut in different sizes or lengths. They lined up and were evenly spaced all the way down the page. Unfortunately, there was no obvious explanation for its function or importance.

Why was it so difficult and complicated to look into the past? I remembered what Doctor Abbot had said as she walked us to the door, unhappy we were leaving and taking Uncle Jack's walking stick with us. She'd reminded us she had not one, but two doctorates, one in history and one in economics.

"An impressive accomplishment though it sounds brutal," I'd said.

"Yes, it is," she'd agreed, with no idea of how pompous it sounded. She'd gone on to say it was vital to understand human behaviors in both economics and in history. Only when we had an appreciation for the way people responded to conditions, situations, and stresses could we hope to avoid making the same mistakes in the future.

I'd known Craig was curious about her financial situation, so I wasn't surprised when he'd asked her if it would have been more financially rewarding to stay in economics than become a historian.

I remembered her answer. "Possibly," she'd said with a glint of a smile, but then it faded. "Unfortunately, the world of finance was and continues to be an old boys' network. The guys on Wall Street do a lot of bonding over martinis and cigars. I enjoy a good martini." She'd shuddered. "But I cannot abide cigars. Being a historian is much more civilized and certainly less frenetic. One cannot lose a million dollars of one's client money because one slept in on a Thursday morning. Don't misunderstand me. History can be messy, but one has the luxury to think, research, and consider different situations."

That was before. New questions were bothering my brain.

What situation made Joshua hide this holey piece of paper in his walking stick? Unlike the historian, I didn't have the patience, nor the background to carefully consider the facts. I had the one fact that could unlock secrets: I knew about the man who owned this walking stick. He was many things. The presence of this historical antique suggested there was still more to discover about this man. Did he play a role in the war? If so, what did he do?

I heaved a deep sigh. The holey piece of paper went into a baggie to protect it. Now, how was I going to find out? I needed help. The answer might be in the Waterwood House, but I'd already wandered around and been overwhelmed by just the possibilities I could dream up. I needed an expert. It meant the library and the Maryland Room in Easton, the place I'd found so many answers in the past. But there was a problem. I needed to get there.

CHAPTER TWENTY-THREE

"The future is no more uncertain
than the present."
—*Walt Whitman*

TJ poked his head just inside the kitchen door. "Emma, are you here?"

"Yes!" I called out. "Come in."

"I knocked at the front door, but there was no answer. I saw Maureen's car leaving. She sure has a spiffy ride and knows how to handle it on a curve."

"I hope so. She spent a bundle on driving lessons at the Porsche training track down south. She learned her lessons well. When I'm riding with her, I feel comfortable."

"Not holding on to the chicken bar?" he asked with a wink.

"No," I said proudly. "I'm getting braver every day. And, speaking of the day, how was yours?"

"To be honest, I'm exhausted."

"Why don't you sit down and catch your breath?" He looked a little pale, his face drawn.

He pulled out one of the kitchen chairs and fell into it. "I've been working since sun-up and still have to fill out some paperwork before I can hit the rack."

"Why don't I give you some dinner? As usual, Maria has made enough for an army."

He didn't waste a second. "Thanks. I'm starved." He rubbed his face with his hands, working hands, but they weren't calloused and scarred. With a nod of his head, he gestured toward the patio outside. "I see they took down the police tape. Are they all done?"

"I think so. This has been quite a day." I was beginning to fill him on the details when I noticed his eyes had closed, and his breathing was regular. I quietly busied myself getting dinner ready using some of the things the housekeeper Maria always left in the fridge or on the counter for my meals. When I'd first come to the Shore, I couldn't cook or clean for myself and needed her help. Now, I was more independent, but I didn't have the heart to let her go. Besides, she was a much better cook than I could ever hope to be.

Was it my gentle nudge or the delicious aromas rising from the plate I put down in front of TJ that woke him? A little groggy, he said, "Oh, this looks great!" He grabbed a fork and food began disappearing. While he ate, I nibbled. I was always astonished at the amount of food he could put away and still look trim. Hours of physical farm work and fresh air must have balanced it.

While he ate, I told him of my discovery of Uncle Jack's great find which was probably the reason of the professor's murder. I told him of our visit to Billy Bob's auction house, his weird cousin Wendell, and how a random question led us to another university professor. TJ almost choked when I repeated her words, *You may call me Doctor*.

After I cleared away the dishes, I retrieved the

gentleman's walking stick from its hiding-in-plain-sight hiding place. "Let me show you what we found." I unscrewed the shaft from the top to reveal a flask. TJ was impressed. I reunited the pieces and ran my hands down toward the tip, gripped, and twisted again.

When the two pieces came apart, his eyebrows shot up in horror. "You broke it."

I laughed. "No, it was made to come apart."

"I've heard of some canes having a secret compartment, but two? And you found it. Good for you. Was there anything inside?"

I screwed the second section back together. "Yes, there was something, but it's baffling. I'll get it." I returned the cane to the hall umbrella stand, picked the paper sheet of tiny windows, and took it to the kitchen along with the towel I'd used to carry the walking stick.

When I laid the paper on the table, TJ drew his eyebrows drew together. "I don't understand. What is it?"

"I don't know."

"Are you sure it's important?" he asked. "It looks like an old piece of paper with a bunch of holes cut into it. What does it mean? There's no pattern I can see." Baffled, he looked up at me. "Do you see something I'm missing?"

"No, it's a mystery to me." I said, nodding my head. "When I first saw it, I thought it was a torn piece of paper, but look closely. Every hole had clean edges. Nothing was torn. The paper was cut intentionally."

I sat down, a little sigh escaping my lips. "I don't know what it all means, but I believe Uncle Jack knew." Into the silent grief in my heart, I whispered, *Uncle Jack, I know I say this every day, but today, I really mean it. I wish you were here.*

"It's all very interesting, I'm sure, but I'm too tired to work out any puzzles right now. If it doesn't have something to do with me, Waterwood's fields or my custom farming business, it will have to wait for another time." TJ glanced at me and frowned when he noticed I was sitting silently with my lips squeezed together. "You look like you're trying to keep something from escaping from you."

I shrugged half-heartedly with one shoulder.

"Come on, out with it. I said I'm too tired to play games." His tone was a little sharp, not normal for this mild-mannered man.

I was so eager to tell him, then felt guilty for bothering him when he was tired and now, I'd pushed him to snap at me. I'd better just come out with it. I relaxed my lips and felt the tingle of warm blood rushing back into them. "I think the walking stick belonged to your ancestor, Joshua Collins."

He jerked up in his chair. "Emma's husband?" He was referring to Emma who'd lived during the Civil War, the daughter and later the mistress of Waterwood. "This fine piece of wood belonged to that no-good—"

I held up my hand for him to stop. "It's true."

TJ sank back in his chair like a deflating balloon. "How can you know…"

"His initials, JTC, are carved near the top where the shaft meets the silver handle. They're small, but they are there. I may have to go back to Waterwood and look around some more. Didn't Joshua have a library or study in the house?"

TJ sat silently watching me. It almost looked like he was in pain. Maybe he wasn't following the logic.

I jumped up. "I'll get it and show you."

He waved me back in my chair. "I believe you." He drew in a jagged breath. "You're saying this all has something to do with Waterwood and it's important, right?"

A pained expression clouded his face. I knew he cared about Waterwood. Nothing was closer to his heart. But in my excitement, I hadn't considered his feelings. Now, I had a chance to smoothe things over and keep it light. "Yes, it's important, but you don't have to *do* anything. Just know I found something of interest..." I slowed down my speech when a strange look came over TJ's face.

He made a grumpy sound. I didn't think he believed me.

"Does this have to do with Craig's murder investigation?" he demanded to know.

"Yes. Well, no. Maybe, in a way. We're not sure yet." I said in a rush. "I'm just doing some research for Craig. I—" A wave of guilt swept over me. TJ had asked me not to get involved. And I had. "It's just research. I can handle that part." I dearly wanted him to agree.

Instead, his face tightened into a stern expression I'd never seen before. "Oh, I have no doubt you can do it all... and you'll stir up a hornet's nest." I started to protest, but he shook me off. "Do you want to know what worries me? You're going to do all this work while there is a murderer running around loose." He jumped out of his chair, almost knocking it over. "Emma, you need protection. I don't have time to babysit you." His voice was louder than I'd ever heard. Normally, he was so mild-mannered, easy-going, but now... "Emma, you need to drop this."

"I'm only helping Craig—"

"You're piecing together the motive for the murder!"

"I'm not in any danger. Craig will—"

TJ wouldn't let me finish. "Craig has a job to do, and it is *not* watching out for you, protecting you every minute of the day. His job is to find the killer."

"Yes, but—" Again, he didn't let me finish.

"No buts. His job description does not read, Protect Emma at all times." Then the true source of his anger and frustration became clear. "I can't protect you while you do your thing. I'm barely here as it is. This is spring planting season, Emma. My job is to keep myself on the tractor. The work I do now takes care of me and Waterwood for another season. I can't do that job if I'm worrying about you. You need to stop and let Craig do his job...ALONE. You have to stop, Emma!"

Was it the way he said my name, EMMM-MMMAAA? Was it the way he was ordering me around? He sounded like my ex-husband who had tried to control me while chasing after other women. I don't know why but my emotions erupted. I jumped to my feet and screamed, "I'll do whatever I want to do, mister. You're not the boss of me."

We glared at each other.

Then he let out a breath and sagged back in his chair. "No, no, I'm not, Miss Emma." He took in a deep breath. "And a good thing, 'cause you're a handful. And I don't have the time or energy to deal with you now." He grabbed his napkin and slapped it down on the table. "Thanks for the dinner. Good night!" His words bit the air as he stormed out of the Cottage.

I put my hand on the table to steady myself and stared at the door. Was it still vibrating from the moment he'd slammed it? I could barely breath. Every ounce of energy drained away and I collapsed in the chair. TJ...

CHAPTER TWENTY-FOUR

"I hate commas in the wrong places."
    —Walt Whitman

The next morning, I was glad to see Maureen drive up to the Cottage. I didn't want to tell what had happened the night before with TJ. I didn't even want to think about it. But it flooded my mind. I had picked up my phone a dozen times to text him. No, I should call him. No, a text would be better. But each time, I put the phone down. I couldn't think what to say. I think I was too busy piecing my heart back together. At least she would distract me from thinking about him. I went to the door to meet her.

"Good morning," I called out as she lifted a tote from her back seat. "I didn't think we had a writing session this morning."

"We don't. I brought you a few writing books to leaf through. See if something catches your eye."

I took the tote and was a little surprised how heavy it was. "Do you want to come in? I have coffee."

Maureen was shaking her head. "No, thank you. I'm going to Easton. Do you want anything?"

I paused for a moment, unsure if I should ask or...

Maureen was inspecting my face. "There's something going on in that head of yours. Out with it."

After what happened the night before, I didn't want to lose another friend. When I didn't respond immediately, she held her arms out wide and let them drop to her sides. "If we can talk about something as personal as an Internal Editor, we should be able to talk about anything."

"I don't want to impose," I began hesitantly. "And if the answer is no, it's okay."

She folded her arms and stared down her nose at me. "Out with it."

"Could I hitch a ride to the library in Easton? I can probably get a ride back with—"

"Nonsense. I'll take you to Easton and I'll bring you home. How long do you need to get ready?"

"About three minutes," I called out as I headed up the steps.

When we were in the car, I relaxed to enjoy the ride, but Maureen wasn't one to waste time. "Remember the book I gave you called *Bird By Bird* by Anne Lamont?" I nodded. "It tells you how you're going to write this book, bird by bird... or one step at a time."

"I mean..." Now, my face felt really hot. "Do I begin by using a pen and paper or do I use the computer?" I didn't want to admit to her neither way was satisfactory for me.

Maureen laughed. "You have no idea how many people want to know how a writer writes. Use whatever method is comfortable for you and gets the job done."

"But what if..."

"You fail?" Maureen chuckled. "This is your first novel. Do you know how many authors bury their first novel or their second or even their third novel in the bottom drawer of the desk?"

"Why?"

"Because they are much better writers today than when they started. You will learn your craft by studying but the real key to accomplishment is writing every day! Will you write about the people who lived in Waterwood House, your namesake Emma?"

"No, I don't think so. I feel it is Emma's personal story. I need to come up with a story involving my own characters and how they are affected by historical events. Then it will be my story." A little laugh escaped my lips. "I could use some of the research I have and set the story in the mid-19ᵗʰ century. Yes, I think it would be fun."

Maureen burst out in a fit of laughter. "Please," she said when she finally got her breath. "Please write it down on a piece of paper and put it in a prominent place."

"Why?"

"As you go through this process, you will need to remind yourself you accepted the challenge and thought it would be fun. Trust me, you're going to need the reminder as you go along, because writing a novel is hard work. There will be times you will want to quit but yes, it is fun."

I felt like it was the first day of school for my kindergarten class. New challenges, new experiences, new memories. Everything was possible.

But Maureen wasn't finished. "It will be fun, except for the little voice in your head."

I almost panicked. Did Maureen know about Daniel and Emma? "Who...who do you mean? I'm at the Cottage alone."

"You're never alone when you're writing," she insisted. "You start writing a description of a place in the story, or a sketch of the main character. And BAM!" Her palm struck the steering wheel. "Your worst enemy shows up."

My eyes grew wide. "Who?"

"Your Internal Editor, the little voice inside your head saying you're not good enough. Everybody has one. They just might not realize it." Maureen chuckled. "A writer's Internal Editor is always looking over your shoulder, ready and eager to point out what you've written is terrible, childish, wordy... Ah, the list can go on and on."

I was a little confused. "How do I know if—"

"Your Internal Editor is in the room? If you're working on a computer, you type and type then your fingers pause over the keys. A little voice whispers, 'You can do better' and you hit the delete button. Same thing happens if you're writing with a pen, except you scratch out what you have and make a big mess. Sound familiar?"

My mouth was hanging open. "How did you know? I figured it was because I'm new and should keep going back until I got it right."

"How did I know? It happens to everyone, newbies, experienced editors, published authors."

I burst out laughing. "Oh, if you only knew..."

"Oh, but I do. My Internal Editor shows up every time I sit down at the computer. The difference is I have found a way to make him be quiet."

"Oh, please tell me your secret."

"You'll develop your own technique to tone down the negative voice. I gave mine a name, Franco, because he sounds like a little dictator. Only he liked it. Gave him more power. Then I started using the nickname, Frankie. He hated it. Thought it was disrespectful." Maureen roared with laughter. "It was, but it made him go away to pout and he left me alone!" She wiped a tear from her eye. "Don't worry, you'll learn when to listen to that little voice."

Not only in writing, I thought, but in an investigation as well.

CHAPTER TWENTY-FIVE

*Mission of an Historical Society: To promote and encourage
historical research; to acquire preserve, and protect sites
records, relics, and other things of historic interest;
and to promote public knowledge of
local and national history.*

I walked into the main county library building and home of the Maryland Room, the curated reference room held stacks for all things Maryland Eastern Shore. People crowded around a special desk by the entrance.

A librarian, carrying an armful of books, stopped to say, "Oh, we just put out our seed library. With the weather warming up, everyone is thinking about their gardens. Spring is in the air. Isn't it wonderful?"

Wonderful? Hmmm, I wasn't so sure. The flower beds around the Cottage could use some attention. With a strong and healthy leg, I realized I should add gardening to my to-do list. But not right now. It was time to visit the Maryland Room for some answers.

Charles, the dedicated research librarian, greeted me warmly but in hushed whispers, of course. The man was careful and precise in his work, and still as skinny as the first time I'D met him. His fascination and curiosity with the past often made him forget to eat. He was devoted to the books, manuscripts, letters, newspapers, everything placed in his charge. If only he would handle the present the same way he organized and protected the past. As usual, a small white towel hung from his belt so he could wipe his hands before he touched any item in his care. Oil and dirt were his enemy.

We caught up and then he asked, "What kind of challenge have you brought me today?"

I looked around the room and thankfully we were alone. "Let me show you." We sat down at a library table, so I didn't have to crane my neck to talk with him. He was the tallest man I'd ever met who didn't play basketball. I pulled a plastic baggie containing the holey piece of paper from my big tote. "Any idea what this is?"

His eyebrows shot up toward his receding hairline. "Something my granddaughter would make if we allowed her to use scissors?" he said with a weak chuckle. "But I don't think it's what you wanted to hear, is it?"

"No, afraid not." I straightened the baggie to make sure the paper lay flat. "The only thing I know is it has historical significance and probably dates back to the Civil War."

I jumped when a soft voice spoke from behind me. When I turned, a bland-looking woman was trying to peer over my shoulder. She was short, a little soft around the edges. Salt-and-pepper hair was pulled back in a bun at the nape of her neck. Brown eyes sparked behind thick bifocal glasses.

"Oh, I'm so sorry. I didn't mean to startle you." Her apology was honest and sincere, but there was a note of urgency. "I get excited when I come across a rare, historical artifact. If what you have there is what I think it is, I'm excited."

Charles made the introductions. "Emma, meet Pamela Ridgley, well-known historian with the Talbot County Historical Society." He introduced me as an amateur history buff. If this woman was an actual historian and we talked too long, she might sense I had unusual sources. She gave me the impression she would not back away from anything that piqued her interest. I feared she would be full of questions if she suspects I had unusual sources.

"You may be right about your artifact. It could have some historical implications," she said as she pulled out a pair of white cotton gloves and held out her hands to me. "May I?"

"You know what it is?" I asked, a little incredulous as I handed her the baggie.

She took a moment to examine it, holding it close to her thick glasses. "I'm not certain, but it looks like a Cardano Grille." She looked up and saw both Charles and I were lost. "Sorry again. A true Cardano Grille is a piece of paper or leather with small rectangular windows or boxes cut out. When laid over a written letter, words or portions of letters would reveal a secret message." Spoken like a teacher. Her information was helpful, but her next question threw me. "Do you have the correspondence?" She smoothed down her blouse of royal blue that matched a color in her bright print skirt. "There should be a letter with it."

"I haven't found anything yet," I replied, a little nervous.

Her shoulders sagged. "Oh dear, then this grille is just a curiosity. Without the letter, it is well..." She shrugged her shoulders as her words trailed off.

"I'm still looking," I said quickly. "I haven't found any correspondence, yet." My last word snagged her interest again.

She brightened. "Oh, you have someone to help you. That's good, but if you need—"

"Thank you, I'll let you know." Just what I needed, another expert crawling around the Cottage. I had to stop being so interesting. "I'm so glad you're here now. You've sparked my interest. How does this grille and letter thing work? Why would someone use it?"

"Ah, now it gets interesting." Her eyes sparkled. "A Cardano Grille was used to hide secret messages. If I remember correctly, a man named Cardano, an Italian mathematician, developed it in the 1500s, but the concept may date back to ancient China. A dark history is attached to the grille. Cardinal Richelieu might have used it for much of his correspondence. Even George Washington had spies who used the technique during the Revolutionary War."

Captivated, Charles asked, "How would it work?"

"Both the sender and recipient had to have the grille with small rectangular windows or boxes cut out at certain intervals. The sender begins by laying the grille over a blank sheet of paper and writing the secret message in the boxes. Now comes the tricky part. The grille is removed, and the sender must fill the rest of the page, so it appears to be an innocent letter. The recipient who had a matching grill would be able to read the secret message."

Charles burst forth. "It's ingenious and so simple."

"It might sound simple, but it was hard to do. The sender had to compose an innocent letter, the more boring the better, around the words and letters of the message. And penmanship was important."

"Why?" I asked, caught up in this intriguing way of passing intelligence.

"Remember, the correspondent wrote the secret message first. Then the rest of the innocent letter was written around those words. If the handwriting wasn't smooth, if it looked choppy or inconsistent, anyone reading it might become suspicious, the last thing anyone in a spy network would want."

"What kind of information would they pass?" I wanted to know.

She took a breath. "The short answer is anything and everything. There is the obvious, of course: troop movements, troop complements-how many men in a particular unit, the cost of flour and other necessary commodities, shortages, and the like. Anything to weaken and defeat the enemy."

"If this spy network existed and the correspondents kept using the same grille, wouldn't someone catch on?" I asked.

"Ah, here it becomes truly ingenious. The grille could be used in several different ways." She reached into the computer bag hanging from a strap over her shoulder and took out a piece of paper and a pen. "Pretend this sheet has boxes or windows cut out here, here, here, here..." She quickly drew several boxes across the page. "...and here. Imagine you have blank letter paper underneath. You can write your message using the grille this way or..." She turned the page of inked boxes upside down. "This way or..." She turned the page over. "This way..." She turned the page upside down once again. "or this way. Four different ways to write a secret message with one grille."

Both Charles and I gazed silently at the grille, lost in our own thoughts.

"Oh, there's one piece of advice they shared with people who used this system. Plan on writing the letter three times to be sure the handwriting and wording of the innocent letter was smooth and natural."

"Wow, who has time to do that?" I blurted out.

"People made time. Those involved in espionage and used this system in the 16th, 17th, 18th, and 19th centuries probably had servants to cater to their daily needs and/or a military staff. They had the time to try to get it right." She paused for a moment and thought. "You know, the Maryland Eastern Shore was a hotbed of confederate activity." She reiterated the reasons for Southern sympathizers finding a home here, information I already knew, thanks to Charles's briefings. "People suspected there was a Confederate spy around here who was the link to a well-placed Confederate spy up North and Richmond, the Confederate capital. This grille may have belonged to him. Who--"

Her revelation caught me off-guard, and I started coughing then choking. Charles had to pat me on the back so I could get my breath.

"Easy, there. Are you okay?" she said. "What I said didn't upset you, did it?"

I shook my head, trying to stifle another cough. "No," I struggled to answer. Once I could breathe normally again, I asked, "Why would it be important to identify a Confederate spy here on the Shore?"

"It would be a coup," she said with a light laugh. "Historians would want to know who the person was, the kinds of information passed, the origin of the information and –"

"Pamela, slow down," Charles insisted. "You're going to overwhelm the poor dear. She just asked a simple question."

"Charles, you know as well as I do a simple question rarely has a simple answer." She flashed him a broad smile. "But you're right, my friend. I do get carried away."

She turned to me. "To give you a simple answer, it could change an historian's career. The discovery alone could suggest new research inquiries. For example, if the spy was identified, who else was part of the network? Was it larger than two people? Another question to address would be, what was the impact of the information? Was it reliable? How much weight was it given? Did it play a role in the decision-making process of how the war was conducted? Did it a difference in the outcome of a battle? I could go on."

"Those are the, oh…" I turned to Charles. "What do you call them?"

"Avenues of academic inquiry?" he suggested.

"Yes, those. But my question concerns the effect the discovery would have on the historian?"

She smiled. "The historian would be very busy. There would be research papers to write for peer review. It is part of the process to make sure the research and findings were valid. Then there would be presentations to prepare and, of course, The Book to write, bringing together all the information, background, and the historian's conclusions."

Her demeanor changed slightly. Her eyes narrowed a little and she peered at me as she leaned forward a bit. "Do you know something?" She pointed at the grille lying innocently on the table. "Where did it come from?" She leaned forward a little more to be sure she heard my answer.

My palms felt damp. I was right. I had to be careful what I said. If I made the slightest error, gave her the least inkling about Daniel, Emma, and the plantation desk, she would pounce to find out the truth. Casually, I raised my shoulders to show I didn't know. "I found it among my uncle's things. He passed away not long ago and I'm going through his things."

Hearing of the loss of a family member, she backed off. "I am so sorry. My condolences."

"Thank you," I said softly as I cast my eyes downward. I hated doing it, but I had to be careful.

"Then I wouldn't let it concern you. In the past what, 160 years, no concrete evidence has come to light to prove those spies ever existed. Frankly, if it hasn't happened by now, it's probably a local legend. Everybody wants to get in on what they think is the glamour of being a spy." She winked, then pulled a large envelope out of her computer case and handed it to Charles. "Here is the information I promised to bring you. This has been fun. Thanks, Emma, for the trip back into the past. If you need anything else, call me. Charles has my number. Gotta run. Thanks again."

I mumbled a good-bye and watched her make her way through the people congregating in the reading room. "That was amazing, Charles. Who is she?"

"Her name is Pamela—"

"I know, but *who* is she?" I asked again.

"Oh. She is a credentialed historian with all the appropriate degrees. One time at an historical society function, she hinted she retired from an agency on the other side of the bay where people liked solving puzzles." When I didn't react, he leaned closer and said under his breath, "NSA, the National Security Administration." He stood straight again and spoke in a normal library reference-room tone, "Now, I'm not sure but…" He tapped his nose.

Secrets. I was surrounded by secrets.

CHAPTER TWENTY-SIX

"The real war will never get in the books."
– *Walt Whitman*

I saw Maureen in the parking lot. As I crossed the street, the gray clouds that had gathered while I was in the library began to leak on the thirsty landscape. We didn't get much snow here on the Shore over the winter and there was no such thing as snowpack here on the flat peninsula.

I yanked open Maureen's car door as the heavens opened. She said, "Good timing."

"Yeah, I wouldn't dare get your car upholstery wet!" After I chuckled, I met her blue eyes, always filled with warmth and caring. "Thank so much for waiting."

"Glad to do it. I like driving around here. Can't stand the hectic traffic of the city." She started the car. "Did you get what you needed?"

I had to think for a minute. Had I made progress on my quest? "Yes, I guess so."

She shot me a quizzical look. "Not exactly a ringing

endorsement."

"No, I guess not. Maybe it's because I got some good information, fascinating even, and walked out with even more questions." I watched the raindrops try to collect on the windshield only to be slapped away by the wipers. If only my worries about the murders and the reasons for such crimes could be swept away as easily. Better to stay in the here-and-now. "Do you get nervous driving in the rain?"

"I'm fine as long as there isn't a tornado or flood warning. The driving school taught me how to handle most situations. Don't worry. Just sit back and relax."

"Okay," I tried to sound relax, but my stomach was tying itself into knots. I'd told TJ the truth. I was getting more comfortable being in a vehicle, especially driving with Maureen, but rain and slick roads were another matter. It had been raining when the semi-tractor trailer had crossed the median and headed for my car. I would be better able to hide my anxiety if there was conversation.

"Why don't you tell me what you did while I was meeting with our esteemed librarian?"

As she launched into her tale of shopping in Easton and how it compared with shopping in New York, I stared out the passenger window. Meeting Pamela, the historical society lady, in the Maryland Room had been sheer luck. Understanding what a piece of paper full of holes could represent had turned my brain inside out. The possibility Joshua Collins was a spy... well, it took my breath away. I thought he might have had sympathies for the South, but I never got the feeling he'd been politically motivated at all.

My first introduction to Joshua was in the ghostly letter from Daniel, son of Waterwood's plantation manager and Emma's close friend. Joshua was described as the son of the despicable owner of a neighboring and almost bankrupt plantation. Before Emma's father left on a trip south, Joshua's father proposed they join their children—Emma, heir to the

SUSAN REISS

Waterwood fortune, and Joshua, his only son—and their lands in a marriage bond. Wisely, Emma's father rejected the plan. Or maybe it wasn't so wise. Joshua and his family became even more desperate which probably led to a fatal confrontation.

When Daniel went with Emma's father on a trip to Southern Virginia to deliver supplies to the Confederacy, Joshua secretly followed them. What happened after they crossed the river was murky. I could only wonder if Joshua followed them with hateful, lethal thoughts in his heart.

Once Emma's father returned to Waterwood alone and worn out by what he had seen, he accepted Joshua to be Emma's husband. From what I knew of the man, Joshua as motivated by one thing: money. After the marriage and death of her father, Joshua left Emma in charge of Waterwood and traveled extensively. Did he position himself to pass secret messages to the Confederacy? The excitement of being a spy might have appealed to him more than dealing with the day-to-day issues of running a plantation. I wondered—

"Emma?" Maureen's voice pulled me out of the past and back into the present. "Where are you? Everything okay?"

"Yes, yes." I repeated and realized the car was stopped in front of the Cottage. "Oh! We're here already. Do you want…" I began, but what could I offer her? I wasn't ready to share my wandering thoughts with anyone yet. I needed some quiet time to think.

"No, I don't want anything, thank you. I'll run along if you're sure you are all right?"

I smiled. "I'm fine. Just lost in my own head and tired."

Maureen released the brake. "Then get some rest."

I waved as she drove away, certain there was no nap in my immediate future. I was staggering under the weight of so many questions. Before I could think about resting, I needed some answers, or, at least, some reliable information. And I knew how to get it.

148

CHAPTER TWENTY-SEVEN

"I exist as I am, that is enough."
–Walt Whitman

I stood at the kitchen window with my hands wrapped around a hot mug of Lady Grey tea. I knew it would help slow down my galloping thoughts. A thin veil of rain fell, more like a spring shower than a threatening storm. I could see the Lone Oak tree across the creek. It had stood there for more than 200 years, maybe more. It had seen countless storms, everything from gentle rainfalls to ferocious Category 3 and 4 hurricanes. It was tall and strong and in the passing years, it thrived. So much time had passed. So much had happened under its branches. My thoughts wandered back to the time when Emma and Daniel had lived here at Waterwood Plantation. A time in the mid-19th century when life was not simple or easy. When issues were not clearly defined or understood.

It was a time marked by the Civil War. People had to take sides though their choices were often complicated. The

Maryland state legislature had been to vote on a proposal to secede from the Union. It was narrowly defeated. But the ties to the Southern way of life and economic model were strong.

In the eastern third of the state, known as the Eastern Shore, plantations of thousands of acres had existed from the Chesapeake Bay to the Atlantic Ocean. Landowners had strong ties to the South and needed cheap labor to farm what had been their main crop since the 1600s: tobacco. Though some people opposed it, slavery came to the Eastern Shore. There had been clashes. Many had to walk a fine line to live their lives.

Living at Waterwood, a large and profitable plantation, Emma could not escape the financial and political realities of the time. When her beloved father implored her to marry Joshua, her life and the fate of Waterwood were sealed.

Looking back, even with a 21st-century perspective, thoughts of Emma's love story and how a young woman's heart was given no choice, made me shudder. Thanks to the connection established by Daniel, one of Emma's letters guided me to her secret room and diaries where I discovered so much more to her story. Now, after my conversation with the historian, I realized I had even more to learn.

What had started with a simple gentleman's walking stick had become a mystery that might lead to the discovery of an unknown spy network of historical significance. Standing here at my kitchen window during a spring shower, I resolved to follow the clues to see if I could prove the existence of the network. It meant wrestling with a long list of questions meant to reveal more of Waterwood's secrets.

I had a unique way to begin, and it was time to use it. I had to write a letter to the mistress of the plantation with whom I shared a first name. Carrying the fountain pen Uncle Jack had given me, I walked down the path, muddy from the recent rain to the cabin. When I graduated from college, he had offered me the top-of-the-line black Mont Blanc fountain pen. Lovely and expensive, but when I'd tried it at the local pen store, I found it was too fat my hand and so heavy, I could barely control it. The proprietor of the tiny shop had a vast selection of fine pens and the patience to help me find the perfect one for me. It was a black Waterman Expert Fountain Pen with gold trim. Nothing ostentatious, just a quietly strong statement that I knew what I was doing and honored the words I was writing. Uncle Jack was right when he had said every young lady should have a fine pen to use when she had to write something important or sign a document. It was appropriate for me to use this pen whenever I wrote to Emma.

My Dearest Emma,

I hope all is well with you and Daniel and your existence together is everything you hoped it would be.

I also want to express my deepest gratitude to you for coming to our assistance in a most dire situation at the cove. You saved us from a man who meant us deadly harm. The little girl who was with me on that darkest of nights had just lost her mother and was in danger of losing the glorious light of childhood optimism and hope. As the weeks and months have gone by, I have visited with little Rosie and am pleased to tell you her light is burning bright once again. She talks often of the lovely lady who appeared above the water.

I remember the day she first saw your portrait in the foyer of Waterwood House. She was filled with delight and admiration. I credit you with not only saving our lives but her spirit as well.

These two words do not express the depth of my gratitude, but still, I say, Thank You.

Now, I hope I do not presume but I am writing to you about another matter. My Uncle Jack came into possession of a gentleman's walking stick. It bears the initials JTC on its shaft. Sadly, I am not able to ask him where or how he procured this lovely piece. Are you familiar with it? Do the initials stand for Joshua Thomas Collins? Was it one of your husband's possessions?

Upon close examination of this walking stick, I discovered not one but two hidden compartments. The first and most obvious one was for a flask, a common hiding place for a gentleman's restorative.

But at the other end of the shaft, I discovered another secret compartment. An unusual piece of paper was rolled up inside. It is the size of a regular piece of fine writing paper, but there is a series of small windows cut out of it.

I've learned from an expert it is a significant piece of paper. It is called a grille, an instrument of espionage. It would be laid over a page of a book or letter to reveal a secret message embedded among innocent words of a story or a missive.

May I ask, do you know anything about this grille? Did your husband have a favorite book?

What I am about to write may sound outrageous to you, but I hope our friendship and our experiences together have built a strong connection between us.

Your answer may lead to an important historic discovery in my time.

Based on what I have learned, the existence of such a grille hidden deep inside Mr. Collins's walking stick suggests he was part of a Confederate spy network during the War Between the States.

Are you shocked?

I have also become privy to some other background information. When you guided me to the attic in Waterwood House, I discovered trunks with the initials JTC. Their battered condition suggests Mr. Collins traveled a great deal. Considering your family's social position, his destinations would have brought him into contact with individuals who may have played key roles during the war. He may have gleaned information valuable to one side's war effort.

I ask your help in discerning the meaning of the grille and the possible importance of your husband in the war effort.

In advance, I send my gratitude for your assistance.

With warmest regards,
Emma

I put the cap back on the pen, pleased with the flow of words. It was so easy to write, to say just the right thing while sitting at the plantation desk and using the pen. I didn't have the trouble I'd experienced when trying to write my novel at the computer. Was it because this was only a letter? Who was

I kidding? The letters left here on this desk were more important than any first draft of a novel!

Why? They were read by a ghost!

If they weren't worded just right, there could be long-term ramifications. Wasn't history filled with stories, real and imagined, of angry ghosts, vengeful ghosts, haunting a place, making life miserable for living, breathing humans? TJ's concerns about upsetting Emma and Daniel from the 19th century were valid. They could make life unbearable at the Cottage and Waterwood House.

But when I sat at this desk and composed a letter to Emma, the words had flowed from my mind to the pen and onto the paper. Maybe I should ditch the computer for now and try another method to get my story down on paper? I shook my head. If I wrote my story longhand, it would take me forever to finish the first draft. Then how would I edit it? No, there had to be another way.

Should I bring my computer here to the cabin? I closed my eyes and sighed. No, it wasn't an option. No electricity. I'd be running back and forth, interrupting the word flow to recharge its battery.

No, I would have to wait for another inspiration. In the meantime, I would enjoy the golden light peeking through the trees, making the raindrops clinging to their leaves sparkle. Here on the Eastern Shore, there was comfort and beauty all around me. I needed to take the time to enjoy it.

CHAPTER TWENTY-EIGHT

Why are keyboards laid out using the QWERTY design?
It was first used in 1874 to spread out the most commonly
used keys so they were less likely to jam
when a fast typist was using a typewriter.
–Tenrandomfacts.com

I took Maureen's comments about the Internal Editor to heart. I had thought about her suggestions and avoided the computer...the past few days.

I had to work in the dining room. Originally, I wanted to work in the den so there would be a little separation from my regular living area. When the movers had found the plantation desk in the garage, I wanted to use it as my writing desk. They set it up in the den, but life had a different plan. TJ had renovated the cabin so the desk could be moved there. It would make a comfortable work environment. Since then, I had searched for another desk to fill the empty space, a desk where I could work comfortably. I'd gone to a couple of antique stores. I searched online, even Amazon. Desperate to have something, I bought a desk that took forever to put together. It should have worked, only it made me feel like a child with her first school desk.

Writing in the den was not going to work. I set up my computer at one end of the dining room. I put my notes on one side of it and my coffee on the other. I was ready to start my first writing session on my new novel.

The session lasted two hours then I went upstairs and threw myself down on my bed. What a disaster. I couldn't concentrate. My mind shot off in so many different directions, I was getting dizzy. I bounced out of my chair so often I felt like a basketball. When I ordered myself to sit in the chair and work, I ended up staring at the blank document on the screen with the little blinking cursor. Whoever designed it hadn't realized what kind of an impression the blinking line made. The only thing missing was the sound of the computer's fingernails clinking on the table, impatient for me to get on with the work. What was I going to tell Maureen?

I never had this kind of trouble when I was writing papers for school or developing lesson plans for my classes or writing evaluations of my students. This should be easy. I was in charge. Everything was coming out of my brain. I had complete control, only I had no control at all.

I was sprawled on the bed, feeling sorry for myself, when the familiar prickling behind my eyelids warned that tears were about to fall. No, a crying jag wouldn't help at all. I got up, went downstairs, and headed down the path to the cabin. I wasn't there to leave a message for Emma or retrieve one. I just wanted to visit the desk where I had once dreamed of writing my novel. When I'd first seen it in the garage, I knew it would inspire me. I had oiled it several times to bring out the patina and grain. The large writing surface could accommodate a laptop computer and notes. Above, there was a large door hiding cubbyholes, slots, and shelves for everything from research books to paperclips. Seeing the desk, I felt this was the place I should be writing my novel, not at a dining room table or on a flimsy particleboard desk that swayed when I typed. If I was going to write about people during the Civil War, what an inspiration this 19th century desk would be.

Then my good old Internal Editor spoke up. *There is no electricity here for your computer.* I realized with a sigh he had finally said something worthwhile. It was true. There was no need for an electrical line in the cabin. I had read an article about some famous authors who used a pen and a pad of paper to draft their novels. I could do it if I tried.

Feeling lighter and more positive, I locked the door to the cabin and meandered down to the Cove where I'd brought my books as a child. If I wrote longhand, it would probably take me years to complete the first draft of my novel.

Disheartened, I trudged back to the Cottage. There had to be another way. Inside, I wondered back to the den and remembered Uncle Jack working on various projects like his research book and college lectures. He hadn't had a computer. He hadn't written everything out longhand.

He'd used a typewriter.

An electric one wouldn't work in the cabin, but a manual typewriter would.

If it worked for Uncle Jack, maybe it could work for me. Did they even make manual typewriters anymore? Was I going to waste even more time hunting through antique stores looking for one in good condition, good enough for me to use to type a book with tens of thousands of words? There was one best option: Check Amazon.

I found a variety of brand-new typewriters of assorted styles and colors. The mint green or red or purple one would be distracting. I didn't particularly care for the small sleek model. I didn't need something lightweight. Hopefully, I would set it up on the desk and leave it there.

There were so many options, even an external typewriter

keyboard to connect wirelessly to my computer. It had another unique feature. It had the keys of an old-fashioned typewriter. It even sounded like a typewriter. The design combined the old with the new, including all the function keys. It was tempting.

Finally, I opted for a new black typewriter in the old-style of the early 20th century. The keyboard wasn't flat but staggered in rows and would take some finger dexterity to use. I also ordered a couple of reams of paper, because this old-school unit didn't use a monitor. I was glad the site had reminded me to order typewriter ribbon. This was really old-school. I was eager to get started, but I had to be patient. It would be a long, two-day delivery. It would be worth it. I just knew it. I wondered what TJ would think of my plan. I missed his visits, our chats over coffee. But I didn't need his help to make this decision. For me, it was the right thing to do. I shrugged to myself. What could go wrong?

CHAPTER TWENTY-NINE

*The American Civil War was also known as
the War Between the States, War of the Rebellion,
War of Secession, and Great Rebellion.
To Confederates, it was the War for Southern Independence.
Frederick Douglass used the term Slaveholders' Rebellion.*

The next morning, the air was scrubbed clean, and the trees and plants looked rejuvenated – almost sparkling - - from the spring rain the day before. After breakfast I walked, down the path to the cabin, stepping around the puddles that still remained. I came around a bend in the path and saw the cabin nestled in a grove of crepe myrtle and wild grasses, as it had been since Emma's time. I dialed in the combination and freed the lock from the door. TJ had recently changed it in case we lost the key or someone else found it. As I opened the door, I prepared myself to be disappointed. Emma hadn't had enough time to respond to my letter. But, maybe…

The massive plantation desk stood opposite the door. It was about three feet wide and six feet tall. When the movers discovered it in the garage covered by a blue tarp, its dark wood was scratched, and the dull finish was thirsty for some furniture polish and oil. I'd gone to work almost immediately to restore its condition and now, kept up the regimen on a regular basis. The slant top opened to make a large writing surface for a computer and notes. Above, was a large door hiding cubbyholes, slots, and shelves which I filled with everything from reference books about punctuation and pens to paperclips and blank notebooks. This was supposed to have been the place where I would write my first book. That had been the plan until Daniel's letters arrived and the desk's true importance became clear. TJ thought it would be prudent to renovate the crumbling cabin by the creek, Emma's favorite place where she loved to spend time with Daniel. And we moved the desk out here permanently.

There, on the writing surface, lay Emma's response to my letter. I wanted to sit down and read it, but I had disciplined myself to take any letter from Emma or Daniel, photograph it, and transcribe it into a Word document immediately. Why? In a short amount of time, the words written in black ink would mysteriously disappear. I didn't know why but they did.

I hustled back to the cottage, preserved the communication and settled down with a printed copy of her letter.

My Dearest Emma,

I am delighted to receive another missive from you. Please, you are not disturbing me. Time has no meaning here. Daniel and I only revel in being together for eternity.

I was intrigued to read about your discovery of the gentlemen's walking stick. I knew there could be a secret compartment inside the shaft, but you found two! Was it unusual?

I wish I could help, but I have never heard of a grille for a book or letter. It sounds ingenious. And to think you suspect he might have been a spy! It is unbelievable.

Now, I must think what information will help you.

You are correct. He traveled a great deal, most often without me. Do not fret. I was happy to spend my life at my favorite place in the world, Waterwood. It was important to me to keep the plantation running so it could adequately care for its people, both my family and the slaves.

My husband did not have the same commitment. It disgusted me when he did not treat them as human beings. They were only property to him. They were the basis of our wealth which he thoroughly enjoyed.

Regarding the war, my husband did not seem to be particularly engaged by the issues. He was more concerned with maintaining a privileged lifestyle. That being said, I lean towards the idea he aligned himself with the Confederacy.

If he was involved in espionage, it wasn't for his political beliefs. I am embarrassed to say he would have sold his talents and position in society to the highest bidder.

For a man whose attitudes did not agree with Unionists and abolitionists, he traveled extensively in the North, enjoying their company. He spent time in Washington, Baltimore, and New York City, but his favorite place was Philadelphia. I found travel during the war exhausting, unreliable, and fraught with danger. During those years, I was happy to stay at home.

Emma, I am glad you are the only person reading this letter. Someone else might think less of me because I am speaking ill of my husband. At the time of our marriage, my words would have been severely criticized. I would have been accused of being disloyal. I am comforted that you understand, for you have read my diaries.

Now, I want to thank you. You may have answered a question about something that happened in the first years of our marriage, those being the years of the War Between the States. When he was home, he would disappear into the library for hours. Sometimes, he would ride out early in the morning and not return until dusk. Could he have been involved in some kind of disreputable activity?

One night, I walked into the library to find him at the desk surrounded by candlelight and correspondence, scribbling on a piece of paper. Do you think he was working on a secret message?

When he saw me there, he was so angry, it was frightening. He accused me of spying on him. I was never allowed to enter his library again without an invitation.

His library? My father designed and selected the books kept there. I should have been the one who was angry.

I never saw him use the grille you described. Therefore, I must use my imagination. You suggested he might use a book, but I almost never saw him with one. How would he know which page to use to decode a message?

Your idea of using the grille with a letter sounds more logical. Many letters flowed into Waterwood House during the week. He kept in contact with people he met on his excursions even though paper became scarce.

My correspondence was with ladies, most of whom resided here on the Eastern Shore. I also exchanged letters with friends and family in Baltimore. I did not have a wide circle of friends. We often discussed topics concerning the proper management of the home, our children, the best ways to deal with illness, and social comings and goings. Please do not think me vain when I tell you we also exchanged opinions and ideas about fashion. I truly cannot imagine he would use letters addressed to me.

You should know that unless a letter was valued because of its content or the dearness of the letter writer, I disposed of many missives after I read them.

Dearest Emma, I hope you find some help or a clue in these words to assist you in your determination *of an answer to the question you raised. I hope you will share with me the truth of what you find and your determination about whether my husband was a spy.*

With warmest affection, your faithful friend,
Emma

In a way, Emma's reply was disappointing. I had hoped she knew about the grille for passing sensitive information in what seemed to be a normal letter or a favorite book. Her comments confirmed my belief that Joshua was a man who cared for himself alone.

Emma continued to impress me with her wit and common sense. She raised an excellent question. If the grille was meant to work with a page of a book, how would you know which page to use? Maybe the conspirators could decide in advance the first message would be written using page 15, for example, and then the next message would be written using page 29 and so forth. It was a possibility, but the conspirators would need an excellent memory or have to write down a special series of numbers.

I would have to find a letter that, when using the grille, would reveal a secret message. It would be the only way for me to prove Joshua was a spy for the Confederacy.

I heaved a deep sigh. Where was I going to find such a letter? It was possible Joshua had burned the letters with secret messages. But, I argued silently, if the letters appeared to be innocent correspondence to the casual, uninformed reader, he might have kept one, some, or all of the letters. If he kept them, he might have put them in a secret place.

So many *ifs*. After all I'd learned about Waterwood and its people, I feared this time, I might fail to find the true story. I pulled myself out of the chair, folded the copy of Emma's reply, and put it into the file with all her correspondence. Yes, it was possible I would fail, but if I didn't try, the possibility would become a certainty.

TJ should have this background. It involved his family. I remembered how angry he'd been about my *investigation* into the professor's murder, as he called it. I wasn't working the case the way the police were. I was only looking at the historical perspective which made this case complicated. The killer's motivation was tied to the past. My efforts might help Craig understand the connection and help him name the killer quickly.

I wished TJ understood the true value was learning more about his ancestors. He had been interested in what I'd found before. We had even worked together. Why was he so touchy now?

I didn't feel I could stop my investigation, as TJ put it. After all, I was trying to find out if Emma's husband, his ancestor, had been a Confederate spy. And, yes, help identify a killer. It was worth the effort.

I needed to find the letters Emma had mentioned in her reply if they still existed. She had said Joshua had spent a lot of time locked in the Waterwood library. He must have kept them there. I had to go back to Waterwood House. Considering it was mid-morning, I wouldn't run into TJ. That thought brought conflicting feelings of relief and sadness. I missed my friend, but never again wanted to hear his harsh words about my actions.

I spilled out the remnants of my coffee in the sink and headed out to the driveway we shared. This adventure wasn't as easy as following Emma's suggestions in her diaries. I figured I could probably write her another letter asking for clarification and search ideas, but I got the sense from her reply she really didn't know much about Joshua's activities during the Civil War. This time, I had to step up to meet the challenge.

As I approached the back of Waterwood House, I saw TJ's truck which meant he was home. I didn't want to bother him, so I walked around to the front of the house and slipped in through the door there. I wanted to make my way quietly to the library without disturbing him. Instead, a pretty woman, a stranger, walking down the main staircase met me. She was carrying a large silver tray.

CHAPTER THIRTY

A Proper English Tea Service: Teapot, Sugar Bowl, Creamer,
Hot Water Kettle, Waste Bowl, Tray,
and if desired, Coffee Pot.

Seeing an attractive woman walking down the main staircase of Waterwood House brought back unhappy memories. Last fall, when I walked into Waterwood House, a petite young woman, with long strawberry blonde hair pulled back in a ponytail, had bounced down those steps, carefree, and sucking on a lollypop. I'd thought she was TJ's girlfriend only to find out she was the prettiest *handyman* I'd ever met. A wave of sadness came over me as I remembered what had happened to Dee and her twin sister, Belle.

But this young woman was different. A mass of auburn curls framed a heart-shaped face of pale skin and freckles. Her emerald-green eyes flashed in my direction. Then she smiled which made her even prettier. TJ certainly knew how to surround himself with good-looking women. Was this his girlfriend? It wasn't my place to ask. This wasn't my home, and he wasn't my boyfriend.

Instead, I said, "Hi, I'm Emma Chase. I live in the Cottage down the driveway." I pointed as if she could see it from here which was stupid because we were inside the house. I kept quiet so I wouldn't make any more embarrassing mistakes.

TJ walked in carrying a big box. "I got it all in here. I'll —" He looked up and saw me. "Oh, Emma," he said in surprise. "I see you've met Abby."

"Actually, we haven't met yet," the girl with the auburn hair said. "I'm Abby Strickland and it is great to see you, but I can't stop to talk. I'm late for an appointment at Fair Winds. TJ, I found the tray that belongs to the tea set. Could you put the box in my car?"

"Sure thing."

"Nice to meet you, Emma." She followed him back to the kitchen and out the door, leaving me standing alone, like a fifth wheel, in the foyer.

My feet seemed stuck to the old oak floor, so I was still standing there when he returned. I wanted to ask if she was a new girlfriend, but I didn't dare. I had no right to ask. Instead, a boring comment tumbled out of my mouth. "She seems nice."

"Abby?" He turned his head towards the kitchen. "Yeah, she is."

Maybe he was as nervous as I was. Finally, I couldn't stand it anymore. "Who is she?"

He turned and gave me a quizzical look. "A friend," he barked, as if I'd asked him a deeply personal question.

I almost jumped back at his tone of voice.

"She's helping me out with something. You're not the only one curious about old things here at Waterwood House." He took a breath as if he realized his words stung. In a softer tone, he continued. "I couldn't sleep one night – too many things rolling around in my head about the house, the farm. So many things. I thought about your interest in the past and your amazing finds in the attic. I wandered up there with an industrial-size flashlight and found the old ledgers from the 1860s. They must have been in the plantation desk originally. I guess Jack wasn't interested in them and we stored them in the attic for another day. That's when I saw something glint in the flashlight's beam. I backtracked and found an ornate tea service just sitting on the top of a dusty dresser as if someone had put it down for a moment on their way to serve tea in the parlor. I have to admit, it was creepy. The set must be part of our family history and might even be worth some money. Whatever the case, it needed attention, so I brought it downstairs." He shrugged. "I was going to try to clean it up myself, but I remembered all the care you put into dealing with Emma's things in her trunk. It deserved some tender loving care by someone who knew what she was doing. I didn't ask you, because I knew you were busy with your *investigation*."

Did I detect a note of contempt when he said the word *investigation*? I hated being confused by my friend who I'd once relied on, valued, and... Too much was coming at me. I didn't say a word to him now, not wanting to say something I didn't mean.

He continued. "I called Abby. She is an expert when it comes to sterling silver. She is so good at what she does, that Miss Lorraine over at Fair Winds hired her full-time and gave her a cottage. I knew Abby would know what to do and she was nice enough to come by. She lives at Fair Winds which is on the other side of St. Michaels."

My brain rushed to process all this information: He knew this young, attractive woman, knew where she lived, felt comfortable having her in Waterwood House. And he had never mentioned her. I didn't know what to say. I didn't know what to do with the feelings bubbling up inside me. Words blurted out of my mouth. "Is that what was in the box, a tea service, or were you two looking around for other things?" I felt awful grilling him like this, I couldn't seem to stop.

"No, just the tea service." He seemed to have missed my prying attitude. "I had to find a big box. There were so many parts to the set. Who needs more than one teapot?"

"Anyone who is also serving coffee," I responded in a snarky way that wasn't necessary. This time, he didn't miss anything. His jaw tightened and he shifted the way he was standing so his body language screamed he was annoyed with me. I tried to move the conversation to more neutral ground. "My mother's friend had a formal tea service with a huge tray like the one your friend was carrying. The set probably has a teapot of course, coffee pot, creamer, sugar bowl—"

"Yes, there are a lot of pieces." The words came out clipped. "Abby..." He gave her name some emphasis. "...is going to look at them all and let me know about its background and what it might be worth." He pulled his baseball cap out of his back pocket and settled it on his head, a clear signal our conversation was over. "Now, if it's okay with you, I have to get back to work."

"Me, too. I'm just going to..." But my words, as sweet as I'd wanted them to sound, met with his back as he escaped to kitchen and out the door. There was a definite chill in the air. It wasn't from the presence of a ghost. It was from the cold shoulder from a friend, someone I cared about. Maybe more than I realized.

I felt my face grow hot. Was I blushing? I didn't want to know. I was sorry I'd found Abby there. Were there other women who visited Waterwood House? I gave my head a strong shake. I didn't want to know. I wished I hadn't come. The encounter with TJ had been hurtful and left me confused.

This is ridiculous, I lectured myself. TJ is a friend, a good friend. He— I stopped. He was...what? What was he to me? I had to figure out what I felt for TJ...*BUT now is not the time,*

I ordered myself. There is a killer out there right now and I may hold the key to what is driving him.

With a promise I'd think about TJ tomorrow or the day after, I marched into the parlor and over to the library. A smile crept onto my face. I had actually repeated the words of Scarlett O'Hara in *Gone with the Wind*. "I'll think about it tomorrow." I was becoming rooted in the Civil War period. It would be serious if I ever thought of exchanging my jeans for a gown with a hoop skirt.

CHAPTER THIRTY-ONE

Nineteenth century portraits were painted in a vertical orientation when the subject was in an upright position. Landscape paintings were done in a horizontal orientation to include more of the vista.

With a sense of purpose that ignored what I might feel for TJ, I walked through the parlor and stepped into the Waterwood library and the sunlight streaming through the tall windows. Golden velvet draperies, hanging from ceiling to floor, framed the vistas of Waterwood's rolling lawns that ran up to the wall of evergreens standing guard against the outside world. It was easy to feel protected and safe here. Inside, shelves of books covered the library walls. They created a cocoon of warmth and safety to surround the reader with knowledge, entertainment, and adventure.

Art was well-represented, too. An oil painting over the fireplace was a portrait of Waterwood itself. The wide array of greens and blues captured the color pallet of its landscape and its waters. The honey-colored oak of the large fireplace, the bookshelves, and the large desk held the warm light of the sun that made the plantation's crops grow. Then I glanced up and my breath caught. The ceiling was nothing if not magnificent. I'd learned from my random readings it was called a coffered ceiling made in a pattern of beams and sunken areas to give the illusion of height and formality. This was a hallowed place of learning. A place where one could think and reflect in safety and comfort. But to one man, was it something else?

Had Joshua sat in one of the comfortable wing chairs flanking the hearth and thought about ways to undermine the Union and bolster the Southern cause? Had he sat at the grand oaken desk and deciphered secret messages? Had he analyzed the information and sent it on to Richmond? It was what I had come to find out.

The air in the room was stale and threatened to make me cough. TJ preferred the kitchen as a place to work. I opened the windows to let in a little fresh spring air, before gravitating to the massive desk near the center of the room. Its top was almost the size of a small dining table. The silky patina of the wood, the crackled condition of the leather inserts, and a few slightly worn places along the edge suggested it dated back to the mid-19th century. There were enough desk drawers to rival the space provided by a small chest. I sat down in the desk chair and pulled on the center drawer. It wasn't locked. It moved easily which was a testament to the quality of its original construction. Though I was pawing through some papers there, I didn't feel like I was violating TJ's space. He had put together a modern computer desk and set it up in a little space just off the large kitchen. It was better than working in the formal library *with all those leather-bound books,* he'd said. It made sense to work where there was warmth in the winter and good cross-ventilation in the summer.

Most of the papers I found in this desk were bills and notes from previous decades, probably from the time TJ's uncle had run Waterwood. I reached deep inside the drawers and touched the nooks and crannies of the desk, hoping to find a latch or spring to release a hidden compartment? Ever since I'd come to Waterwood, I'd spent a lot of time uncovering secrets. Today, nothing came to light, no matter how hard I tried.

A question came to mind, and I stopped what I was doing. Would Joshua conceal critical messages in a piece of furniture that could be moved out of the room, even out of the house? No, he would probably pick a hiding place in the house.

I glanced around the library at all the shelves filled with leather-bound books and realized there could be a secret hidden among all those leather-bound books. Any one of them could be hiding a latch or a pressure point to open a secret compartment. Any of them could be a fake, its hollowed-out middle filled with letters. I would have to search every volume hoping to discover a secret stash.

The mere idea threatened to crush my resolve. But this was for Uncle Jack. I took a deep breath, pulled myself out of the comfortable desk chair and went to work to find out what Joshua had been trying to keep secret.

I began by pulling two or three books at time off a shelf then probing the wooden shelf area for a release to expose a secret storage area. My hand holding the books got tired and I had to work with one volume at a time. These books were heavy. Their covers were of superior quality leather and embossed with gold leaf lettering and designs. I needed to use muscles I hadn't used very much for a long time.

I put a moveable set of the antique mahogany spiral library steps next to the shelves. At first, I was hesitant to use it, but it seemed studier and the tall carved pole in the center of the spiral gave me something to steady myself.

After finishing one section of books, I took a moment to catch my breath. I looked around the room. I had a long way to go. My enthusiasm for this project was weakening but my impatience to know the truth about Joshua was getting stronger.

I moved the library steps and climbed up to reach a high shelf. When I grabbed a volume, it was stuck to the volume next to it. I widened my grasp, but I couldn't budge the books. Thinking they were stuck, I gripped three books and pulled hard.

And I almost fell backwards. I didn't need much strength to dislodge the books, because they were fake book spines designed to hide what lay behind them. There was an oval metal piece surrounding a keyhole... with a key sticking out. It was the only indication there was a door built to match the fine wood of the bookshelves. A locked door to a secret place to protect something valuable. I'd found what I hoped was Joshua's safe hidden behind several fake book spines.

I wanted to do a happy dance, but I didn't dare while I was standing on one of the top library steps. I pulled out my phone to document the disguised door and whatever I might find behind it. I held my breath and turned the key. The door to the safe swung open easily to reveal three drawers, one of which spanned the width of the safe.

Certain I was about to find the missing correspondence, I opened the large drawer. Inside, there were two stacks of letters. Carefully, I pulled out the full drawer, climbed down the library steps, and took it over to the library desk.

Standing over the drawer from the safe, my nose twitched at the musty smell drifting from it. I poked the letters with my finger. Some were tucked in their envelopes, slit open at the top. Many were loose. Some were written on fine stationery; others were on a cheaper stock. Charles, the librarian, had said paper was in short supply during the war. The historian believed the spy would be a well-placed member of society. People of lesser means probably wouldn't have access to information about troop movements, foodstuffs, or supply schedules. They wouldn't know about the inventory and availability of ammunition, the location of cannon, or the availability of guns.

The dust in the room was starting to get to me. I kept clearing my throat and coughing a little. It would be easier and more comfortable if I could spread out on my dining room table. I gave myself permission to move everything to the Cottage.

As I was moving the letters to a box I'd found in TJ's kitchen, a letter written on good quality paper grabbed by attention. The handwriting was fancy and feminine. I opened the folded pages to find a letter. Surprisingly, it was not addressed to Joshua. I sifted through other letters and envelopes and found two more like it from the safe. None were addressed to Joshua.

They were all addressed to Emma.

CHAPTER THIRTY-TWO

"This is the city, and I am one of the citizens.
Whatever interests the rest interests me."
— *Walt Whitman*

At the Cottage, I put the box of letters on the dining table and tossed my light jacket on a chair. I didn't want to waste the time hanging it up right now. I needed to go through everything carefully to be sure of what I'd read in the library.

I shuffled through the letters and envelopes, looking for the three letters and one envelope addressed to Emma. Where were they? Everything had shifted in the box during my walk back to the Cottage. They should be easy to find. They were on fine quality paper. All I seemed to find were cheap sheets addressed to Joshua. Finally, my fingers touched smoothness and thickness of quality.

With a sigh of relief, I lined up the three letters, their envelopes set off to the side. Yes, all three began, *Dear Emma*. In the upper right corner, the sender had written,

Miller House, Philadelphia, Pennsylvania. Then, I turned the pages until I got to the end. The same person signed every letter: *Annabelle.* No last name. Frustrating, but then I noticed the third letter dated April 13, 1861 was signed *Annabelle Jennings Miller.* Was that significant? But first, the goal here was to find out if there was a secret message nestled in what appeared to be an innocent letter.

Maybe these were innocent letters. I looked at the stack of letters addressed to Joshua, compared to three measly letters addressed to Emma. If Joshua was the spy, wouldn't it be his correspondence hidden in the safe?

Then a strange notion entered my mind. No. Surely not. Was Emma the Confederate spy? The letter that had fit the grille was from Annabelle in Philadelphia and addressed to Emma.

No, she would have something in her letter. Wouldn't she? There was no reason for her to lie to me, even if it was a lie by omission. It wouldn't matter to her if I knew she had been a spy, right? This uncertainty was not productive. It was time to find out one way or the other.

After putting on the white cotton gloves, I picked a letter to Emma at random and laid the first page flat on the table. Then I took the grille and placed it on top, so it covered the letter exactly. This was the decisive moment. I ran my eyes over the grille's boxes and ... the letter "a" appeared in the center of one box. The letters "ly" at the end of word were in another box, sort of. Part of another word was half in another box, but I couldn't tell what the letters were.

As I removed the grille and turned the letter over, I thought this was a lot of work for nothing. Again, I placed the grille on the letter. Again, I scanned the boxes. This time, there was no match up at all, not even one letter. I turned it this way and that, the way the historian had described but still no great discovery. Okay, two more pages to check. Might as well check them. I had nowhere else to be.

A combination of frustration and disappointment made the placement of the grille sloppy. There was no other word for it. When I straightened the letter and grille, words popped into every box.

Okay, I thought, this was luck. Then I saw the little black dot at the bottom of the overlay. Did it mean this was the right position? Yes, letters appeared in each box randomly placed down the page, but they didn't make sense. I removed the grille and deciphered the handwriting. I knew from reading Emma's diaries and letters she'd received from friends, not everyone in the 19th century wrote with a clear hand. Once I got used to the loops and embellishments on the capital letters, the page was easy to read. This Annabelle from Philadelphia wrote about her friend's little boy in a sailor suit, playing with a toy ship and a train. They were from Baltimore. What did it have to do with the Civil War?

I put the grille over the page and wrote down each word or letter that appeared in each box. When I read the message on the pad, I gasped.

Arms shipment to Baltimore 2 stop train four 1 9

Baltimore? Train? There was something... I checked the date on the letter. March 18, 1861. I jumped up and started to pace. I knew there was something. I just didn't know what. Did Emma say something? Had Daniel written about...? This was it. Daniel had mentioned confrontations between Union soldiers and Southern sympathizers. But there was more.

I paced around the table and headed to the kitchen. There was something, but it was just beyond my reach. I headed back to the dining room and the computer. Google would have the answer. My hands paused above the keyboard. What would I type? The wrong search words might send me down a rabbit hole. I jumped up again and paced.

I am too young for dementia, I told myself. Just think. Be calm. Let it bubble to the surface.

I took a deep breath and walked slowly to the kitchen. A cup of coffee might help. Slowly, I popped a single serving coffee brew into the machine. I wanted to pace but forced myself to relax. Slowly, I opened the cabinet and reached for my favorite mug, sitting right next to TJ's mug. And my hand stopped in mid-air.

TJ. He had told me a story about Baltimore. Coffee forgotten, I rushed back to the computer. I typed Baltimore Train. But wait. What was the meaning *four 1 9?* Maybe my search would explain it. And there it was. The story of the Baltimore Riot of 1861!

An overwhelming majority did not want to go to war against their brothers in the South. Only a tiny fraction of the people of Baltimore had voted for Abraham Lincoln in the recent presidential election. They wanted to stop the reinforcement of Washington City with troops from the North on April 19th... *four 1 9*.

The date on the letter showed the arms shipped to Baltimore was before the attack. The Confederacy would have needed to know about the availability of weapons to attack the Northern soldiers. This message would have been confirmation. The covert plan must have come together. The first blood spilled in the Civil War, declared more than two weeks earlier, was on that date in Baltimore.

Was there another letter dated before April 19, 1861? I gently shuffled through the papers and found only one. Using the grille, I read:

Train vulnerable between 2 tracks

I checked Google again. The train tracks from the North did not join the tracks running South. There was a gap between the two lines. Passengers from the North had to walk several blocks to join a southbound train. Annabelle had pinpointed the best place for the attack!

I plopped into my chair and tried to take in the importance of the secret messages buried in these letters. But why... There was a piece missing out of this picture. There was a man who could fill it in, if only he was on duty. I grabbed my phone and dialed. It rang and rang and...

"Hello, Maryland Room. This is Charles Tompkins, Reference Librarian."

"Charles! You're there!" I said in a rush.

"Ah, yes, I am. How may I help you?"

I quickly identified myself and apologized. Then I asked my question. "Charles, tell me why it was so important for Maryland to stay in the Union and Baltimore stay out of the hands of Southern sympathizers?"

"Ah, you're making progress with your research, Emma. Wonderful. I thought—"

I hated to interrupt, but I did anyway. "Charles, I'm so sorry. Do you know the answers to those questions?"

"Short on time? I understand. Let me give you the highlights." He cleared his throat and I braced myself for a lecture. "Second answer first," he began. "Baltimore was a major shipping port. Having it in the control of the enemy could have crippled the North... shipments of food, supplies... troop movement and more."

I grabbed a pen and scribbled notes.

"Now, your first question. It was vital for Maryland to stay in the Union. As you know, Virginia is just south of Washington, D.C., the capital of the United States. Virginia seceded from the Union and Richmond, its capital, became the capital of the Confederacy. If Maryland sided with the South, the Confederacy would have completely surrounded Washington. The war would be over."

I thanked Charles profusely and promised to visit with him again soon.

I had the rest of the story. If the Confederacy could coordinate actions in Baltimore, the result might have been very different. The men in Richmond needed this information. The professor and Dr. Abbott were right. These secret messages could be important additions to the historical record. Before I got carried away, I needed to check my work.

CHAPTER THIRTY-THREE

The chocolate chip cookie is known as a Toll House *because Ruth Graves Wakefield made up the recipe in 1930 when she and her family moved to a new home between Boston and New Bedford, Massachusetts.*
Built in 1709, it was known as The Toll House Inn, *where travelers rested there, changed horses, ate, and paid tolls.*

I was concentrating so much on the letter, it barely registered when the driveway gravel growled under someone's car tire outside. When it did, I froze. I wasn't expecting anyone, but someone was here.

TJ? Craig, the detective?

My throat tightened. No one was here, except me.

Had the killer come back? Dragged back from the past so quickly, I sat in my chair, not moving. But one thought took over my brain. The person knew where I lived. I closed my eyes and whispered like a mantra or a prayer, Go away, Go away.

I only had to look out the window to see who ... but I couldn't.

A car door closed. I tensed, waiting for the knock at the

door or the jiggling of the knob. But another car door slammed shut. My eyes trailed to the window then closed.

The key scraped into the lock. The door opened. Maria, my housekeeper, called out. "Miss Emma! I'm here!"

I let out the breath I hadn't realized I'd been holding. And a new panic set in. Maria would pick up on the littlest thing, touch everything trying to keep the Cottage neat. She was caring and sweet, but sometimes, her fussing could be a little irritating.

"Hi! I'm in the dining room," I called out while quickly pushing the letters and envelopes together into stacks. When she came into the room and saw the mass of things on the table, she frowned. She thought of the dining room as an extension of her domain, the kitchen. And her kitchen was always immaculate even when she was cooking a big meal. As she stood there, loaded down with bags of groceries, I marveled at the amount of food she brought into the Cottage. Except for an occasional dinner with TJ, Maria was cooking only for me. Was I really eating all this food?

Maria... Funny lady, committed to making me comfortable here at Uncle Jack's Cottage so I could recover and heal. She kept the cottage spotless. She kept the kitchen stocked with delicious meals I only had to reheat. She made it feel like home. So, why was she always complaining? One time, she said she liked working at the Cottage though I had lost count of the number of times she complained about one thing or another. Secretly, her complaints made me laugh. Was it such a terrible thing her delicious chocolate chip cookies, meant to last all week, were gone in days? Any other baker would've been thrilled. Not Maria. Could it be she wouldn't allow herself to get too comfortable here because this job would come to an end at some point? It wasn't a thought I relished, but I had to admit it was true.

She always shooed me out of kitchen, but we would chat whenever she brought me a hot coffee or warm cookies on the patio. That was before I'd found the professor's body slumped in the chair, dead. Now, we both avoided the patio.

Standing in the doorway, she looked around the dining room table and frowned. "What is all this? Another project?"

I looked at the dining room table through her eyes. The letters in neat piles might look like clutter on the dining table large enough to seat six people. But right now, I needed a large work area to keep the letters organized. If I was going to prove Joshua Thomas Collins was a spy for the Confederacy, I needed proof. It had to be in one of these letters from his safe or it had gone up the library chimney in smoke.

This was not the time for her to see my concern so, I plastered an excited smile on my face. "Yes! I'm on the trail of a new discovery about TJ's family."

"Again?" Her frown deepened. "What about you? What about your family and your life?" She adjusted the heavy bags she still held.

"It involves my Uncle Jack, too. In fact—"

"I thought maybe I'd make a nice dinner for you and Mr. TJ. I could set the table here, in the dining room, with your uncle's fine china, crystal, and silver. I thought it might be nice…" She lowered her head and sighed.

Her disappointment worried me. She had been through so much with me. We had grown to be friends, family.

"What a lovely thought. We can do it," I said quickly. "Just not right now. He is busy. Maria, I'm sorry. Let me finish this project first, okay?"

"Okay," she mumbled as she headed to the kitchen.

It broke my heart to see her so disappointed, but it would have deeply upset her if she knew what I was thinking.

I didn't think TJ would come.

CHAPTER THIRTY-FOUR

Chili Controversies: Beans or No Beans. No Meat or Meat:
Ground Beef, Sirloin, Brisket. Chicken, Turkey, Venison, Elk.
Style: Con Carne, Vegetarian, Texas Red, Cincinnati, Verde,
White, Cajun, Black Bean, Five-Alarm.
BUT one ingredient is always needed: Chili Powder.

While working quietly in the dining room, Maria appeared from the kitchen, looking a bit distraught. "I put everything away, but I forgot something."

"Is it important, because—"

"I need it for the chili I'm going to make. The good news is I don't have to go all the way back to Easton. I can get it in St. Michaels. But I have to go to St. Michaels. I'm sorry, Miss Emma. It's not like me to forget something. Everything seems to be off kilter." Her eyes fell and she trudged back to the kitchen.

I was worried about my housekeeper, my friend. Forgetting some ingredient was no big deal, but she was acting like she had committed a firing offense. We'd had conversations about her work here at the Cottage. We both knew it would come to an end at some point. I would be independent again but not quite yet. As long as Uncle Jack's small legacy covered the Cottage upkeep and Maria's fees, I'd be okay. TJ thought she liked working here and didn't want to leave. She didn't want to make a mistake and be forced out ahead of schedule. It was a ridiculous idea, but people would get an idea in their head and...

"Maria! I'm so glad you have to go to St. Michaels. Could I catch a ride? There is a package waiting for me at the post office. I've been waiting for it. It would help so much..." She frowned. "It will only take a minute, I promise."

Her face lit up with a big smile. "If it will help you, Miss Emma, I'll do it."

In minutes, we were in her car and headed down the driveway. I'd never ridden with her before. I hoped it wouldn't be an adventure. I distracted myself by focusing on the trees pushing out their buds for the new season. Among the brown and gray branches that had survived the winter, there was now a hazy suggestion of color: light green in a line of birch trees with white-gray trunks and dark burgundy on branches of maple trees. It was a sign that spring was here.

In the town of St. Michaels, Maria dropped me off by the church so I could use the crosswalk and drove off to the only grocery nearby. As I rushed into the main door of the post office, I almost collided with a woman coming out. She looked familiar, but why eluded me.

She recognized me and touched my arm. "Emma, isn't it?" I nodded. "I heard the news. Is it true? Someone murdered my patient, Professor Kincaid?"

Of course, she had been the professor's nurse in the hospital. "Yes, I'm afraid it's true. I'm so sorry. You took such great care of him."

Her eyes glistened with tears. "I should be used to losing a patient. It happens sometimes, but he was so interested in life and going forward. We talked about ways for him to better manage his diabetes. It was going to be difficult for him." She sighed. "But to lose a patient to murder. It's more than I can take in."

"He talked to the police. Did he say anything while you were with him that might help the investigation?" I wondered. "When he was in a half-awake-half-asleep zone, he rambled on about how he had found the love of his life here on the Eastern Shore and then he lost her." She sighed. "It sounded like a story of Romeo and Juliet. It's sad. It's all so sad."

"He didn't mention anything about knowing someone here on the Shore, except Uncle Jack, when I talked to him in the hospital."

"Sometimes people say things when they are in recovery, though he sounded pretty insistent. In fact, I thought it might be his wife. Asked him if I should call her." The nurse's shoulders sagged. "He cried. Tears ran down in face. I didn't press him. I always try to avoid topics my patients find upsetting. It's not good for them." The church bells rang to mark the half-hour. "Oh, I have to run. Nice seeing you. It's just so sad," she mumbled as she hurried away.

I waited at the desk for the worker to bring my package. YES! My typewriter had arrived.

When we met in the parking lot, Maria felt better, too. She told stories about her young nieces and nephews all the way home.

Maria wanted to lug the heavy box into the dining room but doing it myself was so satisfying. She watched as the packing materials came out of the box and piled up on the floor. It felt like the Christmas. Once she saw what was in the box, Maria gave a disappointed grunt and headed back to her domain without an avalanche of questions. I wanted the typewriter's purpose to be my secret.

I slipped out the front door with the machine and headed

down to the cabin. The online product description read fifteen pounds. Every step down the path seemed to add a little more weight. It took a while to get things set up and organized on the plantation desk. For a brief moment, I wondered if Emma would ask for typing lessons. Then, still smiling, I made a list of what else I needed, like extra paper and typewriter ribbon. Right now, the typewriter—my writing instrument—looked great on the antique plantation desk.

CHAPTER THIRTY-FIVE

"The glory of expression and the sunshine of the light
of letters is simplicity."
—*Walt Whitman*

The morning sun shone into the bedroom as an early morning wakeup call. I was eager to sit at my new typewriter and get to work. Craig was busy in Baltimore with the crime lab people so, I could get my writing place set up. The days were getting longer but working into the evening would require some source of light in the cabin. Maybe a kerosene lamp? Normally, I'd ask TJ. Not this time. I wasn't ready for him to find out what I was doing. And he wasn't exactly available.

I bolted down some toast and my first cup of coffee. Armed with a fresh cuppa, I headed down to the cabin with paper and ribbon in hand. Soon, I faced my new writing instrument. It was satisfying to roll a blank page into the carriage and a relief not to have a blinking cursor awaiting my eloquent words. Yes, this just might work.

Eager to begin, I typed Chapter One at the top of the page. With a moment's hesitation, I swiped the carriage return lever twice, hit the tab to indent, and typed.

```
The early morning sunlight fell on a
Maryland plantation that was already
awake. Women were carrying baskets of
laundry or scurrying in and out of the
cookhouse, preparing breakfast for the
white folk still asleep on their smooth
               cotton sheets.
```

I leaned forward and read the words on the snowy white paper. The letters were clean. The typeface called Courier was old-school. It looked strange. My first inclination was to reach for my mouse and click to change the font, but I couldn't. The typist had to change, not my typewriter. If this was part of the price to avoid the cursor and to disarm my Internal Editor, it was worth it.

I reread the words and decided it was a good start. Then I typed,

```
The men were already out in the fields,
 sweat glistening on their black skin.
 Their backs aching from leaning over,
 digging in the soil, and planting the
 seeds to grow the cash crop, tobacco.
```

Hmmm, what else would they be doing in the field? What were they wearing? It became painfully obvious this story needed research already. Silently, I vowed the next time I picked up a novel, I would quietly thank the author for all the work he or she had done. People said it wasn't easy to write a novel. How true. It might be more complicated than I'd anticipated, but it was okay. I hit the Caps lock on the keyboard and typed out a note about the research needed, unlocked the key and went back to the story. Time flew by as I filled one page after another. I kept reaching for my coffee mug. Since coming to the Cottage, hot coffee was available all the time. What a luxury! While teaching, I'd had to wait until I got a little break, or lunchtime in the staff room. Now, work would stop while I made the trek to the coffee machine at the other end of the path. I'd been so spoiled. But it would be good to move around.

When I returned to the cabin with a fresh coffee, I found the first pages of my draft sitting on top of my typewriter. I had put them in a stack to the left of the typewriter. Had TJ come to the cabin? Had he read the first pages of my first draft without asking me?! I felt like someone had intruded on my privacy. Why would someone do that? It was my work, and everyone would have to wait until I thought it was ready to be read by others.

But there was more. There was a note next to my typed words about planting the tobacco seeds. Someone had written in black ink:

With all due respect, this is not how it was done at Waterwood.

TJ was the only farming expert I knew. How could he... And I thought he was out, working hard for other farmers. No, he was skulking around, following me, correcting my work. Indignation burned inside. I grabbed the page and marched to the door. I was going to track him down, show him he'd been caught him red-handed, and tell him to mind his own business.

As I reached for the door handle, I hesitated and looked at the handwriting again. It was familiar. My hand shook, making the paper rattle in the silence of the cabin. The words were written in copperplate script. I had a writing partner.

Emma.

I would recognize her smooth, elegant handwriting anywhere.

TJ's worried words rang in my mind. "Remember, Emma and Daniel are ghosts. We don't want any trouble. So far, we have been on friendly terms. We have to keep it that way or there is no telling what could happen. We don't need vengeful ghosts at Waterwood."

No, we didn't. I had to be careful. Emma might be bored or looking for a new challenge. She must have thought the pages of my novel's first draft were meant for her to read. I didn't want her or anyone else to read it, not yet. There were only two choices: move my writing place back to the Cottage or politely tell Emma to back off. Oh, that was a scary thought. I looked at her comment again.

With all due respect, this is not how it was done at Waterwood.

Then I noticed her additional comment at the bottom of the page:

You have a printing press. How exciting!

She still had a sense of wonder about the world. But first, I had to check Google to find out how tobacco was planted then. If she was right, her input would be valuable. Before I did anything else, I had to find out if her notes were correct. My computer and gateway to Google were at the Cottage. I grabbed my typewritten pages and headed to the internet, pleased I had some time to work on this project. I smiled to myself as I headed up the path. I always had too many projects going at the same time.

The internet reported that Colonial Virginia farmers scattered tobacco seeds on the soil in the fall so sunlight could start the germination process. Then they used wood ash or animal manure to fertilize the seedlings. To protect the young plants from frost, the farmers covered them with tree branches and left them alone until spring. I had mixed emotions about what I found. Happy she had saved me from making a big mistake. How awkward to think she was looking over my shoulder.

I felt I needed to acknowledge her comments. I had always treated Emma with respect. I shouldn't stop now. On a clean piece of paper, I wrote:

Dear Emma,

I was surprised to find your notes on the first pages of my novel. Thank you for your advice about planting tobacco. I will make the needed changes to the manuscript.

Please know this is my first attempt at writing a book. You might have been disappointed by the first draft you read. My friend, who is a writing coach, said to just write the first draft. It will not be perfect. A writer can always fix things in the edit.

If you want to wait until I have a more polished manuscript, it would be acceptable.

Thank you again for your assistance in the details.

Respectfully,

Emma

My letter lay on top of the typewriter when I locked the door to the cabin. Hopefully, it wouldn't offend her.

CHAPTER THIRTY-SIX

SPY: a person who secretly collects and reports information on the enemy's activities, movements, and plans. Also known as a secret or enemy agent.

I t was a new day and this one started at the dining table, the work area for not one, but two projects. Both were critical, but in different ways. Writing a novel was important to me. There was a long road ahead. The only way I'd reach my goal was to follow Maureen's advice: Write Every Day. Only, there was the investigation into the murder of Professor Kincaid.

The murderer could not escape the consequences of his or her actions. Her? Was the killer a woman? It was possible. The professor had been weak. It wouldn't take much to overpower him. Had he brought Dr. Abbott to the Cottage for our appointment? Why were they on the patio? Had she come up close to him, whispered in his ear, and plunged the steak knife into his chest, all the while setting me up as a suspect?

The officer had said it wasn't as easy as one might think. The rib cage helped protect vital organs. The professor had been stabbed multiple times, but it had only taken one stab to the heart to kill him. It took some force. Dr. Abbott was an avid gardener. All that weeding and pruning, planting, and hauling required strength. Did Craig consider her a suspect?

Detective Craig Mason was following the evidence, as they said on TV cop shows. It was the core of police work. His staff was looking into the professor's life in Philadelphia and at the university in case the murderer had followed him across the Bay. Craig was committed to getting justice for a victim. Whenever assigned a case, it was more than a job to him. If someone took a life, someone would pay the price… and the detective was coming to collect for Professor Kincaid.

That was why the man himself was knocking on my front door. Now that he was back from meetings in Baltimore, I'd let him know if I found a letter among those taken from Joshua's library that fit the grille.

"A grille?" he asked.

"Yes, it was used to mask out unnecessary, extraneous words that had nothing to do with the secret message," I explained.

He made a little joke: "You unmasked the mask."

Thankfully, his investigation skills were better than his jokes.

He bypassed the offer of coffee and sat down at the dining table in front of a letter to Emma lined up with the grille.

"Now, you can read the secret message," I explained.

He looked over the missive silently and peeked underneath at the innocent letter. "This is amazing! The letter is about a little boy and the message confirms an arms shipment." He looked at the letter again. "It is addressed to Emma. I thought Joshua was the spy. Did you get it wrong or did Joshua have an accomplice?"

The question caught me off guard. I couldn't tell him the real story in Emma's letter. I had to avoid sparking his inquisitive sense or he would start questioning me. It couldn't happen.

"I'm still putting the pieces together," I lied. "The historian who works with the Historical Society has been helpful and she has more to share." I hoped my response would satisfy him, at least for now. "What is important thing is this letter proves there was a Confederate spy at Waterwood who was passing along messages to the Confederate generals. In the academic world, it could be a motive for murder, crazy as it sounds, but true."

"I'm fascinated how someone could write a letter with a hidden message," he said.

"Good question. Charles introduced me to a historian at the library who explained how spies used it during the Civil War. Let me show you. The letter writer put the grille over a blank piece of paper and wrote a secret message in the little boxes. Then, and this is where it gets complicated, the writer had to build an innocent-looking letter around the secret message. When it was done, the letter was sent by mail or courier, no one being the wiser. The recipient would have the same grille and do what we did here. The letter would lay flat with the grille over the words and the secret message would appear."

"Why would such a letter come to Waterwood?" He asked. "Maryland did not secede from the Union."

"You're right, but a Confederate spy who lived up north couldn't send a letter to a Richmond address. Remember the Federal government controlled the mail. Anything addressed to a Confederate state that had seceded from the Union was probably confiscated."

"Okay. How did he get it to the Confederacy?" he asked. "Wouldn't they have closely watched the borders between Virginia, Washington, and Maryland?"

I smiled. "I had the same question. I searched and searched on Google until I found an exhibit online at a small museum in Stafford, Virginia. Let me show you." I brought up the Stafford County Museum site on my computer. "The Confederate spy network ran something called the Secret Line used by couriers to carry encrypted messages from as far away as Canada, down the East Coast to Richmond or other Confederate centers in the South. Look at this map." It was the Chesapeake Bay region from its northernmost part at Havre de Grace, Maryland, south to Norfolk, Virginia. Heavy black lines snaked over the area. "Most of the routes linked towns on the western side of the Bay. Look here. This is Seaford." I put my finger on the dot marking the town in Delaware and followed several lines south. "These lines show routes down the Eastern Shore. This route came close to Waterwood. Joshua could have met the rider or left a message in a covert location."

"Where would that have been?"

I leaned back in my chair with a sigh. "I don't know. I haven't gotten that far."

His eyes were bright with appreciation. "Emma, you've done a great job here. Must be in your genes. Your uncle would have been very proud of you," he said with a grin.

A smile touched my lips. "Thank you. Yes, I think he would have been proud of me. But it's only part of the story though. There is a missing connection. How did he link up with the courier?"

Craig stood up stretched out his back. "I don't know. However, there might be someone who could help you. It's time to talk to the good *You Can Call Me Doctor*," he said with mockery. "She is part of this elaborate scheme."

I brightened at the suggestion. "You really think she'll help?"

"It doesn't hurt to ask, especially when you have

something to trade. Can you put the grille back in the walking stick?"

"I think so."

"Do it and bring the walking stick. We're going for a ride."

CHAPTER THIRTY-SEVEN

A German study found weather can affect
a person's mood in many ways. A small change in
temperature, cloudiness, and humidity can also affect it.
– Study Leader: Jaap Denissen, Humboldt University, Berlin

I t was a gray afternoon. Heavy clouds threatening rain blocked the sun. A typical spring on the Eastern Shore. TJ said he spent a lot of time looking up, trying to guess what the weather was going to do. Of course, he used weather apps and reports, but he often said doing it the old-fashioned way was more accurate.

I remembered one time when we were going out somewhere that I brought an umbrella. He wanted to know why. I had told him the app's weather map showed an incoming green blob indicating rain.

He looked up at the gray clouds and shook his head. "There is rain in those clouds, but it's not going to come down here. You can leave your umbrella at home."

I kept it with me, but he had been right. Not a drop fell at Waterwood, the Cottage, or in Easton where we went.

I looked up and thought about TJ. What was he doing now? It had been a while since I'd seen him. He was busy with the spring planting of his fields as well as the fields of his customers. Since he owned the heavy farm equipment designed for specific tasks only done once a year, he had built up a thriving custom farming business. That meant he rented out his equipment and himself to other farmers, so they didn't have to invest thousands of dollars in the specialized attachments, or the time needed to use or maintain them.

TJ had helped me so much, especially when I had first come to the Cottage. He was stretched almost to the breaking point. I wondered if there was something I could do to help him. I might suggest he train me during one of his downtimes so I could help ease the strain during his busy seasons.

Of course, it would depend on what I decided to do with the rest of my life. Did I want to give up Big City living? Did I want to continue teaching? If I stayed here at the Cottage, what would I do? What did I really feel for TJ? Could we have a life together?

It would all depend on what path I chose and if our friendship survived and blossomed. I wondered what he would say if he knew I was sitting in Craig's unmarked police car going to a stranger's house to follow up another possible lead in the homicide investigation.

TJ had made his feelings known the night he'd stormed out of the Cottage. I hadn't meant to upset him. Whenever I thought of his caring ways and how he worried about me, a smile played on my lips, then faded when I felt conflicted. I was doing the right thing helping Craig with the investigation, but TJ was concerned for my safety. But it was my Uncle Jack who was at the center of this awful business. It was his discovery that had triggered the professor's reactions which led to his murder. I was sure Uncle Jack didn't mean to set off these events, but I felt it was my responsibility to help find out the truth. I was sorry TJ didn't understand. Plus, there was one not-so-minor detail. I was still a suspect.

That was why I was sitting in Craig's unmarked police car, on our way to see the Doctor. Was she a suspect? In the detective's mind, she was a source of information for now. Looking out the window at the passing landscape turning a verdant green, I wondered if she could have murdered the professor. She hadn't contacted the police when news of his murder hit the media outlets. She was clever in avoiding direct answers to his questions. I wondered why she was reluctant to share information to help Craig in his investigation. She was comfortable talking in detail about the antique gardening implements on her living room shelves but sidestepped his questions about her relationship with the victim.

When she had inspected the walking stick, she'd found the compartment hiding the flask, but how had she missed the second compartment? Had she known it was there and didn't want to tell us? It bothered me that she'd kept suggesting she should come to the Cottage and look at Uncle Jack's things, suggesting he might have hidden something else there. Something I was too stupid to find. She didn't exactly say it, but it was implied. She must know something key to the investigation. I didn't have long to wait to learn more about the Doctor. We were pulling up to the front gate of her garden and the walk leading to her front door.

But the door was open.

"Emma, you'd better wait in the car—" Craig began to say.

"No, I'm coming in. I'm part of this."

Unwilling to waste the time fighting with me, we headed up the walk. "Stay behind me and don't touch anything." He pushed open the door and called out, "Doctor? Are you here?

It's the police. Detective Mason. Are you..." He stopped when he heard me gasp.

"Dead," I breathed. "She's dead."

He focused his attention down the hall and up the staircase. That's why he missed what I saw. Her body, sprawled on the floor of the living room. She lay in a sea of red the same color as her sofa.

"Stay right there!" Craig ordered. He looked and listened then went to crouch next to her body.

I couldn't turn away. I couldn't stay where I was. I'd spent time with this woman, talking about unusual antiques. True, I didn't like her, but I hadn't wished her dead. As much as a I wanted to look away, my eyes were glued to the collapsed body on the rug. I tiptoed into the room and watched as Craig searched for vital signs. His mere movement sent her delicate sunshine-yellow scarf fluttering. When it settled, it landed in a pool of blood that was thickening and turning dark. My stomach flipped over, and I covered my eyes. I could not, would not throw up.

Craig continued to search for life. How could he think she was still alive? There was so much blood.

Feeling a little better, I dropped my hands from my face. Something metal caught my eye. Something metal by her neck. In her neck. I took a step closer.

"Emma! Outside!" he ordered.

I ignored him and spun around, scanning the bookshelves. Did someone kill her with

"Emma!"

It wasn't there, the strange-looking implement once used in the orchard. It wasn't anywhere. I forced myself to look at the body again. "Craig..." My voice came out like a croak. I cleared it and tried again. "Craig, I think the killer used the antique apple picker."

Craig's finger hovered over the screen of his cell phone and looked at her neck, the source of the blood.

I went on. "Its points are like little knives. They used it—"

He waved me off. "I know. I remember what she said about it."

"This time, the killer didn't come prepared. It wasn't planned. He must have lashed out and..."

He dropped his head. Was he wrestling with the same thought I had? If we had come earlier, we might have interrupted the scene and saved her life. Or we might have seen the killer leaving her house.

"Emma," he said softly. "Wait outside. Please." It was a plea to separate me from the killing we might have stopped.

I did the kindest thing I could do. I walked lightly to the front door and stepped outside. Now, maybe Craig could forget the *what if* questions and get on with his police work.

CHAPTER THIRTY-EIGHT

The Two Faces of Annabelle*: Sweet grace and beauty and the
doll in a white wedding dress that brings terror.*

I waited in Craig's car and watched the first officer drive up
to respond to the 911 call. Of all the people in the world, it
was the one'd who hassled me about the professor's murder.
When he got out of his cruiser and saw me, he said with
contempt. "You, again."

I wasn't going to get into it with him. I just pointed to the
open front door.

As other people arrived—ambulance crew and police units
—I was grateful nobody stopped to talk to me. Craig had
offered to have one of the officers drive me home, but I was
willing to wait, at least for a while. The sky had cleared. The
air was warming up with a light breeze. If it could only blow
away the awful sight we'd found in the Doctor's living room.

Waiting gave me time to process the scene we'd found
inside the house that was meant to be a tribute to beauty. The
place she was in control, until now. Seeing the darkening

blood on the light rug was a vivid reminder of the blood leaking out of the professor's chest on his light blue shirt.

I opened the car door so I could take several gulps of clean, salt-favored air. Maybe if I focused on why someone had killed her, my nerves and stomach would settle down. My first thought was almost a joke. There was a point that I suspected she had killed the professor. I was sure this wasn't a suicide. So, who killed her? Was this a game of dominos? One killer murdered by another? Then another? Or was this a game of winner take all by killing everyone else involved?

Was there a link between the two victims? What could it be? I had to think. Craig always wanted evidence.

Then a new thought swept in with the breeze that brought a dark curtain down around me. Had Uncle Jack died of natural causes as I had been told? Or had someone killed him, too? If that were true, I would not be able to sit quietly and ponder all these questions. I would be scouring the region for his killer. More deep breaths. No, my imagination was out of control. My family, even Uncle Jack's attorney, were comfortable with the medical conclusions. No one mentioned a mysterious historical find. The Cottage wasn't ransacked. No one knew about his find until Dr. Kincaid came looking. No one except him and his killer.

I had to try a different approach. Dr. Abbott had admitted she knew Professor Kincaid. Wendell at the auction house had said she was the woman who was with the professor to their meeting. That was before he'd been killed, obviously. And before he'd became ill on my patio. How long had he been down here on the Shore? I wondered if Craig knew where the professor had been staying. I strongly suspected he hadn't been staying with the Doctor. I felt guilty thinking badly about the dead, but…she didn't strike me as the type of person who would cheerfully welcome a house guest. If anyone was the opposite of Uncle Jack, it was Doctor Elizabeth Abbott, recently deceased.

I realized with a start there was another connection to Uncle Jack: Joshua's walking stick. The two of them had known Uncle Jack had found something they considered important to the academic world. We had shown Doctor Abbott what we believed to be his discovery. The only one who never knew exactly what he had found had been Dr. Kincaid. That was sad. He'd been the one who wanted to declare its importance, research the history it had exposed, and make it public for others to study. He had admitted he wanted to take credit in the beginning, but during our talk in his hospital room, he said he would give Uncle Jack the appropriate credit. It was all very sad.

"Emma?" Craig surprised me out of my daydream. "The crime scene people are packing up for now. And they've taken..."

"Yes," I said, trying to make it easier. "I saw the ambulance load up and leave."

"Do you feel up to coming inside again? I'd like you to look around, see if there is anything else out of place or missing. Can you do that? It would help."

I swallowed and said, "Sure."

After we both put on footies and gloves, we went inside. Walking into the living room, I tried to avert my eyes from the large red stain on the rug. I went to the bookshelves and didn't see anything out of place. Her other antique gardening implements were sitting where they had been before, all except the apple picker. Someone had used it to... I shuddered at the thought.

I wandered slowly around the rest of the room. There was a small antique writing desk by a window overlooking the garden, probably once used by a woman in the decades before email, telephones, or other modern conveniences. A red leather portfolio or book about the size of a regular sheet of paper sat in the center of the desk. There was no identifying title. Using a gloved finger, I opened the cover to see it was a date book, a calendar of appointments. Yes, Craig might find this helpful. But first, I leafed through the pages to the date of Professor Kincaid murder. There, I found a note.

8:30 AM Kincaid at Harbor Inn

I showed Craig the entry and he slid the book into an evidence bag. Neither one of us knew how to interpret piece of information. Was it possible that there were really two killers involved?

CHAPTER THIRTY-NINE

*Antique furniture often has secret compartments: a false
bottom of a drawer or an extension; a secret panel released
by pressing a screw head; a decorative column, known as a
pilaster, pulls out to reveal a slot; a discrete mechanism to
open a side or back; a section that rotates.*

Craig drove me home instead of having one of the other
officers do it. He was thoughtful and considerate,
always. Plus, he recognized I might have something valuable
to contribute to his investigation. He didn't dismiss what I
was trying to do, like somebody else. I had to admit if I'd
followed TJ's advice and steered clear of this police business,
I wouldn't have been in the Doctor's house today, wouldn't
have been shocked by the bloody scene of violent death. It
would take a long time to get it out of my head.

We didn't say much on the trip back to the Cottage. I was
glad Craig didn't want to talk. With all the crazy thoughts and
emotions going through my brain, I wouldn't have made any
sense.

Finding the entry in Dr. Abbott's appointment book bothered me. I couldn't make sense of it. She had an appointment to meet the professor before he had an appointment with me. Had they met for a few minutes, or had she come with him to the Cottage?

When Craig slowed down to drive through St. Michaels and I saw the schools, the dam burst.

I began to think aloud. "If the teaching community is as tight-knit and competitive as we've been led to believe, I could have sworn she was the killer." I held out my hand as if to stop Craig from saying anything. "I know, I know. It's not right to say bad things about the dead, but *really!*"

I turned toward him as much as my seatbelt would allow. "If I were writing a mystery story and needed a murderer, I would have modeled the character after You Can Call Me Doctor."

"But somebody killed her," Craig offered as he shrugged.

I groaned in frustration and turned away to focus on the empty sidewalks of St. Michaels. At least this was something I could understand. It was still early spring. The season for visitors and tourists wouldn't start for another month. Some shopkeepers were setting out planters and doing maintenance on their storefronts in anticipation of the people who would crowd the walkways and clog the streets with traffic. It would be fun to go to the Winefest or the Sea Glass Festival this year, maybe they were better ways to spend my time than dealing with murder.

I guessed we both had needed a little break. As we headed out of St. Michaels and neared the turnoff for Waterwood and the Cottage, Craig picked up the conversation. "You're right." He said it so softly, I almost missed it. "You were right to suspect her. Something about her didn't ring true. Consider her house. How could she afford that kind of home with so much land here in Talbot County? It didn't come cheap."

"And those gardens. They're beautiful, but designing them alone plus all those plants…"

"It costs money to buy the plants and maintain them. How does a retired professor afford it?"

"Didn't Wendell at the auction house say she bought and sold antiques on the side?" I reminded him.

"That's right. I'll have to ask Wendell. Maybe her murder doesn't have anything to do with Dr. Kincaid's murder. Remember how she was pushing for you to let her look through Jack's things. Maybe she pushed someone else, pushed too far," Craig suggested.

We rode along in silence before I reminded him of the appointment book. "What if she was helping Dr. Kincaid figure out what Uncle Jack had found? What if he had invited her to come to his appointment with me? Maybe he wanted her expertise and advice."

He chimed in with more ideas. "What if they arrived early and he led her to your patio to wait. Better than waiting in a car."

"Yeah, trespassing on my property is always a good idea."

He shot me a look and I felt defensive. "What? I can't feel a little resentful? How long do you think it will take me to forget seeing the man slumped over my patio table, dead."

"You have a point," he conceded.

"Then think about this," I said. "What if they had a fight while they were sitting there. She whips out the knife and stabs him. I wouldn't put it past her. She struck me as a woman who always had to be in control."

He screwed up his face then shook his head. "No, that doesn't work. He was stabbed with your steak knife. It had your fingerprints on the handle, remember? There was premeditation."

I sank back in my seat. I think I kept forgetting about that crucial point, because the thought that someone would try to frame me was overwhelming in the extreme. But that was why I was working on this case. I might have forgotten about my fingerprints on the knife, but other people, like Officer Wilson had not.

I tapped my lips, thinking. Then I straightened in my seat. "What if she saw someone else kill the professor..."

Craig finished my thought. "...and that's why she's dead?"

"Yes. How is that for a hypothesis?" I suggested.

"At least it's something I can work with." And he turned onto my driveway and with only a few words, dropped me off. There was too much for him to do now there were two murders to solve.

Inside the Cottage, I couldn't settle. I was too wound up by what had happened. Two murders! I slipped out the kitchen door and wandered down the path. I was tempting to go inside the cabin and work on my novel. At least it was a world I could control.

As I walked along, the magic of the Eastern Shore washed over me, smoothing out my mangled emotions. I could taste the salt in the air from the huge body of water not far away. The geese honking overhead as they lifted for their long flight north signaled the awakening of the new season. Leaves the shades of light green—lime, fern, mint—unfurled on branches bare only a month earlier. And the sweet smell of the air-- full of promise. Yes, it was the beginning of spring on the Eastern Shore, a time of magic.

Feeling revived, I went inside the cabin to find a handwritten letter on top of my typewriter. I couldn't wait, so I captured a picture of it with my phone, then I settled down to read the latest letter from Emma:

My Dearest Emma,

I hope I did not cause offense by reading your manuscript. It is my fault. I'm afraid I was confused. When I first noticed the pages, I thought you had written a long letter to me. When I realized it was not a letter but a story, I grew intrigued. I was drawn into it, which is a sign of good writing, even though you have not polished the manuscript yet.

I pray my comments about tobacco planting did not upset you. A mistake in historical fact might give critics an opportunity to berate your story. Believe me, some people will use even the slightest opening to make negative comments, whether it is a new recipe, a new gown, or a new way of doing something. I do not want that to happen to you as you enter the literature scene. This correction was one small contribution I could make to your success.

I felt confident in making them. Granted, I did not attend a university. Education for girls was focused on the management of the home, dealing with maladies, raising the children, and entertaining. However, Waterwood had an extensive library for its time, thanks to my father. I believe you found my most favorite books of all in my attic trunk. I kept them there for safekeeping. I never wanted to be without those stories.

Raising children and plantation life kept me busy as you might imagine. Books were my constant companions, especially when Waterwood settled down for the evening and I was alone. I read every day, quality literature, informative treatises and opinion works. Yes, I will admit I enjoyed the essays and stories appearing in the ladies' magazines, too.

Be assured, everything I read was appropriate for a woman of my social standing. This extensive reading gave me a strong appreciation of good writing. You, dear Emma, are capable of creating a good story.

With warmest regards and the strong hope you will continue to write,

Emma

With encouragement like that, I had to keep working on my story. While I was here in the cabin, I wanted to write another short note to Emma.

Dear Emma,

Thank you for your kind words. I have only begun to work on my first story, so your words of encouragement are sincerely appreciated.

I have one question for you about something else. I located some letters tucked away in a safe behind some books in the library. I am not sure why they were kept there. You said Joshua made the library his domain. You were only to be an invited guest.

Yet, three letters I found in the safe were addressed to you.

They were sent by a woman named Annabelle who lived in Philadelphia. Forgive my curiosity. Was she a relative of yours? A family friend perhaps?

I await your response.
With warmest regards,
Emma

I hoped Emma would clarify the mystery. There was another question hanging in the air:

If he had been a spy, as I now believed,
how did Joshua get the secret messages to the Confederacy?

CHAPTER FORTY

A Hand Drawn Map is more than an aid to tell people where
they are and where they are going. It is now an art form.
— (www.handmaps.org)

I t had been a stroke of luck to have found the safe in the
library of Waterwood House. The letters inside answered
some questions, but one still hung in the air, unanswered.
How did Joshua pass secret messages to a courier?

I was so disappointed. In comparison, there was no easy
way to find answers to my questions as there had been in my
other investigations. There were no letters handwritten in the
old style appearing on my desk from Daniel. There were no
diaries holding kept secrets so all I had to do was keep turning
the pages until the truth became clear. It helped to remember
that the letters from Philadelphia helped prove Joshua was a
spy for the Confederacy unless Emma confessed to being the
spy. Was that possible?

Joshua had taken over the library and its contents for
himself. He wasn't a man who would acquire fine books. I

imagined he did not have the patience to learn the value of anything. He was a man who liked doing things, not contemplating or planning. An image of his battered trunk came to mind. Joshua liked to be on the move.

Emma had said her father, Benjamin, had built the library at Waterwood and selected the books. The bindings were fine leather, so many with gold gilt, all in excellent condition. The pages of new books had to be cut apart so they could be read. In this library, most of the book pages were cut, which meant they had been enjoyed by someone.

I stared out the window, remembering my search of the library. There were a lot of books on those shelves. I'd gasped when I saw the two volumes of the first edition of *Little Women*. In today's market... I did a quick search on my phone and found them on a rare book website for $2,100, and their condition was not as good as the two books I saw on the Waterwood library shelf. TJ might be sitting on a considerable resource he could use to restore Waterwood House.

Books! I shot up straight in my chair. Books weren't the only thing I hadn't fully explored. I'd been searching Joshua's desk for the letters when I realized the desk could be moved or given away. If that happened, Joshua would lose the letters and the secret messages. So, I'd started searching the shelves, things permanently attached to the house. But now, I wondered if the desk might hold something of value. It was time to find out.

I pulled a light jacket from the hall closet. It was almost dusk and spring temperatures could be chilly. I made a slight detour to the cabin on my way to the main house to see if Emma had replied to my last letter about Annabelle. I was pleased to see a letter in Emma's distinctive handwriting sitting on the desk. I took a quick photograph of it then tucked it in a pocket. I'd read it later. Right now, I was on a mission.

As I neared Waterwood House, my steps slowed. TJ's truck was parked by the kitchen door. My feelings were jumbled. I wanted to see my friend. I'd missed him over the past weeks. He said he was busy, but was he was staying away on purpose? During the fall harvest, he'd found time to text or come by the Cottage every day. Now, I almost never saw him, probably because he was angry about my work on the murder case. Had TJ heard about the murder of Dr. Elizabeth Abbott? It would have really upset him, but I'm not sure he would have understood. He was *out of the loop* by his choice.

I wanted to go back to the Cottage and return tomorrow when TJ wasn't here. I didn't think he would want to see me. He might even be sleeping, exhausted by all the physical work he had to do. I shouldn't wake him.

I turned away then turned around again to face the house. The things I was researching were about TJ's family. He was the one who would benefit from the information I collected. He'd given me permission to use the library. I did not want to harm our friendship but walking on eggshells all the time was exhausting. I walked to the kitchen door, quietly turned the handle, and went inside.

There was no sign of the man. No sign he had eaten dinner. He must have come home and collapsed in his bed upstairs. I tiptoed through the butler's pantry, into the dining room, out to the main foyer... and was shocked by what I saw.

TJ, coming down the main staircase, wearing dark slacks, a light blue dress shirt, and no ballcap. His hair was carefully combed...and he was humming.

I knew I should have gone home, but it was too late to escape.

"Emma," he said in a friendly tone I hadn't heard for a while. "What brings you to Waterwood?"

"Oh, I'm sorry," I stuttered. "I didn't mean to..."

"No, it's okay. I said you could come. Still working on your research?" He gave his head a little shake. "You sure are tenacious."

"Yes," I said, beating down a feeling of indignation. "I'm doing research about *your* family." I had to take a deep breath. This wasn't the way I wanted to talk to TJ. This wasn't the way I—

He cut in on my thoughts. "I appreciate what you've done. You've certainly uncovered some fascinating and surprising pieces of my family's history."

I felt a surge of warmth, happiness. "I'd love to tell you about what—"

He glanced at his watch. "I'd love to hear all about it, but I'm late."

"You're going to work dressed like that?" I wanted to gobble those words back into my mouth.

His left eye narrowed a little. "It isn't work. I'm going to dinner."

I stood there, wishing I could sink into the floor.

"If you must know," he said with an edge on his words. "I'm making good on a deal I made with Abby. If she evaluated the silver tea set, I'd take her to dinner. She did the work, now, I have to do my part." He looked at his watch again. "Sorry, I've got to run."

Run, he did, down the hallway, calling over his shoulder, "We should talk soon." And the kitchen door slammed.

Dinner. Abby. She seemed nice enough... Dinner. To talk about a silver tea service.

My stomach hurt. What was I feeling?

I wanted to go home, crawl into bed, and pull the coverlet over my head. But my feet wouldn't move as my brain was rocked by waves of emotion. My brain and my heart. Was this jealousy I was feeling? I had spent so much time working on Craig's investigation, I'd ignored what my heart was now telling me I wanted, wanted more than anything.

It was the price I had to pay for doing what I thought was my responsibility: to help with Craig's case since I still believed Uncle Jack's actions and discovery were at the core of it. I heaved a deep sigh. It didn't seem to matter anymore. What was the point of figuring out how I truly felt, what I wanted? It was too late. He had found someone else, someone who made him happy, made him want to dress up and go out for dinner when he was probably dead on his feet. I had missed my chance.

He'd been so kind to me over the past months. The least I could do now was finish my research. I hoped it would yield more information about his family. I made myself move. It wouldn't be good if he found me here when he came home later, especially if he didn't come home alone. Slowly I turned toward the parlor and shuffled my way to the library.

CHAPTER FORTY-ONE

A coffered ceiling incorporates sunken shapes or panels to create a 3-D effect. A room feels more spacious while, at the same time, cozy due to the sound cushioning of the ceiling.

I opened the heavy door to the library. I remembered my first glimpse of the room and it still took my breath away. The high oak coffered ceiling, the walls of leather-bound books, the marble fireplace were not enough this time to distract me from my feelings of misery and gloom. TJ was out with a lovely young woman who gave him her attention, who took time to make herself attractive. Here I was doing what he asked me not to do: research sparked by a murder investigation. I felt like a *schlump*. He'd seen me wearing jeans, a light shapeless sweater, and one of Uncle Jack's jackets at least two sizes too big. I was in TJ's house, researching members of TJ's family with no TJ. I didn't know quite what to do with it all.

As I slipped the jacket off, I remembered Emma's letter, folded into one of the pockets. At least I had a valuable consolation prize. I slipped the letter out of the pocket and flung myself onto the gold upholstered settee opposite the broad hearth. I unfolded the letter hoping to find solace and distraction.

My Dear Emma,

Here is a quick note to answer your question directly.

Annabelle Jennings Miller lived in Philadelphia. She always signed her letters to me with both her maiden and married names. We are not that formal here on the Shore when we sign our letters. I thought it might be the proper thing to do in a big city. When I asked her why she did it, I learned I was wrong. She wrote, in confidence, she grew up in the South and her heart would always be there. She thought I would sympathize. She signed her maiden name, Jennings, because it was recognized and highly regarded as a Southern family name.

Her strong feelings for the South were a little odd since she was the wife of Richard Miller, a wealthy man and an important figure in the federal government.

I never met her in person. Shortly after we were married, my husband suggested we correspond. He believed I could benefit from her experience and guidance as she was older. Perhaps if we had talked face to face, I could have learned more and better understood. Alas, it was not possible. When we began our correspondence, the war was raging, and it was too dangerous for me to travel to Pennsylvania.

In the early days of our marriage, she and her husband were good friends of my husband. Many times, he felt it necessary to travel across the Chesapeake Bay to better secure the fortunes of Waterwood. He did business with Annabelle's husband though I cannot tell you the nature of their exchanges.

When my father was alive, he always made certain I understood how interactions affected Waterwood. He worried something would happen to him before I had a husband who would take over the management of the plantation. Mr. Collins should have felt comfortable sharing information with me about business arrangements for the plantation, but he did not.

Instead, Mr. Collins was more concerned about my lack of female companionship and instruction. It is true I grew up without a mother, who died giving me life. My father decided early on not to marry again. He felt it would be unfair to any bride, because his first wife had truly been the one love of his life.

Let me be clear, dear Emma, I did not grow up deprived of knowledge of the feminine ways and responsibilities. I had my dear Sally, the slave woman assigned to care for me the moment I entered this world. She nursed me through all the childhood ailments, grave and minor. Even if I sustained only a skinned knee, she was there immediately with a soothing balm, a clean hankie for my tears, and a hug.

Between my father and Sally, I learned all about the duties and responsibilities required of the mistress of a plantation like Waterwood. I carried the mantle almost from birth.

After I became Mrs. Collins, my husband arranged for this woman in Philadelphia to correspond with me about things required of a lady of the house, such as how to act in polite company, proper entertaining skills, the latest in fashion, and the like. In many cases, she wrote to me about things I cared nothing about or were not appropriate to life at Waterwood. Even when I pointed this out to Mr. Collins, he insisted we continue our correspondence. In fact, he took exceeding pleasure in reading her letters himself though, for the life of me, I cannot imagine why. Occasionally, I would have to slip into the library to find a recent letter from her so I could respond appropriately.

That is all I can tell you about the mysterious, but oddly, good friend of mine, Annabelle. I hope this sketchy information satisfies your curiosity.

With affection,
Emma

How curious. The circumstances surrounding the correspondence sounded credible. Then again, wouldn't it have been the responsibility and the privilege of the local ladies on the Eastern Shore and her family in Baltimore to provide such guidance? Wouldn't the lifestyle in this rural community have varied wildly from the social whirl of Philadelphia? I too was puzzled why this married woman would include her maiden name in her signature at the end of a personal letter? How prominent was her family?

I grabbed my phone and searched the name and a few keywords. Nothing came up to suggest the name Miller would have a political connection. Then I searched the name Jennings. One of the hits was a site listing the names of prominent Southern families. The name Jennings was on the list. Was this Joshua's link to a well-placed Confederate spy in the North? Was this the reason he removed Annabelle's letters from Emma's possession? Did her letters hold secret messages?

The possibilities were so exhilarating I could no longer sit on the settee. I wandered within the walls of the library surrounded by bound tomes of the world's intelligence, imagination, and scholarship. Excitement sent rejuvenating energy through my body. And how appropriate to put together these pieces of the puzzle in this room where I'd found the letters from Annabelle Jennings Miller tucked into Joshua's safe hidden behind some fake books.

I felt like dancing until I remembered there was still an answer needed to bring everything together. I still didn't know how Joshua got the secret messages to the Confederacy?

CHAPTER FORTY-TWO

Reading 19ᵗʰ century letters and documents handwritten in the Spencerian style can be difficult. The words were fluid and somewhat decorative. Impediments such as ink spots, smears, and paper deterioration from age do not help.

Daylight was fading to evening. I flipped the switch and the overhead library chandelier burst forth with heavenly light. The four-foot-wide chandelier had such grace and elegance I figured Emma's momma must have selected it when she was a bride early in the 19ᵗʰ century. The white glass lampshade in the center reminded me of the opal with its gentle pastel colors. The nine electric lights must have once held enough candles so someone could read both books and letters comfortably.

Enough gawking. I had to finish my search of the desk before the night shrouded my way home in darkness. The last full moon was weeks ago. Starlight wouldn't be enough to navigate the driveway. I check my phone and my battery was almost gone. It wouldn't be good for my phone's flashlight app to die on the way home. I'd need a flashlight... I'd look for one later. Now, I needed to search the desk.

My fingers explored the top and edges of it. Was there a button or secret spring to release a door or drawer somewhere in the desk? An indentation gave me a moment of excitement until I realized it was the place where a man might place his elbow to support his chin while he was reading.

I stopped and thought, IF there was a secret hiding place in the desk, it must be inside the drawers or underneath.

I began my search again but, this time, with the large top drawer. Someone had stored the standard items there, pencils, pens, paperclips, and more. My fingertips wandered around the inside of it. Maybe a touch would activate some hidden mechanism. Nothing. I repeated the process with the top drawers on either side of it. Again, nothing.

Uncle Jack would have called this a fool's errand. Only one more drawer to check.

I pulled out the bottom left drawer... and it almost dragged me out of the chair. The drawer lurched downward about 3 inches. Had I broken it? I tried to push it closed. No way. As I was getting down on the floor and crawling into the kneehole, I wondered how I was going to explain to TJ I had broken his library desk?

Looking at it from underneath, it didn't appear broken. It just didn't have anything to support it. If I held it up a little, the drawer closed smoothly. The users of the desk must have known and handled it correctly.

Wait a minute. When the drawer had sagged, did it...? I ran my fingers along the edge. Yes, there was a gap. And in the gap was a rolled-up piece of paper.

I had to tamp down my excitement and move carefully. A tear might destroy whatever it was. Only I couldn't see what I was doing. I laid down with more than half my body underneath this heavy solid wood desk. What if it…? No, no negative thoughts.

I closed my eyes to better visualize what my fingertips were telling me.

Easy. Gently. Got it!

The scroll fell onto my face, along with decades of dust.

Coming out from underneath, I hit my head lightly on the center drawer. I was coughing, but triumphant. I had the rolled-up paper tied with a gray satin ribbon in my hand.

I wanted to unwrap the scroll, but this wasn't time. This wasn't the place. Night was moving in. TJ could come back at any time. It was time to go home.

I jiggled the bottom drawer and slid it closed. Everything else looked the same way I'd found it. I clicked off the light, but before leaving Waterwood House, I headed to the mud room off the kitchen and found a flashlight. TJ was always prepared. I headed home, wishing I could share the excitement of my find with him.

In the Cottage, my dining room chandelier wasn't as grand as those at Waterwood House, but it gave off plenty of light to see what was on the old, discolored paper. I unrolled it with care. Thankfully, it did not crack or disintegrate as it revealed lines, not words.

It was a map. A map with two heavy Xs in black ink. I used some little things from around the room to hold the map open while I took a picture then let it snap back into a scroll. Looking at it closely after sending it to the computer, my jaw dropped. Unless I was totally wrong, it was a hand-drawn map in black ink of Waterwood Plantation.

I recognized the shape because of I'd spent a lot of time studying the large, framed map of the little place near the Cottage where the water had created my favorite cove. The place sheltered by a grove of crepe myrtles in all shades of pink and ringed by tall pines. The place where the renovated cabin stood. The place Emma had loved the best.

Someone had made some rough illustrations to represent certain landmarks inside the heavy boundary lines of Waterwood. I zoomed in on the largest landmark near the center. It was a crude rendering, but it represented Waterwood House. A slow smile spread over my face. This was the missing piece of evidence to prove Joshua was the spy.

CHAPTER FORTY-THREE

"Whatever satisfies the soul is truth."
–Walt Whitman

The next morning, I wanted to skip down to the cabin. I wanted to greet TJ on the path and have us set out on the quest together. Things were falling into place. The map showed clues to places where Joshua had passed messages to the Confederacy. The big, black Xs marked specific places on Joshua's map. But I would have to put in the time and effort to find what I thought were the meeting points. I felt a little empty inside. A little lonely having enjoyed TJ's company on past adventures. But I couldn't let those negative thoughts stop me. I had to set them aside, set my feelings for TJ aside right now so I could move forward. It was an important lesson I'd learned the hard way in rehab, learning to walk, learning to live again.

I would have to fill that empty place with something else that was important to me. That was why I was glad Maureen was coming to the Cottage today to give me her feedback on the first pages of my novel.

My novel. Those words were thrilling and scary. Questions started to bubble up in my mind: What if I don't finish the book? What if it is terrible? What if...? Thanks to Maureen, I understood where these confidence-destroying comments were coming from... my Internal Editor. I was getting better at shutting him up, but he still burst into my mind without warning. It didn't matter. Not today. Maureen was coming. I couldn't wait to talk with her about what I'd written.

Maureen's lecture about the Internal Editor and the shift of my work area to the plantation desk in the cabin had made a real difference. The typewriter was like a magic trick. Yes, it had been inconvenient to retype my pages into the computer, but I could make small corrections and add a better word. Emma's notes guided me through certain corrections. I couldn't wait to tell Maureen about my workspace. But could I? She would wonder why that beautiful desk had been relegated to a small cabin where the woods met the creek's shoreline. TJ had made it clear Emma, Daniel, and the desk had to remain our secret. No, I decided, we could share the work but not the mechanics of where and how I did it.

When Maureen arrived, I felt like a little kid. We met in the living room to avoid the stacks of Joshua's Civil War letters, notes, and printouts on the dining room table. She pulled out my draft she had printed out from my email. I had my copy, and we began. But not the way I thought we would.

By mistake, I had also brought the photos of Emma's comments that I'd printed out for later reference. I put them off to the side and squared up my pages in front of me.

Maureen never missed a thing. She leaned over and pointed to them. "What are those? May I see them?" She held her hand out for them. "It looks like you have another reader commenting on your writing."

I closed my eyes for a moment and thought, my dear

friend, you have no idea. "Oh, these pages? I didn't mean to bring them to our meeting. They are just an early version of what you have."

"But there are some comments written on them."

"Yes, I scribbled some thoughts when I was reading," I said slowly, trying to put together a believable response. "I incorporated them in a later version, so they really have no bearing on our meeting today." Mentally, I crossed my fingers and hoped she would drop it. She didn't.

She wiggled her fingers toward them. "If you'll let me see them, it will help me better understand your process. It's the only reason why I want to look at them."

There was no way I could avoid the situation without being rude. I handed her the pages Emma had corrected.

Maureen's eyes grew wide. "Oh! I didn't realize you had such beautiful handwriting. Usually, when a writer makes notes in the margin, the script is almost unintelligible. This is beautiful."

I could feel my face getting warm. "Thank you," I said, feeling a little guilty at taking credit. "What did you think of the first part of Chapter One?" I was relieved when she launched into a series of points I should consider until I realized she was critiquing my work. My neck muscles tightened. I admired this woman. I wanted to do my best work for her. And now, she was offering a detailed critique.

We talked for almost two hours. My hand was cramping from taking notes. I was grateful when Maureen looked at her watch and announced she had to go. I stood up to walk her to the door when my phone rang. The caller ID read DETECTIVE. Why was Craig calling?

"Maureen, I have to take this call. I won't be a minute." She didn't look pleased but sat down in a small chair by the door which surprised me.

Why was he calling? Was it more bad news? "Hello?"

"You don't sound very welcoming," he said.

"I'm glad to hear from you. Please tell me it's not…I can't take any more dead—"

"Emma, stop." He gave me a moment to breathe. "Better now?"

"Yes."

"Good," he said. "I'm calling on behalf of your new friend with all the fancy names."

"Who…?" I began to ask. "Oh, you mean Stanley Archibald Holt, well-dressed, dripping-with-money man at the auction house?"

"You got it in one. He is a little upset with you," Craig sounded like a parent talking to a naughty child.

"Why?" I asked, feeling resentful. "I—"

"He said he gave you his card hoping you would call him, but he hasn't heard a peep out of you."

I gave Maureen a weak smile of apology.

"And he called you? This is ridiculous. Look, I'm sorry. I can't talk now. Let me call you later."

"When?" he wanted to know.

"Later. I have someone here right now. I can call you later."

"Make it much later. I'm going into a meeting." And Craig hung up.

With a deep sigh, I turned to Maureen. "I'm so sorry."

"It was something about the murder investigation, wasn't it?" I nodded. "Maybe you should think about writing a mystery novel instead of historical fiction." She stood up. "But that is a conversation for another day. Better get your things."

"Get my things? Why?"

"Emma," she sighed. "Because I'm leaving and I'm taking you with me."

I stood there, staring like an idiot, trying to catch on to what she was talking about.

"The monthly writer's meeting?"

Then it hit me. "OH! That's tonight!"

"Yes, it is tonight and you're coming with me," she announced.

It was the last thing I wanted to do. How could I explain it to her? If only I could work with Maureen alone and not interact with the others in the group. Individually, I guessed they were alright. Who was I kidding? Those women were weird and, together, they were formidable for this fledgling writer. I began to shake my head.

"Emma," Maureen spoke like a mother to a difficult child. "You don't have to show them your pages. You don't have to tell them you have started the novel. If you're asked, say you're working with writing prompts and finding it helpful. You don't have to go into detail."

Her comments were making me feel better, but she wasn't going to let me off the hook. "Emma, it will do you good to be around other writers."

"I'm talking to you, learning from you," I countered.

"But one person isn't enough. If you come home from the meeting tonight with just one insight, one tidbit to better your understanding of the craft, it will have been time well spent," she declared.

"Yes, but---"

"But what?"

I just had to say it. "They're so weird."

She squeezed her lips together, suppressing a smile. "Well, I can't disagree with you." Then she chuckled aloud. "Think of them as characters in a storybook."

I burst out laughing. "That's funny."

"Maybe," she went on without even a smile. "You can learn from them, and it will benefit your writing."

I was listening carefully now. "How?"

"Look for the motivation. An actor always wants to know the character's motivation, right?" I nodded. "If you're going to write a story that keeps your reader's attention, you too have to know each character's motivation. A character who engages the reader is multi-dimensional. Each one should have texture and depth and a reason for doing what they do. It's yet another writing skill you need to develop. The writing group gives you an excellent opportunity to practice, to figure the motivation of each person in the room." She shrugged. "It will even help you in your historical research and this police investigation you're doing."

I thought for a moment, trying to absorb this concept. "Writing is more than putting pen to paper." I added quickly. "Of course, I knew that, but..."

"There is a lot you have to work out before you begin the book with Chapter One," Maureen stated with a smile.

I smiled back and announced, "My learning process tonight begins when the front door opens."

"You've got it!"

Together, we gathered our things and sprinted to her car. If we were late, Gretchen would make our evening miserable.

CHAPTER FORTY-FOUR

A writing group often presents a truth
that no one wants to hear.

We pulled up to the Victorian-style house with the wraparound porch and hustled inside. As we entered the gourmet kitchen, the main gathering place before dinner and the meeting, a woman with midnight-black hair and bangs cut straight across her forehead shot us a dirty look from the other side of the massive island.

Gretchen—our hostess and leader of the group—was not pleased. "Finally," she declared in her normal clipped way of speaking. "I was beginning to think you two had gotten lost and I'd have to freeze your dinners for next time." Her erect posture wasn't the only thing rigid about the woman who spearheaded the monthly meeting of writers. We always met at her house. She always prepared a multi-course dinner and always set the meeting agenda. No one had voted her head of the group. She had us believing she knew what was best for all of us, and we followed her like little ducklings. Even Maureen.

We gathered in what was truly a Great Room with a high ceiling and a wall of windows overlooking a perfect lawn ringed by pine trees. There was room for us to sit at the long table opposite the gourmet kitchen, but we never did. Gretchen always shooed us to her formal dining room.

I looked around at the other women writers. Maureen had called them characters. If someone put them in a story, would readers find them believable? I could feel a smile play across my lips and had to swallow the laugh. I had to be careful. These characters didn't miss much.

"Look at Emma," Frumpy Zelda, in an unflattering green sweater, said. "Something has tickled her." When I just smiled, she made her demand. "Emma, you have to share." She raised her eyebrows forming a straight line above her eyes. "If you don't, I'll call you Giggles for the rest of the evening."

"Yes, share," said Denise, ever the quiet one. Never willing to lead, but always eager to join in... or pile on.

A cold jab of panic hit me. They weren't going to let this go. I had to say something, but what?

Thankfully, Maureen came to my rescue. "I bet I know what it is. I have been working with Emma, helping her develop her craft. We met at her house earlier today and..."

"Oh," cried Denise. "I would have come. Puleeze, can I come next time?"

Oh, no, I thought. *Please no.*

"No, you wouldn't want to be in these sessions," Maureen said. "They are too basic for a writer like you."

Hearing the compliment, Denise squeezed her shoulders up by her ears in delight. Gertrude smiled, too. She was the Mother Hen to her chicks, of which Denise was the neediest. Gertrude guided them as writers, helped them understand how to think, how a story evolved, even how to live sometimes.

Maureen was a crafty character herself in such an elegant way. "Emma must be thinking about the writing prompt I gave her," Maureen continued.

"Oh, tell us," the group chimed in.

All except Gretchen, who gave Maureen another one of *those* looks, but the woman couldn't complain. Maureen's background as a successful writer and advertising creative director made her the star of the group. Gretchen couldn't afford to lose her. So, she said calmly, "Yes, Maureen, you should tell me the writing prompt at dinner and then, together we can decide if we should use yours or the one I picked for tonight's meeting."

All the other women in the room tensed, but Maureen didn't miss a beat. "Of course, but didn't you say in your email about tonight's meeting we would be talking about setting?"

"That's right, isn't it?" Zelda responded looking at Gretchen, wanting to earn her approval. Zelda wanted to shine, but she made it hard to admire or even look at her, with her grizzled gray hair, strange shades of lipstick, and shapeless bohemian dresses in unflattering colors. In a small group of two or three, she could be nurturing. I suspected she had a lot to offer other writers, newbies like me.

Maureen spoke up. "My prompt was about character development. If I remember correctly, we did it last month. Why don't we stick with your original idea, Gretchen?"

In response, Gretchen gave her a tight smile that didn't quite reach her eyes. "Yes, we will." When she went back to stirring something on the stove, everyone in the room relaxed. "I am glad you agree, Maureen. I picked this particular prompt for our writing time in honor of a special guest." Gretchen turned and gestured for a young woman trying to blend into the wallpaper to come stand by her.

She was medium height and rather bland. If I had seen her in Walmart, I probably won't have looked twice, might even have forgotten about her by the time I reached the checkout. Her thin brown hair, parted in the middle, hung straight on either side of her narrow face. She wore a little eye makeup to accent her dishwater brown eyes. The bright red lipstick on her full lips was one thing. The other was attitude. She wasn't thrilled to be attending our meeting, but neither was I on my first night. She smiled, but it was forced and small. Her facial expression defensive and defiant at the same time. Both sadness and pain showed clearly on her face, but she was too young and inexperienced to know how to hide those emotions. So, we had a new character in the group. What was her story? It was more than an interest in memoir writing Gretchen was talking about on her behalf.

"This is Valerie," Gretchen said when she had everyone's attention. "As you know, I volunteer at the new independent living complex in Easton. Valerie works there. She is efficient and compassionate. She wants to do more." Gretchen looked at the girl and cocked her head. "Tell them." She paused for a moment then added, "please."

Reluctantly, she stepped away from a tall kitchen cabinet where she was leaning. Her eyes skittered around the room. Was she looking for a way to escape? Now, I could see she was young, not too long out of high school. She might have a grownup's job, but her clothes were screamed high school: short red plaid skirt, tight black sweater, black tights, and ankle boots. She must have sensed she didn't quite fit in because she asked Gretchen quietly, "Are you sure?"

She received a nod from the leader of the group, quickly followed by encouragement from Zelda. "Tell us what you'd like to do."

Ever meek Denise spoke up. "Yes, tell us and if we can help, we will."

Buoyed with this support, the young woman began to speak, but no one could hear her.

"Speak up," commanded Zelda. "We want to hear what you have to say.

The girl began again, describing a situation at the independent living center with new found confidence. "Each person living there has lived a life. Some good, some not so good. Some rich and fulfilling, some not. Many have joys they want to record so their families and younger friends can know about them. I want to learn how to help them pick the right words and put them down on paper or in an electronic diary."

"Like an oral history project?" suggested Denise.

"Or teaching them how to write a memoir." Catherine said.

Valerie glanced at Gretchen again and said, "Yes, but the point is to help them relive a part of their lives."

As she spoke, she clasped her hands in front of her and pressed her fingers as if she was trying to squeeze toothpaste out of an almost-finished tube. It struck me she was way too nervous for this situation.

She continued. "When the lucky ones make a record of their joys, they are reliving the happy times. Those who have regrets, need a way to atone for what they did or did not do. They may be able to find a way to rectify something in their past."

The depth of her feeling and the gravity of her words made me think there was more going on here than what appeared on the surface. I looked around the room and found Maureen just as she turned toward me. A similar thought must have crossed her mind. I wasn't sure what I was going to learn about the craft of writing tonight, but it was obvious Maureen was right. There was more going on within the group of writers than I'd ever imagined.

I didn't have much time to consider it. Catherine brought up the subject on everyone's mind: Murder.

CHAPTER FORTY-FIVE

"Write what you know." –*Mark Twain*

"Don't limit yourself. Do the research." –*Susan Reiss*

The comments about murder along with speculation about the investigation came so fast, I couldn't follow who said what.

"It must have been awful, finding his dead body and all."

"That poor professor, stabbed."

"And on your own patio."

"He didn't deserve it."

"You must tell me all about it," Zelda whispered to me. "I want to write a murder mystery."

Wanting to remove myself from the mania, I stepped up to the buffet laid out on the kitchen island. "Gretchen, dinner looks amazing!"

She thanked me with a nod, but it did nothing to stop the comments about the murder. I suspected they really didn't want responses, but to hear themselves talk flippantly about such a horrible event.

"I heard he was looking for some kind of artifact and wanted to break into your house."

And there was more. I was surprised at Catherine's comment. "And the police didn't arrest *you* for murder. How curious."

"The newspaper report must be wrong," Denise suggested.

I headed toward the dining room, away from the swirling opinions and comments, when one stopped me in place.

Zelda said, "I know what Dr. Kincaid was going through."

Every head turned toward her.

"It's hard being in academia. It will either drive you crazy or kill you," Zelda stated flatly.

Catherine moved closer to Zelda and put her arm around her shoulders to offer comfort. "Why would you say such a thing?"

"Because I have the scars to prove it. I'm a librarian at the community college." Zelda's eyes glistened as she shrugged. "It is not a bad job. It's just not what I wanted to do."

"Tell me, what did you wanted to do?" Catherine encouraged.

Zelda hung her head as if trying to disappear into her too-big, shapeless, butter-yellow pullover sweater that did nothing for her complexion. "I wanted to teach. I studied economics and landed a teaching position at a good East Coast school. It was all I ever wanted to do, challenge eager, inquisitive students. There was a welcoming staff and a clear path to my doctorate. It was all good. Until I was on track for tenure."

"That's good, isn't it?" Denise looked to Gretchen for confirmation.

"Yes," Zelda responded. "It was the goal. A tenured position at a noteworthy university. When it came clear I was on the track, everything changed. It was so competitive, being invited to coffee and faculty dinners which felt more like job interviews than social events. They grilled me about research questions I was exploring. People made gentle suggestions about articles I should write." Her face screwed up in an ugly expression. "Gentle like a sledgehammer. They tried to manage everything I did. The stress skyrocketed. I guess I pushed back a little, didn't follow all their recommendations. People I'd considered professional friends—you know, fellow academics—began to snub me. I wasn't part of the elite club. My anxiety made it hard for me to function."

"What did you do?" Maureen asked, her face tightened in concern.

Denise and Catherine gathered close to Zelda to give her support.

"I quit." Zelda dropped her eyes. Her normal cocky attitude had evaporated. "I dropped out of my Ph.D. program and left the university. I didn't drop out of academia entirely." She raised her eyes and cocked her head to the side. "I got my master's degree in Library Science. I figured if I couldn't teach, I could help the people who do... and I could teach by helping students one-on-one when they were researching something specific."

"And you do it so well," Catherine declared as she gave the woman a hug. "You helped me so much when I was working on the position paper. I'll never forget it."

Was this what Dr. Kincaid had been experiencing when he heard about Uncle Jack's find? He'd known diabetes was ravaging his body. He'd said he wasn't sure how much longer he could work, how much time he had left to make his mark. Now, I could see firsthand how that kind of academic pressure could affect someone who wanted to focus on giving his students the best education possible, or someone who wasn't part of the elite network. The rest of our group made encouraging comments until Gretchen's rather strident voice rose above the din to remind us to get our dinners and go to the dining room.

When dessert—a scrumptious tiramisu—and coffee were served, Gretchen and Catherine did a joint presentation about writing a memoir for the benefit of our young guest, Valerie. When it was time to move our dishes out of the way and do a writing exercise, I opened my notebook with confidence and was ready to dive in. What a difference Maureen's mentoring had made. Gretchen gave us the writing prompt to briefly describe a place from our past. This was the setting exercise. We wrote our short pieces, read them aloud, and suffered critiques from others. Before I knew it, the house clock struck nine and our monthly meeting was over.

Gretchen stood at the front door, saying good-bye, as the consummate hostess should. I began to thank her for a nice evening when she decreed I couldn't leave yet.

"Oh, why not?" I asked, thinking I had left something behind.

"Isn't it obvious? Your handsome chauffeur isn't here yet," she explained.

Okay, this was awkward. "He, um…"

"TJ is really busy," Maureen jumped in to save me again. "It's spring planting time. He has a jam-packed schedule. I'm Emma's chauffeur tonight." She touched my arm and hustled us out the door. "Thanks for a great evening, Gretchen."

We had almost made it to the car when a voice came out of the darkness. "It's just like him to get everyone on his side."

We whirled around and relaxed a little when Valerie stepped out of the shadows. "I heard them make all kinds of excuses for him. It didn't justify his actions, of messing with people's lives."

"Who? Who are you talking about?" I asked, confused.

"Dr. Phillip Kincaid, of course," she sneered.

Her reaction to the murdered man was beyond disrespectful. There was a history here. Knowing it might help the homicide detective working the case, I turned to Maureen. "Why don't you go on to the car. I'll be there in a minute."

Maureen glanced at Valerie with narrowed eyes. "Are you sure?"

"Yes, yes, I'll be fine. I won't be long." I gave her arm a little pat of reassurance, though I didn't know if it was for her benefit or mine.

When we were alone, I asked the young woman, "Why would you say such a thing about a man who—"

"A man who doesn't deserve your respect or a kind word," she snapped.

I didn't know what to say to such bitterness.

"Don't look so shocked. I can say it because I'm his daughter."

I almost staggered as I took a step on Gretchen's driveway. Daughter? This wasn't what I'd expected. Did Craig know? I took in a quick breath. "His daughter," I said with a little shake of my head. "I'm a little surprised. When I talked to him in the hospital, I asked if there was someone, I should contact for him. He said he wasn't married anymore. His ex-wife wouldn't care where or how he was. He didn't mention a daughter."

"You don't need to be married to have a child," she snarled.

A strange thought hit me. "Did he know you are his daughter?"

"No," she said with a sassy lilt.

"But you know he is… I mean, he was your father?"

"Yes." Her eyes shifted toward the dark woods, not seeing the trees, but a time long ago. Her voice grew soft. "When I was young, I wanted to know about my father more than anything. I bugged my mother constantly. Finally, after making me promise I would never contact him – even made me pinkie-promise—she showed me my birth certificate. His name on it. Mom told me some basic things about him so I wouldn't think he was in prison or a terrorist or something awful. I wish…" Her voice trailed off.

I needed to put facts together. "He lived in Philadelphia, but you live on the Eastern Shore?" It began as a statement and ended up a question, which showed how confused I was.

She looked at me again, coming back to this moment. "They met here. He was visiting a friend and they went to a barn sale. Mom was helping out. They got friendly, really friendly and soon, I was on the way. He claimed he loved my mother but obviously, she wasn't good enough for him. He couldn't condescend to acknowledge me. I was his own daughter, but the world saw me as illegitimate." She started to move around, back and forth, in and out of the pools of light thrown by the spotlights on the house. "I guess he was worried it would put a stain on his reputation of the High and Mighty college professor." She stopped on the edge of where the light met the darkness of the pine forest surrounding Gretchen's house.

Gretchen. Had she seen this side of Valerie? I didn't think so or she may not have spoken so glowingly about the young woman's compassion.

But Valerie hadn't finished her story. "What a loser. He couldn't even step up to his responsibilities. He should have sent Mom some money, at least. She has worked hard my whole life just to earn enough money to take care of us. We were never homeless, thanks to Mom. Always had food on the table, thanks to Mom. But to do that, she was gone a lot of the time. All while he sat up there in the Big City, all high and mighty without a care for the woman he'd claimed to love." The snarl in her voice was back.

I thought about my brief visit with Dr. Kincaid in the hospital and couldn't equate the mild-mannered man there with the uncaring monster this girl was describing.

She was ranting again, and I had to catch up with what she was saying. "...studied and earned good grades in school, always have." She raised her chin in defiance. "Do you know why?"

She waited for me to answer her question., so I said, "Because you're smart?"

"Yeah, I guess, but it wasn't because I got those smarts from my deadbeat dad. I did it for my mom. It made her happy when I brought home good grades. I couldn't buy her nice things. Didn't have the money. But I could bring her my good grades and she loved it. You can't buy them at the store. She was so proud when they read my name at high school graduation, announcing I had made the Honor Roll all four years."

"That's quite an accomplishment," I said. "And now you're working at the independent living center."

Her body deflated like a balloon, and she dropped her chin to avoid my eyes. She didn't want to see my reaction. "Yeah," she said with no enthusiasm. "My mom wanted me to go to college, but I got a job instead. I want to help out, so she doesn't have to work so hard."

Then Valerie stood tall and threw her shoulders back. Her defiant attitude was back. "Why should I go to college? I don't want to be like those snobs in..." She sneered when she said the last word, "...*academia*. I don't want to be like him."

Valerie would ignore any argument I made for the advantages of going to college. I tried a different tack. "If you went to college, what would you study?"

"I told you. I am not going to college," she announced again.

I held up a hand to ward off her angry response. "What would you like to do, if you could do anything?" She dropped her shoulders and took in a breath. I had struck a chord.

Her facial features softened. 'I'd like to be a nurse. Always have, since I was a little girl." Her face hardened again. "But it's not going to happen. You have to go to college and nursing school. It costs a lot of money. I'm not going to put that kind of stress on my mom. I've got a job and I'm helping her out. It's about time someone did. And I'm helping older people make amends."

I stood there with no idea what to say. There was so much anger pent up inside this young woman. Anger and love. I thought about Uncle Jack's good friend. A man who had struggled with a devastating disease all by himself. He and his daughter were two people, blind to each other, wanting the same things, not knowing the other was within arm's reach.

"Well, all I have to say is, don't let *Professor Kincaid...*" The snark was back in her words. "...upset you or ruin your life like he did ours." She shrugged. "At least for you, he will only be a nightmare. Good luck."

She stomped off into the dark, leaving me speechless.

Later, in the car, we rode in silence until I couldn't stand it anymore. I had to talk about what had happened.

"You said the meeting would be a good lesson. I think we learned more than you expected, don't you?"

In the dashboard light, I saw Maureen grimace. "Much more."

"Her emotional outburst almost knocked me over. What was her motivation?"

"Probably the same as Zelda's."

"Zelda's?" That surprised me. "Do they know each other?"

"I don't think so, but their need is the same. Both are carrying hurt running deep in their hearts. Abandonment. Betrayal. Zelda believes the academic system abused her."

"Valerie blames her father," I added.

"She had her mother to soften the situation, protect her. Zelda had to recover on her own."

"But the hurt is still raw in both of them." I sighed, feeling sympathy for the woman who secretly yearned for her father and the woman who wore such mismatched outfits that did nothing for her appearance.

"Yes, sadly. They both have a need for love and to move

on." Maureen's words were soft. "Understanding someone's motivation and need can affect how you interact with her." She glanced at me for a brief moment. "You can't control how Zelda or Valerie feel or what happens to them, but if you had a story character with such deep hurt, think about what you might do in your world."

And I did as I stared out the windshield at the headlights slowly revealing the way home.

CHAPTER FORTY-SIX

St. John's Bay Rum Island Fragrance was first blended in 1838 using St. John bay leaf oils and fine Virgin Island rum. It is still popular today among discerning men.

The next morning, I was still blissfully asleep when my ringing phone jarred me awake. The confrontation with Valerie after last night's writer's meeting had sapped my energy. I should have turned off my phone. I extended my arm from under the covers, grabbed it before it vibrated off the nightstand, and touched the green button. "Hello?"

"Hello Sunshine," Craig said with a razor-sharp edge to his words. "I was beginning to think you were blowing me off again. Any reason why I should forgive you for not *calling me back* yesterday like you promised?"

I wanted to pull the covers over my head and chalk this up to an early morning nightmare. How in the world did I get on the wrong side of two important men in my life?

"I didn't get home until late. It was too late to call." I was not going to say I had forgotten.

"Oh, I'm sorry." The sarcasm dripped through the phone. "I didn't mean to intrude on your social life. I'm only trying to solve two cases of murder." His voice was tight. "I don't have time to run errands for some wealthy personality from the Western Shore ..." I pulled the phone away from my ear. I'd never heard Craig shout before.

"Look, I am truly sorry." How could I soothe him? He sounded so frustrated. "What can I do to help?"

"You can call the man!" He bellowed.

Stanley Archibald Holt had poked the beast and I was paying for it. "Tell me why he called you?" I asked softly. "Why did he think he needed a police detective to track me down?"

"I can thank Wendell for giving him my name and..." I could imagine Craig sitting back with his eyes closed, the way he did when a case was exasperating, and he needed to calm down. He took in a slow, deep breath. "The point is the man wants to talk to you. He asked for your number, but I offered to make the call, in keeping with police procedure."

"Is that a thing?" I asked.

"Yes, it is." His voice was tightening up again. "Since you met Mr. Special during an active homicide investigation, I thought I should be in the loop. Any complaints?" he grumbled.

"No, not at all, Detective. Thank you."

"It may have something to do with the case since you met him at Blue Crab Auctions." He paused for a moment then continued by making a little joke. "Or he wants you as arm candy at some fancy event." A little joke that fell flat.

The image of me at a high-class social event, wearing some designer's gown with flawlessly applied makeup, the center of the media attention, being used by a distinguished, wealthy older man. *Arm candy.* Not me.

"Emma? Are you there?" Craig wanted to know.

I sat up in my bed, bracing myself. "Why do you think he

wants to meet with me?" What is with these men wanting to meet with me? First, Professor Kincaid and now, Stanley Archibald Holt. Would I find this older, attractive man dead on my patio tomorrow morning?

"Emma? Are you there? Is the signal dropping?" Craig wanted to know.

"No, I'm here. Tell me more." I suspected Craig knew more than he was saying. And I was right.

"He knows Jack found something special. Something with a connection to the Confederacy will write a new chapter in the history of the War Between the States. Wendell blabbed to him that Jack had found *something interesting* that you had in your possession and now the man wants to see it?" Craig sighed. "He said he would make it worth your while, whatever that means."

"It means he probably wants to buy it. Only I'm not interested in selling it to him or anyone else," I declared, feeling stronger, more in control. I knew what he wanted.

"It's your choice, Emma. All you have to do is call and tell him. That conversation should go well." Craig chuckled, but there was no humor in it. Just sarcasm.

This was such a weird way to start my day. "Do you really think so?"

"No. I think this guy is a certified weirdo," Craig declared. I perked up. "Why?"

"He said you might say you wouldn't sell *the thing* to him, and if you did, I was to ask you to let him examine it, hold it in his hands." Craig cleared his throat. "Does that sound normal to you?"

"No…"

Craig sighed. "Do me a favor, call the guy and tell him no-go, so I can go back to work. Do you still have his card?"

"Yes, but I have a better idea."

"Oh boy, this should be good. TJ warned me about you and your ideas."

Hearing TJ's name, hearing he had talked about me, threw me off.

"Emma, stay with me here or I'm going to hang up," Craig threatened.

"Okay, okay. You're the one who called me at whatever hour of the morning this is. I bet you've had at least one cup of coffee. I haven't. I'm having trouble keeping up, okay? And for the record, I wasn't out socializing last night. I was working." I did not wait for a comment. "Since we met Stanley at the auction house, and we feel the walking stick may be at the center of the investigation—"

"*You* think it is," Craig interrupted. "I'm still on the fence."

"It doesn't matter. What if I meet with him, ask him some pointed questions, see what—"

"Why would you do that?" Craig was suspicious.

I shrugged one shoulder. He couldn't see it, of course, but maybe he could hear it in my voice. "Oh, I don't know. To help you…"

"And…?"

"There's something about him, something that reminds me of Uncle Jack."

"What?" My comment had caught him off-guard. "What reminds you of your uncle?"

"He has manners, the old-fashioned kind. He is respectful."

"He must show it to all those sweet-young-things we saw in the photos online," Craig shot back. "because he doesn't extend it to the police."

"Don't be so cynical. Just because he has money—"

"A lot of money."

"Okay, a lot of money, it doesn't make him a bad person." Or did it? Craig knew more about these things than I did, but I hoped… "Plus, he has a mop of silver hair like Uncle Jack and … and there's something else. It's… it's…" I thought for a moment. "Yes, he wears St. Johns Bay Rum aftershave, just like Uncle Jack did. Yes, Craig, I'll meet with him because he knew Uncle Jack and reminds me of him. And he might lead us to the killer?"

"Wait one minute! You are not doing this on your own, are we clear?" Craig roared.

"Of course not. We'll meet in a public place. Let's say the Blue Crab Antique Center, we can meet in Wendell's office....and..."

"And what?"

I swore the man had the patience of a flea sometimes. "And you'll be there, too."

"Because I'm leading the investigation." He sounded pacified.

"No," I countered.

"Then why am I at this meeting?" he demanded to know.

I cringed, hoping he wouldn't scream or hang up. "I need a ride. I don't drive, remember?" I smirked. "Since he likes talking to you... and he may say something important, do you want to set up the meeting for this afternoon... if you're free?"

"Okay, I'll make myself available." And he hung up with a huff.

CHAPTER FORTY-SEVEN

Christmas Ferns – Three-foot long leaves bring dark
evergreen color to the woods year-round, especially
in the wild shady spaces of the Eastern Shore.
        –Maryland Native Plant Society

I dropped the phone on the comforter and covered my eyes
with my hands. What a way to wake up, especially after
last night. The writers in the group made me laugh, wanting to
know the details about finding a dead body. Zelda chalked up
her hunger for specifics to her desire to write a murder
mystery. So, she had an honest excuse for asking questions,
none of the others wrote mystery stories. They were more like
drivers who rubberneck as they pass an accident. At least the
good wine Gretchen served had helped take the edge off.

And then there had been the confrontation with Valerie...
or should I say, Valerie's confrontation with me. There was so
much sadness in her. I wished the adults in her life had made
different choices. Her mother could have told the professor
about the baby. She could have introduced the girl to her

father, maybe encouraged a relationship. He could have helped them financially, maybe even become a family. So sad. I had to shake off the feeling. There was nothing I could do about the past. But I might be able to help Craig find the killer who had taken away her father forever. Though the lead from the past seemed farfetched to Craig, I needed to follow where it led. Now that I had rejected the possibility of Emma being the spy, I needed to figure out how had Joshua gotten the secret messages to the Confederacy?

After I dressed and ate some breakfast, I went to work. First, I printed the drawing I'd found online of the Confederate Secret Line used by Southern couriers and laid it on the table. Then I printed out the picture of the land map of Waterwood with the black Xs retrieved from the library desk and put it next to the drawing. Using Google Maps, I compared the two.

I was right. Two routes came close to Waterwood. It was time to find the places marked with black Xs.

I raided Uncle Jack's front closet again for things to use on my search for Joshua's Secret Line. An old pair of rubber boots, rubber gloves, and a heavy slicker would keep me dry in a sudden shower and offer protection from branches and twigs in the thick parts of the woods. Fortified with a water bottle and the maps, I headed out on my quest.

It wasn't long before I felt beads of sweat rolling down my skin. Making my way through the woods was hot work. If I could have taken off this jacket, it would help, but carrying it would be worse than wearing it. The rubber boots were hot, but they allowed me to walk off the path, through grasses and wet spots, finding my own way to key spots on the map.

Up ahead, there was a place where the trees filtered the sunlight falling into a wide area covered with ferns. Their slender leaves hid the forest floor. I could almost imagine fairies and other magical creatures living here. When I took two steps into the glade, reality hit me. The ferns were thriving there because water had collected in a dip in the land. Even here on its edge, the water almost topped my boots. Carefully, I backed out and retraced my steps. What was I doing? No one knew I was out here. Cell phone coverage was spotty. I turned back into the shadows of the trees to continue my search in another direction.

As I trudged through the undergrowth, it felt like I was getting close to water. Not the kind collecting in the glade of ferns, but a finger of the Chesapeake Bay. I could almost taste the salt on my tongue. A little breeze of cooler air was another good indicator of being close to a body of water.

The undergrowth thinned out. The trees were not growing as close together as they did in the thick woods behind me. Dried leaves from last fall crunched under my rubber boots. I could hear the gentle lapping of water against the land before I saw it. Holding on to the strong tree trunks to steady my walk down the slope, I made my way to the water's edge. I kept my eyes down so I didn't trip over an exposed tree root or a hefty branch from the tree canopy above. Soon, I raised my eyes from this narrow strip of land to take in the scene of water widening into the Chesapeake Bay. If I squinted, a thin strip of green seemed to appear miles away. Even at the narrow point where they had built the Bay Bridge, the Bay was more than five miles wide. The Miles River at St. Michaels was a good mile and a half across. You had to love the water if you were going to live here, and I did.

It was still early in the season, but soon, the long white boats would dot this vista. Local watermen would be busy pulling blue crabs from the local waters. From here, cradled in an environment to keep them alive, the crabs would be taken to restaurants here and across the Bay to Washington, D.C., Baltimore, Philadelphia, even New York. Many would be flown from Baltimore-Washington International Airport to eager chefs and gourmet market owners all around the United States and Asia. But it wasn't time yet. The crabs who had wintered in the deep mud of the southern part of the Bay were working their way north to mate. For now, the blue heron standing like a statue in shallow water nearby could fish in peace.

I checked the map. This had to be the spot Joshua had marked by the water. I needed to look around in case some remnant of his activities still existed. I stepped carefully along the shoreline I was sure had belonged to the Waterwood Plantation in the 19th century. Up ahead, there was a place where suddenly something like a wall rose up about five feet, covered with vines and leaves. It wasn't natural. Someone had made it. As I got closer, gray stones, weathered by time, about the size of a loaf of bread, appeared under the vegetation. I check the map and the location of the black X by the water. This place corresponded with it.

I pulled away the vines from what looked like a small well. Looking down, I saw it wasn't a well at all. The bottom was at ground level, covered with ashes and pieces of rotted wood. This was a fire pit, built a long time ago. It was possible it could have protected a fire Joshua used to signal a courier working the water route. It was easy to imagine someone familiar with these waters rowing a small boat at night. Seeing the fire signaling a message was waiting, would row to shore, jump out and pull the bow up on land. He would retrieve the message from its hiding place then he would push his boat back in the water and row away, swallowed by the darkness.

I could imagine it all happening. My eyes filled with tears. If only Uncle Jack were here to share this moment.

CHAPTER FORTY-EIGHT

"Real Italians use only their fork and the plate to twirl pasta
like spaghetti or angel hair, but only enough to fit politely in
your mouth. Using a knife (shudder) is *improprio.*"
–*An Italian Friend.*

S atisfied I had confirmed another piece of the puzzle about
Confederate messages, Joshua, and the Secret Line, I
headed back to the Cottage. When I had it in sight, my phone
rang. Craig, again. "Good afternoon, Detective."

He sounded irritated. "I've been calling you. I thought you
weren't going to ignore me?"

"I'm sorry, no. I—" He didn't let me explain.

He pressed. "You do realize we have a bad guy out there
somewhere, don't you?"

"Yes, I do. I was—"

"Emma." He took a breath.

"What?"

"I can understand why TJ worries about you."

He does? Does TJ care anymore? I wondered.

"At least I can keep an eye on you, so you stay safe." He sounded relieved.

I was puzzled. "Craig, is this what you called to tell me?"

"No, of course not. I wanted to tell you I've arranged the meeting with the man of many names, but when I didn't reach you, I kept calling and worrying."

"I get it, Craig. Sorry, I was out of cell phone range." I didn't want another lecture. "Tell me about the meeting."

"I talked to Stanley Archibald Holt. He is eager for the meeting. I don't know which he wants to see more—you or the walking stick."

"Did *you* tell him about Uncle Jack's find?" I was a little exasperated, feeling like I was losing what little control I had over the situation.

"No, Wendell was the one who got the ball rolling. He gave Holt a detailed report of our visit to his office. Anyway, the meeting is tonight."

"Tonight? Why the rush?" It sounded a little odd to me.

Craig's voice was flat, obviously resenting like the role of errand boy. "He wants to see the walking stick and they want to talk with both of us before the auction."

"Auction?"

Craig sighed. His patience was running out. "Tonight's auction includes a number of items from the Civil War period. They thought you'd find it interesting."

"I've told them, I am not selling the walking stick." I thought for a moment. "And why do they want both of us to come?"

"Both Stanley and Wendell seemed anxious to talk with us. We have to go to find out why."

I looked at the clock on my phone. I would have time to take a shower to get the dirt and sweat off my body. "Is all this supposed to happen at the antique center?"

"Yes, Wendell is more than happy to allow us to use his office." The sarcasm was trickling into his voice.

I wished I had time to make sense of all this, coming so fast. Why did these men who were so interested in Civil War artifacts, eager to see both Craig and me? Why was this particular auction important? Were they trying to get me caught up in the auction excitement, so I'd sell the walking stick? They could dream, but it wasn't going to happen.

I had a new thought. They weren't interested in me. They wanted to know if Uncle Jack had made any more important discoveries. They knew of his interest in history and artifacts. His interest had influenced his decision to buy the Cottage here on the Eastern Shore. After his retirement, his interest in history had become his number one priority, second only to spending time and caring about me. Yes, framed items hung on some of the Cottage walls. Some old items sat on bookcase shelves and side tables, but none of them had any major financial or historic value. Or he would have told me about them long ago. But the one thing I believed was important was the gentleman's walking stick, hidden it in plain sight in an umbrella stand. Maybe I'd have to reevaluate those other things in plain sight, but not now.

I had to deal with the walking stick. "You said, *us*. Are you willing to go?"

"If it will help my case, yes. We might pick up some bit of information to get me closer to the killer. Neither the medical examiner nor the crime scene reports gave me much to go on."

I felt relieved I didn't have to deal with these men on my own. Why? There was nothing scary about them. They acted like perfect gentlemen. Still, I was glad Craig would be with me.

"What do you say? Um, I can pick you up at four. I mean, if you'd like, we could grab dinner on our way. Um, together, I mean. Or you could—"

Was Craig asking me on a date? I knew he was divorced

with a young son, but no... Except this was the first time I'd ever heard him hesitate.

Emma, you're spending too much time entertaining romantic notions. We are two people who have a long evening ahead and two murder cases to solve. It is smart for us to eat more than doughnuts and coffee, the standard fare at an auction. We needed to eat a good meal so we could stay sharp. This wasn't a date, was it? No.

I said to Craig, "It's the least I could do for the man who was so polite to make the arrangements with those auction hounds. And it wasn't even part of your job. Thanks, Craig."

"No problem. This evening might yield the break I need."

Ready, though my hair was still damp, I went downstairs to pick up the walking stick. As I reached of it, strange feeling came over me. I was suddenly the center of attention, and it made me uneasy. I picked up the grille still in its baggie. Stanley would want to see the piece intact, but I didn't want to take the chance of damaging the grille by rolling it back in the secret compartment. I almost took one of Emma's letters to show them how the grille worked but hesitated. I wrapped the towel around the stick, leaving the letter behind.

Craig arrived on time. In all the time I'd spent with Craig, I'd never given much thought to how my hair looked or what I was wearing. Silently, I ordered myself to focus on what was important, finding the killer of Professor Kincaid and Dr. Elizabeth Abbott.

I slipped into his car and opened the window. The air still held the day's warmth and could finish drying my hair. Sitting back, enjoying the ride, a thought came to me. "Craig, do you think the person who killed the professor also murdered Dr. Abbott?"

"I certainly hope so," he sputtered. "I mean, the thought of two people running around the county killing people is almost overwhelming. We're having enough trouble understanding the motive of *one* person, let alone two."

SUSAN REISS

"We're scheduled to meet *two* people later. Do you think—"

"That you have upset my stomach before I've had dinner?" he said with a weak smile. And nodded.

"Oh no, I'm so sorry," I said quickly. "I didn't know you had a sensitive tummy—" I stopped, horrified by what I'd said. Then I burst out in gales of laughter that brought tears to my eyes. All the tension and emotion pent-up inside from finding two dead bodies, tromping through the woods in search of a spy's lair, and seeing another woman in Waterwood House came flowing out. What an embarrassing moment. The hurt look on Craig's face made me want to explain, but I couldn't catch my breath.

I held up my hand, signaling for him to give me a minute, as he turned into the restaurant parking lot. Now worried how we would ever get through dinner, I gasped for air, trying to settle.

Embarrassed, I reached for a clean tissue in my purse to wipe away the mascara and eyeliner must be staining my face. When I raised my eyes from the black-marked tissue to look at Craig, a calm man who was always in control of his emotions, a gifted analyst, an uncompromising investigator, I saw the hurt in his brown eyes. I felt small. I didn't belong in the world of adults. I should go back to the classroom. "Craig, I'm so sorry. I wasn't laughing at you. I'd never laugh at you. I respect you too much to even think of making fun of you." I cleared my throat. "I'm embarrassed I referred to your upset stomach as a tummy."

"I know what a tummy is." He sounded grumpy.

"It's a children's word, one I used with my little students. I taught kindergarten, remember?"

He nodded.

The truth began to dawn on him as I continued. "It's fine to talk about a five-year-old's tummy, but an adult man like you…" Another wave of laughter began to threaten, as I tried to imagine this man, champion of the law, as a little boy in short pants.

This time, it was Craig's turn to chuckle. He got it. And I joined in with more giggles. Finally, we got it out of our systems and settled back, relishing the moment.

"Wow," he said. "That felt good. Homicide is such a serious business. I sometimes think I've forgotten how to laugh. Thank you, Emma."

"I didn't mean to make fun. Am I'm forgiven?"

He drew his eyebrows together in a stern expression. "Absolutely not."

Had I really, truly offended him?

"And as your punishment, you have to make me laugh again when we've solved this convoluted case!"

It was my turn to give him a serious look. "Yes, sir. I accept my punishment."

Now relaxed, with a warm feeling of friendship, we went inside to enjoy a delicious meal. I was relieved we were at a different restaurant than the steak house TJ and I visited often. At least, we used to. Remembering the steak knife with my fingerprints on it sticking out of the professor's chest, I ordered a simple pasta dish I could eat with a fork.

CHAPTER FORTY-NINE

MURDER:
An act born of envy, jealousy, hatred,
pride, anger, fear, revenge, even love.
The result, whether premeditated
or in the heat of the moment, is a body lying lifeless.

It felt good to take a break and sit down in the warm atmosphere of the restaurant. The food was good. The conversation was relaxing and entertaining. I guess it shouldn't have surprised me to learn Craig was a referee for young boys' soccer games. He wanted to coach, but his schedule didn't allow it. His stories about the parents who thought their eight-year-old children were the next Manchester United stars were hilarious.

Back in the car, driving down Route 50 toward the Auction Center, I felt like we were going back to work. I watched the landscape whiz past my window and wondered what we might learn from Wendell and Stanley. One thing was certain. I was not going to tell them about the Secret Line map and my trek through the woods.

Craig interrupted my thoughts. "You asked me before if I thought we were dealing with one killer or two. I think it is an appropriate question since we're on our way to meet *two* men directly involved with the victims," Craig said. "What motive could each have? Or do you think they were working in tandem?"

"Wendell and Stanley?!" My head came off the comfort of the headrest as I sat up in surprise. "Oh, no. I don't think Stanley was involved in any of this mess."

"Why not?"

I stared straight out the windshield. I truly didn't think Stanley had anything to do with either murder. It wasn't the evidence that convinced me. The truth was, Stanley reminded me of my beloved Uncle Jack, at least in some ways. And Uncle Jack wouldn't hurt anyone.

"Come on, Emma. He makes a good suspect. His name alone makes him suspicious: Stanley Archibald Holt. It appears he has a lot of money, fills his time with philanthropic pursuits, and likes adding to his collections, especially his Civil War relics and arm candy."

Craig was referring to the pictures on the internet of the older man posing with young model-type companions. And I didn't like it. "Stop referring to arm candy, please."

"Why?"

"Because I don't like it." I looked straight ahead again. "It offends me."

"I'm-I'm sorry."

It was an honest apology, but still, I didn't like it. "I like the other two as killers, if there were indeed two killers."

"Who and Who?"

"Dr. Abbott and Wendell."

"Okay," he said slowly. "Tell me why."

"Let's start with the professor's murder. What if Uncle Jack told Wendell what he'd found?"

Craig's eyes grew wide.

"They could have made a pact to work together. Uncle Jack would do the research on the walking stick, show its connection with a previously unknown Confederate spy, and write the book. It would carve Uncle Jack's reputation as a historian into the annals of academia. Then Wendell would sell the walking stick to a private collector or even a large museum, maybe making them both some serious money in the process."

Craig nodded slowly, evaluating the possibility. "Go on."

"Then Uncle Jack died suddenly, before he finished the research. Wendell knew circumstances had changed. He could still make a lot of money, even more now because he wouldn't have to share. But where was the walking stick? Probably in the Cottage, which was empty. There was no rush to do a search. Then I moved in unexpectedly. The word was I would only stay there for a few months. Wendell could afford to be patient. He didn't want to attract unwanted attention to the walking stick until he was ready... until he knew no one would challenge his ownership he would claim when he put it up for sale." I was warming up to this hypothesis. "He got greedy. He convinced himself there was no reason to share the proceeds from the sale with some unknown relative."

"Then Professor Kincaid walks into his office one day with Dr. Abbott in tow. Remember how hesitant Wendell was to tell you about that visit. He knew the You-Can-Call-Me-Doctor before she walked into his office with the professor. They had history. She might have cheated him out of a valuable piece or made trouble over provenance. She could have stolen one of his clients. She might have cost him a lot of money."

Craig wet his lips. "Okay, though I don't think it's likely.

It is one thing to have a bad business transaction, but murder? That's a little extreme, don't you think?"

"I agree, but with Professor Kincaid snooping around with the pushy Dr. Abbott, Wendell might have started feeling uncomfortable. Maybe Wendell found out the professor had gone through Uncle Jack's university office. It might have set off an alarm. Then Wendell learned the professor was desperate because of his medical condition. Wendell must have assumed the professor would start sniffing around the Cottage for the walking stick. He couldn't exactly break in and ransack the place because I was almost always home. He had no alternative but to slow down the competition. It doesn't sound so farfetched now, does it?"

"No, it doesn't," Craig admitted. "It puts him squarely under suspicion." Craig tapped the steering wheel, thinking. "Then he heard the professor got sick on your patio and you visited him in the hospital. There was ample time and opportunity for the professor to tell you about the walking stick."

"Something Wendell did not want to happen." I nodded.

"Maybe he followed the professor there and had to prevent the two of you from searching the Cottage together."

"Doesn't that sound a little over the top?" I suggested.

"No, I suspect Wendell will do whatever it takes to beat out the competition. After all, he does it all the time at auctions."

"You're right." I sat back. These were a lot of ideas to take in. "Craig, when the professor and I were planning our meeting the next day, he said he had to meet someone before he came to see me. Could it have been Wendell?"

Craig shook his head. "No, it was Dr. Abbott. You found her datebook with the meeting written in it for the day he died."

I gasped. "You think Dr. Abbott killed the professor and Wendell killed her?"

He turned into a crowded parking lot. Only days before had been like an open field. "I think we're getting a little too elaborate." He parked and turned off the engine. "Let's see if we can learn something I can use on this case."

We set out for Wendell's office, but first had to make our way through the crowd of people milling around in the auction space. At the door to the office area, a rock of a man, wearing a vest with a Blue Crab Auction logo stretched over his broad chest, barred our way.

"No entry!" he announced.

I tried to explain I had an appointment with Wendell, but he kept shaking his shaved head. Craig had the one easy solution to the situation. He held up his badge and police ID. The human wall moved, and we made our way to the office.

CHAPTER FIFTY

COVET: yearn to possess; have one's heart set on.

The door to Wendell's office was open. Stanley was sitting at Wendell's desk, in Wendell's chair, lightly drumming his fingers. Wendell was pacing though he didn't have much room. When they spotted us standing in the doorway, Wendell spoke. "Hello! Glad you could make it. Won't you sit—"

Stanley only had eyes for me. "Did you bring it?" His voice flat and wanted an answer.

I looked down to hide my surprise at his rudeness. What else would I bring to an antique center rolled up in a bath towel? In this antique expert's office with shelves of reference books, the towel seemed a cheap way to handle a valuable piece of history. I'd left the Cottage so fast, I just grabbed the towel I'd used to transport the walking stick before... before Craig made the appointment to meet Wendell. Before Dr. Abbott was murdered.

Craig grabbed the moment. "Yes, Emma brought it to

show you. As I understand it, she means to only *show* it, isn't that right, Emma?"

"Yes, I—" I was grateful Craig covered my awkward moment.

"Put it on the desk." Stanley ordered, then realized he had issued a command. "Please. I'm sorry. Please put it on the desk. My excitement at seeing the walking stick has overwhelmed my manners." With little care, he pushed the stapler, pen holder, and phone to the edges of the desk to make room.

I lay my package down and began to unroll the towel.

"I'll do it." He stated as he slipped on white cotton gloves. "You're not properly prepared."

Craig and I exchanged a look. I wanted to brag how I'd already found both compartments and what they concealed but said nothing.

Stanley opened the towel by carefully pinching parts of it between his thumb and index finger. His care seemed a little extreme for a piece of wood. I understood this was a significant piece of wood, but still... I wondered what he would have said if he knew Uncle Jack had hidden the walking stick among a bunch of umbrellas.

When Stanley finally uncovered it, he gasped. Then he ran the tips of his left hand from one end of the stick to the other. Then he lifted the stick with both hands for closer inspection, holding it inches away from his nose as his eyes took in every detail, again from top to bottom. He didn't say anything. Then he moved around the desk, carrying the stick like a butler would carry a tray or a religious leader would carry a relic. His slow steps, one after the other, forced us to scramble out of his way. He stopped when he reached an open area of the floor.

His hand holding the bottom of the cane opened and it fell.

My hands shot out though I wasn't close enough to catch

it. My help wasn't needed. The cane dangled from his tight grip on the top knob. The tip was barely inches above the floor. Contact could have damaged or broken it.

"Interesting," was all Stanley said as I caught my breath. He gently touched the tip to the floor and leaned over as if to use it. A dreamy look came over his face, as if he was back to the time when this walking stick was used.

He shook himself out of the spell, stood up to his full height again, and acknowledged our presence. "Yes, its length also suggests its age. You can see, this walking stick was made for a man much shorter than myself. A man about five feet six inches tall, the average height for a man in the mid-19th century. Its quality is quite fine. Its condition is excellent. Probably custom made for the owner, this JTC who had his initials, small as they are, carved into the wood."

Wendell stepped forward, confused. "Initials? Where are they?"

I wasn't surprised Wendell had missed them when he'd first examined the walking stick. He had been in a rush and had a lot to consider.

Stanley turned his eyes, green as emeralds, toward me. "Have you identified him yet?"

This man was good. He hadn't missed the initials and somehow, he knew I was on the trail of the owner. But I wasn't ready to show him everything I had. "I'm looking into it."

We repositioned ourselves as he walked back to the far side of the desk. He lay the walking stick on the towel again and began to twist the handle. "Let's see what mysteries it is concealing inside."

"You'll find a—" I began, but his upturned hand stopped me short. It became clear we were meant to watch and wait while the expert, the wealthy collector, made his own discoveries. I sat down.

"Ah." Stanley had made his first discovery. "A flask." He

took a whiff. "A brandy of some kind if I'm not mistaken." He screwed the handle back in place. "Yes, it was always good for a gentleman to be prepared with a small libation for himself or to share with a friend."

Stanley's hands moved down the stick, feeling for an almost invisible indication there was another compartment. Then they stopped. A slow smile spread over his face, a smile of satisfaction. He grasped the piece in his two hands and stopped. His eyes flew up to meet mine and narrowed. "Is it intact?"

My stomach tensed. He was testing me.

"Are all the original things here?" he demanded to know.

"Yes." A simple response should have reassured him. It did not.

"Are you certain?" His staring eyes drilled into mine, as if looking for a lie.

Rattled by his reaction, I somehow found a way to steady my voice. "Yes, of course." He didn't have to treat this way. It hurt.

Then the test was over. "Good. Well done, Emma," Stanley declared.

But he didn't take the time to be sincere about his praise so, he missed how his suspicious attitude had hurt me. The businessman/collector was focused and on to the next. He twisted the two pieces of wood apart. My feelings were of no concern to him, which showed the difference between Uncle Jack and this man.

"You would have needed tweezers to pull this out of its hiding place." And I laid the baggie containing the grille on the desk. I leaned back in my chair. "It's called a grille," I volunteered.

His angry eyes met mine again. I leaned back in my chair while a smile of satisfaction spread over my lips. He could strut all he wanted, but, in the end, I owned the walking stick. It was going home with me. I was determined not to offer any more information. This man had reminded me of Uncle Jack, but now, something had changed. Had Uncle Jack been like this when he was doing business, stating his historical conclusions, when I wasn't around?

Wendell sprang to his research bookshelves, drew out a thick reference book, and lay it open on his desk. "I found something. A walking stick with two compartments was commonly used by an architect," he said, running his finger over some lines of text. "In the upper section, he would store a compass, pencil, and drafting tools. In the lower part, the architect could keep a level, straightedge, an elevation drawing, other things..."

While he was reading, Stanley turned the stick and shook it a little. Nothing happened. Then he shifted the wood piece inside his fist and slammed his hand on the desktop, hard. We all jumped.

"There's nothing..." but again, I was wrong.

A slender blade clattered on the desk.

Stanley proclaimed. "Like a dagger." Grinning in triumph, he added, "I thought so."

"Why didn't you show that to us, Wendell?" I wanted to know.

Stanley chuckled. "He likes to leave some things for me to discover, don't you dear boy?" He examined the dagger, then held it so the blade caught the light. It was about five inches long and showed no sign of rust or deterioration. It had been well preserved while nestled in the center of the cane.

"That's amazing," I said.

"That's lethal," Craig remarked.

Stanley resumed his lecture. "It was not unusual for a gentleman to carry some form of hidden protection. It would have been considered crass and offensive for him to openly carry a weapon. The owner was no hooligan."

Stanley stood up straight, stretched his back a little, and

gave us a smile almost blinding in delight. The public image of Stanley Archibald Holt was back in place.

"What an absolutely fine specimen! Well done!" he said, but I wasn't sure who he was complimenting. "Incorporating a flask in the upper compartment was a nice touch. If the owner of this fine walking stick was stopped while involved in illegal spying operations as the grille suggests, the spy could fake inebriation and quickly offer a drink as a distraction. Very clever. It might throw any authority questioning his actions off the scent."

After consulting an open reference book, Wendell noted, "This piece has a high value today, but its original purchase price was not cheap, don't you think?"

Stanley replied, "The owner must have been a gentleman of means and fine reputation." Stanley straightened his jacket. "His manners would have defined him. Presence of the dagger, a deadly weapon, tells us he was a man of courage."

He screwed the walking stick back together. "This is a work of art." Then he raised his eyes to look at me. "Emma, I have a suggestion, but first..." He held the walking stick out to me. "Take it in both hands."

I followed his instruction, not sure what was happening here.

Stanley continued. "Now, close your eyes and let it talk to you."

I closed my eyes and the first vision I had was Craig rolling his eyes. I shook it away and forced myself to keep a neutral expression. *What was this piece of wood, almost two hundred years old, supposed to be saying to me.* I stood still like a statue.

Stanley continued. "You are holding history. It began with the man who ordered the stick. There was the man who crafted it. Then think of all the hands that have touched it, down through its existence. Can you hear the tip tapping the sidewalk of a Philadelphia street during the Civil War? Can you feel the slight movement of the things hidden inside? The slight slosh of the flask of brandy? Maybe the dagger shifted a little as he walked, though it would probably be cushioned by the paper grille. All the elements take you there, back in time, when this JTC walked this earth. The time the spy operated in secret."

I took in a quick breath. I could feel it. Stanley's words brought it alive, all of it, for me. Just as Daniel's letters had reached across time. Just as Emma's diaries had invited me into her mind and heart. But I would never share those connections with these men.

The magical moment blew away when someone knocked on the office door. Stanley groaned as Wendell acknowledged his assistant. The bidding on the Civil War artifacts was about to begin.

Stanley held up his index finger for us to wait. "One more minute, please." He firmly planted his attention on me. "Emma, we have a grand opportunity here. I propose we strike a partnership. You research the history and background of this walking stick's owner, this JTC." He narrowed his eyes as if peering into my mind and soul. "If I'm reading you correctly, you have already begun the research. You know about the grille and how to use it, don't you?"

I nodded.

"Well then, I suggest you complete your work and prepare a manuscript. If there is enough information, we will publish it as a book. If not, it will make a fine monograph or novella."

"We?" My alarm bells were going off.

"Yes. I will make all the necessary arrangements with a publisher and foot any expenses that might arise. You could list your Uncle Jack's name along with your own, putting his first on the cover since he was the one who procured the piece. If it hadn't been for his untimely death, I'm sure he would have gone forward with the research and publication to great accolades. Or you could publish it with your name alone, but you don't strike me as that type of person. I expect you give credit where credit was due."

Craig jumped in to this tidy arrangement with a comment. "And what do you get out of it?"

A slow smile spread over Stanley's lips as he turned to the homicide detective. "I would be the proud owner of this fine and storied walking stick." His head whipped around in my direction. "Fear not, I would compensate you at above market value."

"But I don't—"

Craig turned to Wendell. "Why don't we table this discussion for the moment?" He could be smooth in an awkward situation. "We don't want to miss the Civil War auction lots, do we?"

"No, no, we don't." Wendell glanced at Stanley and upon receiving a nod, he opened the office door.

"Wendell?" Stanley glanced at the walking stick.

The man got the message. "Emma, shall I lock the walking stick in my safe?" he asked, reaching for it.

I cocked my head as if considering his offer. "No, I think I'll keep it with me. Please put the grille back in the compartment." Reluctantly, Stanley did as I asked. I picked up the baggie holding the grille, wrapped the walking stick in its towel, and put it under my arm. "Thanks."

Wendell gave Stanley a shrug. "Follow me."

Leading the way out of his office, he said to the older man, his client. "I'm very glad you're here with us this evening, Mr. Stanley. It's not often you attend the auction in person."

"Oh," I said. "I thought you came here for the Civil War artifacts Wendell finds so easily."

"I didn't say I don't participate. Let me show you." Stanley stepped aside to allow me to enter the auction hall first.

CHAPTER FIFTY-ONE

AUCTION: an ancient tradition of holding a public sale.
Interested buyers compete by placing bids.
The auction item is won by the highest bidder.

W endell led us into the auction hall of the Blue Crab Auction Center. There was a break in the bidding. The noise level was high, and people were milling around. Some stretched out their backs from sitting in metal folding chairs.

Stanley pointed to a long table with eight people sitting in front of laptop computers, papers, and multi-line telephones, many of them with a handset pressed to their ears. One young man had covered his mouth so no one could read his lips. "Normally, you'd find me on the other end of one of those phones."

"You bid anonymously?"

"Oh no," he said with a smile showing his tolerance of my simple question. "The auctioneer and Wendell know I am bidding as does their operator. The people in the room and other telephone bidders do not know my identity. That's important."

"Why?" I was distracted by the behind-the-scenes mischief of an auction.

Something or someone had snagged his attention from across the room. I followed his gaze to see an exotic-looking man with black hair and olive skin, the same one I'd seen on my first visit. Stanley dipped his head as a nod to the man and turned back to me. "I'm sorry. I thought I saw someone I knew."

"If you have to go…" I said, realizing I was monopolizing his time.

"Not at all. I'm the one who invited you here tonight. I want to spend my time with you. Now, what was your question?"

"I asked why it was important to keep your identity a secret?" I repeated.

He waved his hand to flick away my question. "Oh, one just needs to be careful."

A young man wearing an auction house shirt and a serious expression came over to Stanley and lightly tapped his arm. Then he whispered something to him.

"You'll have to excuse me a moment, Emma. Something needs my attention. I'll catch up with you before the bidding begins again." And the young man led him away.

People were everywhere. Two men were having a quiet conversation in the corner. Were they discussing strategy? There were knots of people here and there comparing notes about items coming up for bid or they were updating friends about grandchildren, many of them juggling paper cups of hot coffee and a doughnut. It was the All-American meal at an auction like a hot dog and a beer at a baseball game.

Wendell led Craig and me through the vast number of people hemmed in by rows of metal folding chairs, all facing the auctioneer podium. An employee pulled him aside. With a quick "I'll be right back," he disappeared into the crowd. I shifted the position of the walking stick to use my body to protect it. There were a few raised eyebrows when people caught sight of the rolled-up towel. I got the impression everyone was on heightened alert, afraid to miss something, something important.

"Let's find a seat," Craig said in a loud voice, hoping to be heard over the din of conversation. The metal roof and hard-surface walls did little to dampen the noise.

I saw two empty chairs on the end of the second row and headed toward them. As I slipped into place, a threatening voice stopped me. "Oh no, you don't. That seat is taken."

I looked around to see a stout, grizzled woman, challenging me in a room full of auction lovers. Her raspy voice, probably from years of smoking, added a level of danger to her menacing stare.

I tried to counteract her threat with a sweet smile. "I'm sorry. I'm sorry, I thought these seats were available."

Still staring straight at me, trying to make me disappear, she said, "Everybody knows this is where Miss Sandy sits."

"I'm sorry, this is our first time and…"

"No excuse for ignorance. See the bag on the floor? It's mine." Then she pointed a finger, gnarled by arthritis, to her chest then at the chairs. "Miss Sandy sits here.

I looked down and saw a large, well-worn tote with two knitting needles sticking out of the top. I suddenly had a vision of Madame Defarge knitting at the scene of the guillotine in Paris during the French Revolution. I glanced at Craig and saw his expression that encouraged me to *Go easy* and figured neither one of us wanted to tangle with this regular auction attendee.

"My apologies. I'll get out of your way," I said, hoping she would give me room to step into the aisle. She did, just barely.

After squeezing past her, I scanned the room. Seats were

filling up fast. We were at a great disadvantage. The auction had started hours ago. People had claimed their places while we were in Wendell's office talking. People swirled around us. After the woman's nasty attitude and the bodies shifting around us, I clutched the walking stick to my body and began to panic.

A hand gripped my arm. I whipped my head around and almost swooned with relief when I saw Wendell. "Head to the back," he yelled over the racket of voices.

I looked around and couldn't tell which way to go.

Wendell called out again. "Follow me."

It was a miracle the way he opened a path through the crowd. I didn't dare take my eyes off him and hoped Craig was following us.

As we reached the last row, two auction workers were setting up four more chairs against the wall. I would have preferred to leave this crazy place, but if we had to stay, this looked like a safe place to settle.

"Sit," Wendell ordered.

I plopped into a chair and Craig sat down next to me. Though we sat close together, we couldn't make ourselves heard over the noise unless we wanted everyone to know what our conversation was about. We exchanged silent looks to share our amazement at the auction scene and to quietly observe until we could talk later.

Stanley materialized out of the crowd carrying two cups of steaming coffee. "Black or with cream?" He asked me, holding out the cups.

I took the one with cream which caused him to say, "Good choice. Depending on who makes the coffee, I swear it could take the paint off a car." He offered the second cup to Craig. "Is it a cliché for a law enforcement officer to drink his coffee black?"

"Maybe, but it's the way I like it."

I decided to be brave and took a sip from my cup, expecting the worst.

"How do you like it, Emma?" Stanley asked.

"It's good." I said, surprised.

"It's one of Billy Bob's clever moves. The coffee is almost as good as Starbucks, but strong. It helps keep people awake. It can be hard, waiting through five or ten items until they get to the one you want." He looked around the room. "I don't think he is going to have a problem keeping this crowd's attention." His eyes fell on Craig. "Do you mind moving over one chair?"

Craig looked around. "Sure, I can take the chair on the other side of Emma."

"Ah, no," Stanley said firmly. "Wendell will be sitting there."

Craig glanced at me. The message was clear. They were splitting us up. I winked to show him I understood what was happening and I was okay with it. We had a better chance of finding something, overhearing something, to split this case wide open.

"Okay, I'll just sit here," Craig said as he moved into the vacant chair.

"Thank you," Stanley said as he sat down.

Feeling his arm just touching mine, reminded me of the times Uncle Jack and I would sit in a movie theater, at a sporting event, or at a play. His arm would touch mine just enough to let me know he was there. But this wasn't an arts event, and he wasn't Uncle Jack. There were two unsolved murders. In this crazy atmosphere of churning humanity, it was not surprising I didn't feel calm and content.

CHAPTER FIFTY-TWO

Ways to Bid at an Auction: In Person, By Proxy, On the Telephone, Via the Internet

I n a rush, Wendell appeared and sat down on the other side of me. "Emma, sorry about the chaos, but it is organized chaos. So far, the numbers suggest it's very good for us."

"That's wonderful! This is a new experience for me."

"Then I'm glad we were able to set up chairs here in the back. This is the best place to watch an auction. You can see who is bidding and how. Is the person hesitant or excited, thrusting an arm in the air? Is the person bidding against you, known to the auctioneer so only a subtle movement is needed?"

"Like pulling on an earlobe?" I said with a laugh.

"Well, it may work in the movies, but in a place like this, such a move might be a little too subtle. Over time, you learn who is a dealer and who is a private collector."

"And that is important because…?" I asked.

"A good dealer knows how much a customer will pay for

an item in a shop. He or she subtracts the profit margin needed, sets the limit, and bids accordingly. Rarely does a dealer go over the limit he sets unless he is willing to take less profit." Wendell was in his element. His face beamed. He loved what he did. "If you watch the bidding and see certain people start to fall away, you'll know the bid is getting close to a dealer's limit. If you are bidding for yourself, you might get yourself a deal on a piece you want."

"What does a person like me, who doesn't know all the ins and out of auction bidding, do if she wants something? I asked.

"If you jump into the bidding too early along with other private individuals, the price could soar. If it happens, a dealer will stop and watch as they go crazy, bidding until the price goes sky-high. The excitement is contagious. It becomes a game they must win. You've heard of buyer's remorse?"

I nodded.

Wendell continued. "It can happen at an auction, usually when the bidder goes to the desk to pay and is handed the item. That's when it hits. You can read it on their face, 'I paid *how much* for this?' It's sad and Billy Bob tries to avoid it." His pride for his cousin shone. "If he sees it getting out of control, he'll slow down the pace, even ask bidders if they're sure they want to increase their bid. People here appreciate it."

Wendell moved his hand to reach for the rolled-up towel and the treasure inside. "Do you want me to take the walking stick?"

"No, it's fine." I pulled the rolled-up towel closer. "I've got it." Then I looked out at the room of bidders again. "What you said is a lot to keep in mind when the bidding is going so fast. I've seen auctioneers in movies and shows, in old ads for cigarettes. I can't imagine how anybody can talk so fast or how bidders can keep up."

The sound of the gavel banging for quiet competed with the clamor and soon won some silence for the auctioneer.

Wendell leaned close and whispered, "Wait and see how it goes when Billy Bob gets revved up." He folded his arms over his skinny chest and sat back in his hard chair with a self-satisfied smirk on his face.

I focused on the podium to watch and learn.

Billy Bob spoke into an effective sound system. "Hey y'all, is this thing working?" The man's Southern accent was back, as thick as molasses. He almost didn't need a microphone for the room had fallen silent, people wanting to hear every word. He welcomed us to the next part of the auction featuring items of the Civil War period.

"I know a lot of you have come this evening for these lots," he said. "We at the Blue Crab Auction Center are glad to bring these fine quality items to you. I hope you took advantage of the extra time to inspect these lots. We don't have time to bring them to your seats. That train has left the station." The room laughed. It must have been a popular saying in his banter. "Let's get started."

A man from the auction staff stepped up on a riser in front of the podium so people could see him. He held something close to the left side of his body along his leg and waited.

"Alright, people. I'm not sure how popular this item will be with this group. I know the history of this area, BUT..." He paused for dramatic effect. "This is a fine specimen of a non-commissioned Union officer's sword and scabbard." He paused again.

Billy Bob's helper drew the sword, the scraping sound bounced around the room. He flourished it above his head.

Billy Bob waited then, with excellent timing, he launched into his pitch. "Manufactured by ..."

"Quite the performer, isn't he?" Wendell said with pride.

I dutifully nodded.

Billy Bob continued. "Dated 1864. It was found in an

estate closed out in Dayton, Ohio. Do you want it? What am I bid?"

A flurry of white bidding cards went up in the air.

"He really knows how to get the crowd's appetite whipped up." Wendell grinned.

I was fascinated by what Billy Bob was doing and watched. I had no idea how much a Union sword and scabbard were worth, but the bid of $400 surprised me.

The bidding was slowing down. Billy Bob's banter did, too. "Are you going to let this fine example of an officer's weapon get away from you? I know it belonged to a Union officer, but the quality and condition of this sword and its scabbard should outweigh your sympathies." He took a deep breath. "So, let's get the bid up to where it should be." And he was off again, recognizing new bids.

In only a couple of minutes, he wrapped it up. "All in? All done? Going once. Going twice. Sold for $600!"

When he slammed the gavel, I wanted to clap, but I needed to hold on to the rolled-up towel with its treasure inside. I hadn't realized how caught up I was in the atmosphere of this auction. What a performer Billy Bob was! He barely allowed the group to catch its breath. He was going to build on the momentum with the next lot.

CHAPTER FIFTY-THREE

*A Civil War soldier's quilt held great meaning to remind him
of home. The quilt offered warmth on cool nights If the soldier
lost his life on the battlefield, his body was wrapped in the
quilt and laid in a grave.*

"Now, for the ladies... and for the men who like to stay
warm in the winter..." The comment drew laughter
from the group. Billy Bob waited until it died down then
began his spiel in a lower, more serious tone. "I want you to
know about the quilts we are about to auction off. As far as
we know, they date back to the Civil War." He paused to let
that fact sink in. "My cousin Wendell..." He extended his
hand in Wendell's direction and heads turned. "...is
meticulous about his research and what he'll let me say up
here. He wanted me to tell you about a fine military tradition
of the South. Their women showed their pride..."

On cue, two of the auction helpers stepped up on the
riser and unfolded the first quilt. The diamond-shape pattern
was attractive, and the colors of brown, gray, and cream

were stronger than I expected after so much time had passed.

"Their women wanted to show their support and remind their men of home by making quilts to keep them warm as they moved up to the chilly north. Tonight, we have several to offer you."

The bidding was lively and in a matter of a few moments, the auctioneer cried out "Sold!" There was no break in the action. On the other end of the riser, two more helpers quickly unfolded another quilt. And the bidding began again.

Stanley touched my arm to let me know he would be back in a few minutes, as if we were a couple. I turned my attention back to the next item up for bidding, a child's quilt. It was the same pattern as the previous full-size quilt. Was it from the same family? Would the person who won the first one bid on this one, too?

Craig scooted over into Stanley's seat. "What are you thinking?"

"I can't tell you," I mumbled so no one else could hear. "There is so much going on. So many things to consider."

Craig gave a quick nod in agreement. "Let me tell you what I think."

"Please do."

"Don't agree to anything tonight. Think about your options. Sleep on it. We can talk tomorrow if you want my opinion."

"Good advice. Thank you." I turned toward him and asked in a low voice. "Do you have any ideas about the case?"

He took a deep breath and let it out in a huff. "I'll be honest. I was hoping for some clarification tonight. Instead, it is even more muddled. I'm going to take my own advice and wait until tomorrow to resolve things."

"The night isn't over yet," I pointed out. "You still might…" When I saw Craig's eyes look up at something behind me, I stopped.

"Detective?" Stanley stood there looking a bit irritated Craig had taken his seat. He was holding what I thought was the child's quilt from the auction.

For a moment, I had the unsettling feeling Stanley was treating me like one of his collectibles, but I quickly shook it off as absurd. It was only boys vying for the attention of the only female in the group. I looked up at Stanley to relieve the tension. "I was just telling the detective he still might scc something he'll want to bid on. It's true, isn't it?"

He rewarded me with a warm smile. "Of course, dear Emma."

Stanley held out the small quilt, now neatly folded. "I want you to have this as a memento of this evening and as a more appropriate wrap for the walking stick." He sat down and patted my arm. "It is so much better than that bath towel," he added with disdain. He reached over, lifted the towel-wrapped package from my lap, and wrapped it in the quilt. "There. Shall I hold on to it?

I reached for it. "No, I'll keep it in case you have to get up again or something." Was a little warning bell ringing in my head? But this was not the time or place to figure out what was wrong.

We watched as the auction helpers brought out several more quilts, one after another. Each had a story Billy Bob related to the crowd. They gobbled up every one of his historical tidbits."

I turned to Wendell. "Did you dig up all these historical details?

Casually, Wendell nodded. "Yes, me and my secretary Dot."

"I'm impressed at how much work you've done."

"Thank you," he said, a little shyly. People must not acknowledge his detailed work very often.

A sound came over the public address system that was totally unexpected. Laughter. The auctioneer was laughing. I looked up at the podium and he was leaning over his notes and chortling. I was completely confused and looked at Wendell for an explanation.

He cracked a mischievous smile and whispered, "Wait."

"Excuse me, folks. Whenever we are fortunate to bring to auction a lot in this category, I always get caught between two groups. Those of you who complain we start the bidding too high and the others who demand we treat these pieces not as toys, but with the dignity and respect they deserve." He sat up and his demeanor changed. There was nothing amusing now. "First, we at the Blue Crab Auction Center do not *set* opening bids unless there is a reserve placed by the owner of the item." And then his voice boomed, "I tell you if there is a reserve and why." Confident he had made his point, he brushed down the front of his blue shirt stitched with the name of the auction house over the pocket. "Not tonight. Now, it is you, ladies and gentlemen, who set the prices. Sometimes, I'm amazed at how high the bidding goes when you really want something. At other times, I have to shake my head when a lot goes for a song. Usually, you come within the price range I expect. But it's all up to you."

He looked around the room. "Now, I know there are some toy collectors in the audience tonight. And there are some re-enactors who like to set up tabletop scenarios of battles. I'm going to start the bidding and let y'all duke it out...because this is a mighty fine lot..."

The large screen over Billy Bob's head sprang to life with a picture of a large table filled with small items. "This is the lot many of you have been waiting for... the Vintage Blue Marx Civil War Battle Playset... three hundred and fifty pieces." He drew out the number for maximum effect and got it from several people scattered around the room who ooh-ed at his description. "The set itself is almost an antique dating back to the 1950s." He delivered a rapid recital of how many soldiers were walking, standing, shooting while lying down, and shooting while standing. There are men firing cannons…" He drew in a long, dramatic breath. "And we have soldiers shot in the head, shot somewhere on their bodies, officers with swords…" then he slowed for effect to recapture the audience's attention. "And drummers. Now, I'm going to let y'all set the opening bid for this item. Let the battle begin!"

And it went on and on. I was swamped by the sheer volume and types of pieces offered. It was impossible to keep up with their descriptions. Then there was the rapid-fire bidding. I gave up trying to follow what was happening and leaned over to Wendell and felt like I was shouting in his ear. "How do you think the auction is going?" I asked.

Wendell shrugged then motioned toward the podium. "You're going to want to pay attention to the next lot."

"Okay, listen up everybody," Billy Bob commanded. "You need to give your full attention to this item. It is unique. Something you rarely see outside a museum. And the bid that wins will probably be a high one… as it should be." He gave the room a confident look the bidders would do what was expected, then he smiled and said in a more relaxed tone, "But even if your checkbook doesn't allow you to bid, you should pay attention." He spoke to the man carrying the item from the back. "Charlie, hold it up over your head so everyone can see it. But be careful. This little drum is a gem."

Charlie nodded and raised the next lot high in the air.

"Ladies and gentlemen, this is a Union Infantry Battle Drum from the Civil War." There were several gasps from around the room. "The Union Army used it, but there is more we know about it. Charlie, show 'em the sides." Charlie did as instructed. "You can see there is some wear, but what you see is what is left of the original color and design as it went into the hands of the drummer boy in 1861. It has not been restored. Pretty remarkable, isn't it?

"Show them the Eagle on the side, Charlie. See how it has

the ribbon imprinted with the word Infantry in its mouth. That is why they call it the Union Eagle Battle Drum."

The room was silent. People were too busy looking to talk.

"Now, Charlie, show us the inside." Yes, the bottom drum skin is missing. But this is good so we can see the name written inside the drum: G.W. Barney, 27th Regiment. You don't often find key information written inside a military drum. My cousin, Wendell..." He pointed in our direction and Wendell waved. Many people in the room waved back. It was good to see the star of the show giving his cousin credit for the work he did.

"Wendell went to work and found out there were TWO men who served named G.W. Barney...father and son." Billy Bob was reading from a paper Wendell must have prepared for him. "George W. Barney and George W. Barney, Jr. From what Wendell could find out, the son, all of 18-years-old, enlisted first, in 1861. He was a musician with the infantry. He was discharged on disability about eighteen months later. He must have brought the drum home with him from the war. Then about six months later, his father picked it up again and enlisted with a rank of Drum Major. And both survived the war." He folded the paper and tucked it away. "We'll give you all the research Wendell did and there's a lot of it. It will all go to the person who wins the bid for this rare Eagle Battle Drum. Who will start it off? Anyone? Anywhere?" He pointed from one side of the room to the other."

Suddenly, his hand stopped. "Yes, this gentleman will start the bidding at $100. Thank you, sir." Then Billy Bob dropped his hand and shook his head. "But you should all be ashamed we're starting the bidding so low. I'll take it and let's get it up to where it should be, people."

Now the bids came fast and furiously. "$1,000, finally," Billy Bob said with a dramatic sigh. "Now, maybe we can get down to some serious bidding." He responded to the bidding gestures and fluttering white bidder-number cards in the air. "$1,500. Do I have $1,600?"

The dollar increases were larger now. The casual bidders had retreated to the sidelines, happy to watch the lively action between the more serious and monied collectors.

"$2,000... do I hear $2,500?"

The hands and cards all disappeared at once. Billy Bob laughed, the skin around his eyes crinkling. "Okay, too steep a raise. I get it." He took a breath to give the bidders a chance to reset. Then the fun fell off his face and he was the intense auctioneer again. "Are you interested at $2,250?"

Several hands and cards jumped into the air again. They weren't ready to stop.

Billy Bob pointed at one person, accepting his bid then he lifted his eyes to scan the room. "How about two and a half thousand?"

He pointed to accept a bid from a woman standing along the wall. Then swung his arm around to a bidder on the other side of the room who had raised his hand at the same time. "$3,000?"

The man nodded.

"We're at $3,000," Billy Bob reported. "Who will bid $3,500?"

The man who had bid $3,000 was scanning the crowd, too. Scoping out his competition now. His head stopped pivoting when he saw a man sitting two rows in front of me. New blood. When the new bidder held up four fingers, the other bidder pursed his lips, shook his head in disappointment, and turned away. I'd heard there could be a lot of drama at an auction.

When Billy Bob announced the $4,000 bid, there was a murmur in the crowd with heads swiveling around to spot the high bidder. But the auction wasn't over. The woman at the wall wasn't done. She made a gesture I didn't recognize. Her hand sliced the air horizontally. Billy Bob reacted by playfully collapsing onto his podium. "You're gonna make me work for this, aren't you?" The woman nodded. He straightened up again. "Okay, I'll do it. The bid is $4,250."

The man in front of me made another gesture. The bid was now $4,500.

Billy swung around to the woman. "$4,750?" No reaction from her. "Are you all in? The bid is $4,500. It's $4,750 to you, ma'am." No response. "Are you all done at $4,500?"

I couldn't see the bidder sitting in front of me, but he must have been excited. He sat forward on the metal chair. He seemed to be nodding a little in the auctioneer's direction. Was he encouraging him to slam the gavel?

Then, without warning, the woman held up five fingers. A $5,000 bid.

The man in front of me sank against the back of his chair.

"$5,250?" Billy Bob asked, pointing his gavel at the man, who shook his head. Billy Bob waved the gavel around the room, looking for another bid. "$5,000, going once. Going twice." The gavel pointed solidly at the woman. "Sold for $5,000!" The room erupted in applause, but the woman stepped back and disappeared into the shadows.

Billy Bob put his elbow on the podium and leaned on it, exhausted. "Whew, y'all are tough. What a ride." He pushed himself up into an erect position. "Well, folks, we have finished the Civil War portion of this auction," Then he added in a booming voice, "But we're not done yet. There's more to come. Lots more. Take your potty break. Get yourself some more coffee. We still have some great..." The rest of his words were lost in the conversations erupting around us.

I made my way outside to the parking lot with Wendell and Stanley on either side of me, opening doors and making a passageway for us through the milling crowd busy gossiping and inspecting things won in the auction. Poor Craig trailed behind.

At the car, I turned to Stanley. "Would you like the quilt back now?"

"No, I want you to keep it." His face glowed with delight.

"Thank you, but..." A question had come to mind, and I decided to ask it. "Why? Is there a reason?"

"I want you to remember the Civil War was about people, people who did what they felt they had to do. What they thought was right. Now, I think their story should be told."

"You mean the story of a Confederate spy...?"

"And the people up North who gathered the information he ferried along, yes. People need to know. That's why I made you the offer. What do you think?"

Was he reaching for the quilt or the walking stick? I took a step backwards, hoping to make the movement look natural. "It's a very generous offer, Stanley. I think your idea of writing the book is a good one. It doesn't have to be a literary non-fiction work with footnotes and all. Maybe I could write the story, emphasis on story, like historical fiction."

"Yes, an interesting idea," he said, almost impatiently. "But what about my offer?"

"I'll think about writing the book, but I'm not going to sell the walking stick. It was special to Uncle Jack and that makes it special to me. You know how important family can be." At least I hoped he did. He never mentioned a wife or children when we talked and all the pictures on the internet showed him with many different women. Better to move on. "Plus, I'll need it to write the book, to prove the truth of the story."

"Does this mean you will not sell me the walking stick, Emma?" Stanley stated, as if a jury was listening.

A lamp set high on a post, flooded the parking lot with light and sparked a glint in his eye. Was it hunger I saw on his face when he spoke of the object I carried wrapped in a towel and antique quilt? It was clear this man yearned to own the walking stick. Then the glint was gone. "You have to do what you think is right. My financial offer will stand. It will be there when you're ready to talk."

He sounded certain the walking stick would become his possession and it was only a matter of time before I agreed. That was Stanley's motivation: Possession. But I knew what I wanted. The walking stick belonged at the Cottage, at least for now.

I gave Stanley a big smile. "You've given me a lot to think about. Thank you." Thoughts about slavery, Confederate statues, and marches on both sides of the issues swirled through my mind. I was not going to make any decisions while standing in a parking lot at night. "I will let you know. Good night."

Craig opened the car door, and I slipped inside, safe with Joshua's walking stick in my arms.

CHAPTER FIFTY-FOUR

If you experience rejection, you should learn to accept the situation as it is, acknowledge your role in the final outcome, rid yourself of shame, and move on.

W hen we turned on Route 50 heading back toward Easton and St. Michaels, Craig settled back and talked about the auction. How he was surprised at the size of the crowd, the enthusiasm they had for the Civil War items, the historical information Billy Bob used to get the bidders excited.

"It's Wendell's job to put the background information together, for context." My response almost sounded bored, but I wasn't.

"You sound tired. It's been a long day. An exhausting emotional time," he suggested.

"I'm tired and disappointed. I thought we'd find more on the killer. I was supposed to help you spot likely suspects. All I did was get caught up in the whirlwind of the auction. I'm sorry. I don't have anything to offer you."

"I'm not surprised," he said with a smile. "You were too busy being courted."

My eyebrows shot up. "What?"

"Both Wendell and Stanley were fighting for your attention. Each one wanted something from you. And you weren't cooperating. They forgot I was there until I tried to sit next to you. It was an interesting game to watch," Craig said with a smile.

I didn't think it was interesting or funny. "That's not why I went with you." My voice was hard. "This is serious business." I groaned and gently pushed the thickly wrapped walking stick to the back seat. I'd been carrying it most of the evening and I was tired of it. Tired of the events it had triggered. The emotions it had ignited: envy, jealousy, competition, and anger. A combination turned lethal, not once, but twice. "I'm sorry, Craig. I'm so confused about this situation." I tried to read his facial expression in the dashboard lights. "I can't imagine how you must feel. How do you deal with the frustration?"

He tilted his head to the side. "Don't worry about me. It's part of the nature of the work. Not every case is crystal clear. If it was, I would be out of a job." He chuckled then noticed I didn't respond to his little joke. "Something else is bothering you. What is it?"

"I told Stanley, I wouldn't sell him the walking stick," I said, staring out at road ahead lit by the headlights.

"How did he take it?"

I shrugged. "Okay, I guess. There was something…" I looked out the window, watching the shadows playing along the side of the road. "Never mind, I'm reading too much into it."

We were getting close to the turn-off for Waterwood and the Cottage when Craig asked me an important question. "It's obvious you're worried about Stanley's reaction to your rejection of his offer. I think you're right to feel anxious."

I whipped my head around to face him. "You are? Why? What did you hear?"

"I don't know anything you don't know. It's easy to see the man feels entitled but in a very nice way. Still, he's used to getting what he wants. It probably comes from having a lot of money. You declined his offer and he's not used to rejection. Remember, ownership and prestige are at the heart of his offer."

"You're right. You're insightful." I sighed. "But why do I feel uneasy?"

"Could be," Craig admitted. "Where are you going to keep the walking stick?"

I looked out the window and watched how the headlights played over the empty road. "In the umbrella stand, I guess, where Uncle Jack kept it."

"I don't think it is a good idea. Remember, you've said from the very beginning the walking stick is at the center of this case. He knows you have it. Wendell knows you have it. Probably a lot of other people know, too."

His next words had a sharp edge. "Remember, two people are dead. The killer is still out there. If he or she wants the walking stick…"

He was right. "Maybe I should just sell it to Stanley and be done with it all."

"No!" His reaction jarred me. "I think your reasons for keep the walking stick are valid. It has a lot of value, both historic and sentimental. Only…"

"Yes?"

"Maybe we should have let Wendell lock it up in his safe—"

"No, that would have been a mistake," I insisted. "Wendell is too close to Stanley. The man has a lot of influence over Wendell. He is a good customer, worth some real money in sales to the auction center. By being a client,

Stanley probably enhances their reputation. No, it's safer with me."

"Good point. I could take it to Easton and put it in the property lockup. It would be safe from greedy hands, but I'm not sure it wouldn't get broken by accident. It is an antique and fragile."

"You have a good point." It was my turn to sigh. "What am I going to do with it?"

"It's obvious, isn't it?" Craig turned to look at me. "I think you should put it up at Waterwood House."

I didn't move. I didn't say a word. I tried not to react. I wanted to sink into the car seat and disappear.

"Emma? What do you think?" He tried to gauge my reaction by looking at me while he negotiated a curve in the road. "No opinion?" He paused, waiting for a reaction, but didn't get one. "Does TJ know about the walking stick?"

"A little."

His eyebrows shot up in surprise. "Well, I think it's time you told him in detail so, he can help protect it and you."

"That's the problem. I've become a burden. He is so busy with spring planting and all. He doesn't have time to watch out for me." I looked down at my hands folded together in my lap, the way I'd held them when I was a child and had to confess to my mother, I had done something wrong.

"He doesn't want you helping me with this investigation, does he?"

I shook my head.

"Emma, you have to speak up," Craig insisted. "I can't see you in the dark."

"NO!" I yelled. Then embarrassed by my harsh reply, I apologized.

"Oh boy…" was all Craig said.

"He even told me to my face I'm a handful." I sounded like a whining child, but I couldn't stop. "You said so yourself. TJ told you I had ideas. I'm a handful, always getting into trouble."

"I'm sure he didn't mean it that way. He…" But Craig couldn't make excuses for TJ, because we all knew it was true. The darkness surrounded us as he turned onto Waterwood Road, "Now what?"

"Just take me to the Cottage. I'll be fine." I just hoped I could convince him.

Craig drove along the gravel road and passed the drive to the Cottage. "We're going to Waterwood House. Let's see if TJ is home and we can get this straightened out."

"NOOOO!" I wailed, instantly embarrassed. I cleared my throat. "Sorry, I've probably had too much coffee and sugar. I don't think we should go to Waterwood House."

He almost steered off the road. "Why not?"

I sat back and let out a deep breath. "I think he has a girlfriend. I don't want to bother them."

"No, not true. Anyway, even if there's a girl there, this is more important," Craig insisted, not even slowing down.

I dropped my chin on my chest and silently chastised myself for even looking for Uncle Jack's discovery, his Big Find. It had gotten people killed. It had gotten me in trouble. I had lost a good friend because of it. As we pulled up to the house, I raised my head and saw the first floor of Waterwood house all lit up, at least on this side.

"Is there any way I can persuade you not—" I pleaded.

"No."

I closed my eyes in resignation when Craig honked the horn three times. "Now he will know he has visitors." Craig was out of the car and sprinting up to the kitchen door which was now open. The silhouette of the person standing in the light was TJ.

There would be no way I could stop Craig from talking with him, but I could be part of the conversation. I threw open the passenger side door, slammed it shut, and made for the kitchen door. Then I stopped and retraced my steps. I was in trouble because of that walking stick. It should be part of the conversation, not sitting innocently in the car. After wrestling it out of the backseat, I headed for the door left open for me.

I heard Craig ask about TJ's farming business, but TJ's response was muffled.

I walked into the kitchen and put my precious cargo on the island as TJ said so casually, "This is an unexpected surprise. Beer, anyone?"

Craig didn't hesitate. "Absolutely required, yes."

I nodded silently.

As TJ went to the fridge to get the drinks, he asked, "What are you two up to tonight?" Then he froze and turned around to look at Craig and me in a new way. I suddenly realized he thought we were on a date. TJ started losing his grip on the icy cold bottles. One of them slipped and hit the stone floor, spewing beer, and sending glass shards everywhere. The three of us jumped to do the cleanup, grateful we had something to talk about other than what it looked like when Craig and I showed up at Waterwood House well past 9 o'clock in the evening.

When the kitchen was clean again and we all had fresh, cold beers, we sat down at the big butcher table TJ had reclaimed for eating with friends, spreading out maps of farm fields, and the myriad of papers, all part of the farming profession. Craig took the lead. He told TJ about everything, what I'd discovered about the walking stick, the interest other people had in it, and Stanley's offer to me.

I was glad Craig told TJ everything he needed to know. I didn't have a chance to derail the story with defensive comments or aggravating asides. As Craig told of my research findings, I caught TJ glancing in my direction. At first, I saw a flash of disapproval then resignation. Craig's story confirmed what TJ expected: I had gotten involved in ways I should have avoided. But as the story delved into the historical aspects, TJ's expression changed to admiration and respect.

The only time Craig called for my active participation in this conversation was to show TJ the walking stick and its two hidden compartments. As I unscrewed each one to reveal their contents, TJ's eyes grew wide. When Craig was finished and TJ had examined the contents, TJ looked at Craig, then me, then Craig again with a growing sense of awe and admiration.

"You knew about all this?" he asked.

Craig nodded. "I was with her every step of the way as she uncovered all this information and the secrets. Secrets of *your* family. It was all part of my investigation. Emma has been a big help. And she has more to add to the story." Then he clamped his big hand on TJ's shoulder. "And now, there is something you can do. Emma and I both are a little concerned since Stanley knows she has the walking stick, he might come for it at the Cottage. We need a safe place to keep it, at least for the time being. There are countless places here in your big house where you could hide it, right?"

"Yes, I can do that," TJ sounded a little happy he could help.

"Don't think about it. Just do it, my friend." Craig yawned and turned to me. "You fill in any details I missed. I have to go home and get some sleep. I have an early call tomorrow. TJ, I think you're gonna like what she has to tell you. Take care." And he was out the door. We heard him start his car and listened as it faded into the night.

CHAPTER FIFTY-FIVE

Greek influences in today's world: the weak spot in someone's defenses is an Achilles heel; a Trojan computer virus harkens back to the gift of a horse to Troy which fell to the Greeks hidden inside; the atlas is named for the Titan god who holds up the world.

I felt awkward being alone with TJ. There was no reason for me to feel like this, but it was real. I avoided TJ's eyes. I felt embarrassed, not because of what I'd done to help Craig with his investigation, but I had done it sort of behind TJ's back, especially after he had expressed his concern and worry about my safety.

Then another feeling rose from deep inside. Was it pride? Yes, and a feeling of accomplishment. I had found Uncle Jack's important discovery, researched its significance, uncovered a secret in TJ's family history, and, if I followed the guidelines of academia, would add to Uncle Jack's reputation as an historian. I raised my eyes, buoyed by pride in my actions. What he said to me made me melt.

"Emma, I'm in awe at what you've done. Thank you." He reached across the countertop and covered my hand with his.

After Craig, against my wishes, had told TJ everything, after the hurt of finding out there was another woman in his life, after all the lost time we'd spent apart in these last days and weeks, I felt revived by those simple words. This was a sweet moment to make up for everything.

But we were interrupted by the sound of clapping. It was coming from the dining room and getting closer. A man stepped into the doorway.

"How very touching!" Stanley said with a sneer and stopped clapping. "Do you have every man in your life wrapped around your little finger? I bow to the artist." And he did.

TJ recovered his wits. "Who are you? What are you doing in my house?"

Stanley raised his hand and shook his head to dismiss TJ's concern. "Don't worry. I'm a friend of Emma's, aren't I, dear?"

"H-h-he," I tried again to get my mouth to work. "He is no friend of mine."

"Oh, come now, Emma. You're being harsh." He turned to TJ. "Allow me to introduce myself. My name is Stanley Archibald Holt." He turned to me and held out his arms. "Really, Emma. This is no way to act." He turned back to TJ. "My apologies for her rude behavior, sir. She is rattled, very anxious." He looked down at his blazer and brushed away some invisible lint. "Probably all this murder business. It can be upsetting to find not one dead body, but two."

TJ's head whipped around in my direction, but I had no time to explain or react.

Stanley continued in a casual, nonchalant way. "It's no interest to me. I'm prepared to give Emma a lot of money along with a grand opportunity to add to her uncle's professional reputation. She turned me down. To be truthful, she is in over her head. But I have to give her credit. She has tried to let me down gently, but I don't do *gently* when there is something I want."

It all clicked in my mind. "You, you killed those people, Professor Kincaid and Dr. Abbott, didn't you?"

"No, you give me too much credit. I would never get my hands dirty," Stanley explained.

Had I gotten it wrong *again?* "Then it must have been Wendell?"

"Emma, Emma," he said with deep disappointment as if I was a child. "Stop casting about blindly with false accusations. And please don't belittle dear Wendell. He is such an innocent. He truly should stick to his books and research."

I stared at this short man who believed he towered over everyone else. My eyes sliced into him, looking for the right answer. "But you know who killed those people."

A smile of satisfaction spread over his face. "My dear, have you forgotten my influence and wealth… and the people it can buy?" He chuckled, enjoying every minute of this confrontation. "Since you're so interested in who committed those crimes…" He glanced up at the ceiling, considering his next words. "No, not crimes. I think of them as assignments. Yes, that is the right word." He raised his chin and assumed a proud stance. "You want to know who carried out those assignments? Your wish is my command."

CHAPTER FIFTY-SIX

"Be not dishearten'd. Affection shall solve the problems of
freedom yet; those who love each other shall become
invincible."
—*Walt Whitman*

S tanley raised his voice and called out, "Icarius, *Ella
Etho.*" He looked at TJ. "And for the farm boy's benefit,
it is Greek for *Come here.*"

A man emerged from the shadows, the devastatingly
handsome and dangerous-looking man who should be
somewhere exotic, fighting off the women. Why was he with
Stanley? Were they in business together?

Then I saw it as he moved into the light. A limp, probably
from an accident or birth defect, but still, a disfigurement. A
weakness Stanley must have exploited. I knew there was a
connection. I was sure of it the first time I'd seen them at the
auction center. Icarius was standing along the wall, out of the
way every time Stanley was there. A chill ran through me.
And now they were here at Waterwood House.

"Meet my special assistant, Icarius," Stanley stated. "An unfortunate name, I'm afraid. Pronounced one way, it was the name of the man in Ancient Greece who gave the citizens of Athens free wine. You'd think it would have made him popular, but not so. Someone started a rumor the wine was poisoned, and the mob killed him. If you pronounce the name another way, you'll recognize the name Icarus, the boy who wanted to fly. He made wings from feathers and wax but flew too close to the sun. The wax melted and the boy plummeted to the earth." Stanley shrugged. "Greek can be quite flexible. Either way, it is an unfortunate name, don't you agree?"

TJ took a step forward, anger rolling off of him. "Thanks for the bedtime story. Now, you *both* can get out of my house!"

Stanley shook his head. "I'm afraid, dear boy, I'm not done yet. If I were you, considering what is going to happen, you would want to know the rest of the story."

"What's going to happen?" I tried to sound brave but failed. There were already two bodies in the morgue.

"Patience, sweet Emma. Listen first. I found Icarius washing dishes in a small Greek restaurant. Undocumented. No family here. Very little English, but don't worry. He has excellent reflexes. I am always amazed at how he reads situations and takes action. Perfect for my purposes."

"He murdered both Dr. Abbott and Dr. Kincaid?" I dearly wished I knew the Greek word for murderer so I could scream it at this man. It sickened me to see Stanley turn to him and smile with a little bow of his head in appreciation. The man bowed his head in response.

Stanley looked at the walking stick on the kitchen island. "But that is not the end of the story. When I realized your girlfriend here had Jack's Big Find, I made her a handsome offer. One any normal, rational human being would be thrilled to receive. But not Emma." He sneered, then caught himself and the fake façade was back in place. "Do you know what she had the gall to say to *me?*" Stanley slammed the palms of his hands on the countertop, making us all jump. "She told me no. *Me!*"

Stanley recovered quickly from his fit of rage, wet his lips, and stepped back. Calmly, he continued. "I'm not used to people saying no to me. It almost never happens. When, *if,* it ever does, that person never says no to me again."

"You kill everybody who disagrees or denies you something?" I said, horrified.

He scrunched up his face. "Of course not, you silly girl. I told you; I don't kill people."

"You make other people do it for you," I snapped back. I was provoking him. I knew it, but I couldn't stop. I kept thinking of Dr. Kincaid and the daughter he hadn't known existed. Stanley had destroyed more than a man. He stole their chance to know one another, maybe to be a family.

He inclined his head. "I don't make anyone do anything. The only thing I might do is fire them and make sure they don't work for anyone worthwhile ever again."

"You're a monster!" I screamed and lunged for the man in the nicely tailored jacket.

Stanley took a step away from me. "Temper, temper, Emma. You should be careful." He gestured at the man called Icarius, standing silently with a gun aimed squarely at TJ. "You might upset him. Remember, he doesn't speak English. He responds to non-verbal cues—how someone makes a threat—and he might react." He held his well-manicured hands palms up. "Then I can't help you."

I stepped back.

"That's better." He put his hands in his pant pockets and assumed a casual stance. "Let's be civilized about this. I want what is mine." He walked over to the table, drew out a chair, and pushed TJ into it. Stanley pointed to the rope wound around Icarius's shoulder and mimed the boy should use it to tie TJ to it. "You, dear boy, are going to be my leverage to keep this firebrand in check." He looked straight at me with no warmth, care, or compassion. His face was cold. "Do we understand each other, Emma?"

"Um, I do have one question," I said calmly, as if we were enjoying a hot cocoa together.

Stanley let out a breath, impatient to have this scene resolved. "What is it?"

"Why did you go to all that trouble to get my steak knife from the restaurant, the one you used to kill Dr. Kincaid?"

"It wasn't me," Stanley insisted. "I mean, the idea was mine. I thought if they found your fingerprints on the murder weapon, they'd take you in for questioning, at least. Then I could search Jack's place without worrying about you bursting in on me. But no..." He dragged out the simple word with contempt. "The local yokel police didn't suspect you at all. There you were, happy at home... and in my way." He adjusted the sleeves of his jacket. "Now, if you don't mind, can we finish here?"

My shoulders sagged. "Yes, take the stupid walking stick. It's only a cane... and do you know who uses a cane, Stanley?" I did not wait for an answer. "Old people, Stanley. Old people, like you, who are decrepit in body and spirit. Like you, Mr. Stanley Archibald Holt."

TJ's eyes grew wide in alarm. "EMMA, what are you doing?"

I raised my voice and edged it with razor blades, hoping my words would cut deep. "I don't care. I don't care about any of this anymore." I flailed my arms around in the air as I stomped back and forth. "I don't care about you, Stanley. You're a piece of trash, like an empty old champagne bottle. I don't care what you do, Stanley, BUT..." I whirled around and glared at the old man. "There is someone who cares, someone who cares a lot."

TJ and Stanley both asked the same question at the same time. "Who?"

I pulled my lips a mean smile and glared at him. "The *GHOST*." I raised my voice and repeated, "The *GHOST* cares." I paused and cocked my head. I raised my voice even louder. "The *GHOST* has no patience for injustice." Where was TJ's dog? I'd never known him to be far away from his master.

I had to keep up the ruse. "Stanley, don't you know about the *GHOST* of this plantation?"

Stanley threw his head back. "Oh, this is rich."

"You haven't heard of the *GHOST* who resides here? Pity." I scrunched up my face and shook my head quickly. "Oh, Stanley, you're in for a surprise. We're not talking about a friendly ghost named Casper." I cackled. "No, sir."

TJ had gotten my message and understood what I was trying to do. He jumped in. "Stanley, I have to warn you the *GHOST* is ferocious. *GHOST* hates it when his home is invaded. *GHOST, COME HERE.*" He yelled.

Nothing happened.

Stanley looked around the room, behind him, up to the ceiling, feigning curious anticipation. But there was nothing to see or hear. No scrabbling paws on the wood floors. No heavy thumps coming down the stairs. Nothing.

"Looks like your scary ghost doesn't like to be ordered around." He raised his hands to sides of his face and wiggled his fingers. "BOO!"

Stanley was too busy laughing to notice TJ looked confused and terrified, all at the same time. Where was his dog? What was going to happen to us?

I had to maintain my swagger to persuade these men they were in danger, not us. "Tell me, Stanley, do you believe in a *GHOST*? A spirit? An apparition?" I tried to coolly glance at his Greek puppet. He was watching us closely, but there was no sign of understanding on his face. He had no clue what was going on... in English.

I had to dredge up the word, the right word, Sophia's

parents in our parent-teacher conference when their daughter was so upset about her broken necklace. I had to remember. This was our one shot. I turned and stared right at the man holding the gun. My eyes bore into him. I put all the menace, all the threat I had into that stare and hissed out the word.

"*Phantasm!*"

CHAPTER FIFTY-SEVEN

"Produce great men, the rest follows...
Nothing endures but personal qualities."
        -*Walt Whitman*

I waited, watched, for some kind of reaction, but there was none. I yelled out, *"Phantasm, ella!"*

The gun trembled ever so slightly in Icarius's outstretched hand. His eyes switched from me to the door. Back to me.

I called out again. *"Phantasm, ella!"*

His eyes grew wide, searching the room. He turned away from TJ. I had him. This poor man was truly a good Greek boy. He looked like Adonis, a Greek god and was superstitious. *"Phantasm, ella!"*

TJ caught on and yelled with me. *"Ghost, COME!"*

Stanley let out an ear-piercing whistle. "Shut up, both of you! Enough of this charade. There is no ghost." He looked at Icarius and said in Greek, *"Ohe, fant...*oh, whatever..." He shook his head saying under his breath, "Idiot. You should have just shot him. "

I heard what he said. And it sent ice through me.

Stanley turned, put his hands on his hips, and said in a voice that convinced me the games were over, "It's time for you to put the stick back together and give it to me."

I took a step forward. "NO!"

I slowly started to raise my arms the way they did in the old horror movies when they're raising the dead. I had to try one more time, to put on a good show for this superstitious Greek boy. I lowered the pitch of my voice, so it resonated from deep in my chest. I raised my eyes toward the ceiling and called out, "Ghost, Oh, Phantasma of Waterwood! Come and protect us! GHOST, COME NOW!" I screamed.

"Emma!" TJ's face was white with fear, and he wasn't the only one.

Icarius went mad, waving his gun in the air, ready to shoot anything, but he wouldn't have the chance. TJ, still tied to the chair, rocked it back hard against Icarius, knocking him to the floor. The Greek god went down hard. The gun flew up high in the air. Then came down on the floor far from both men.

A streak of white appeared in the doorway.

TJ roared. "Ghost! BITE! GUN!"

Ghost leapt.

So did Stanley. He lunged right at me. I had no weapon. My hand shot out to the counter and closed on the first thing it touched. The quilt.

I pulled it hard and jumped forward to meet his attack. I swung the quilt at his head and wrapped it around his smug face as tight as I could.

I staggered backward. My chest heaving, desperate for air. The room was fading away.

"EMMA!"

TJ's voice penetrated the fog. My vision cleared enough to see Stanley pulling the quilt off his head, coughing and gagging from all the dust. His face contorted into a mask of sheer fury.

"Emma, I can't..." I glanced over to TJ writhing on the floor, still tied to the chair. Ghost had a firm grip on Icarius, who had tears running down his face in terror.

TJ was still tied up. Ghost was busy. No one was going to save me, but me.

Inspired by Ghost, I stared at Stanley, bared my teeth, and let out an unholy shriek.

It stopped Stanley, but only for a moment. I had to move now. Desperate, my hand shot out to the island, grabbed the lower section of the stick, and put it behind my back.

"You're pathetic," I snarled. "Won't get your own hands dirty. You don't deserve—"

"Emma!" TJ called out, desperate. Terrified.

Stanley started coming at me again. "I'll show you." He sprang. Just as I pulled my left arm from behind my back. His eyes grew wide when he saw the dagger. Too late. He couldn't stop his forward momentum.

TJ yelled out again. "Don't kill him."

I wanted to kill him. He deserved it. All the pain he had caused.

But... I barely had room to twist the angle as he fell on me. The feeling of the Joshua's dagger slicing into his body was like nothing else I'd ever experienced.

Stanley screamed.

He knocked me over. We both fell to the floor.

TJ yelled my name. Ghost barked and barked as if he would never stop.

Lying there with this man's body on top of me, like an elephant on my chest, drove the air from my lungs. I wiggled and jerk to get out from under him or I would be the one to die.

He groaned.

So, I hadn't killed him. "Move!" I gasped, wasting breath.

He shifted enough to look at my face. "You..." he growled as his nostrils flared. There was murder in his eyes.

I still had my hand wrapped around the handle of the dagger. The blade must have shifted when he raised his shoulders. He roared in pain while I squirmed out from under his body

The movement must have pulled it out of his flesh. He howled as blood spewed everywhere. On my face, in my eyes, in my mouth. I spit it out, sent it flying in his face. The spittle landed right between his eyes and dribbled down over his eyelashes, his cheeks, his nose. His face screwed up in disgust.

I flashed the dagger in his face. Don't try it, or I'll stab you again and again and…" I stopped when I saw the flash of fear in his eyes.

"Emma." The rich voice, like melted chocolate, spoke from across the room.

"TJ!" Hearing my name broke the trance. I jumped up and ran to him, lying on his back still tied to the chair. "Are you alright?"

Gasping, TJ nodded.

Ghost barked. He still had the Greek boy down on the floor, but for how much longer?

"We need help," I said. Nothing like saying the obvious.

"Hey!" Stanley bellowed. "What about me? I need help!"

I grabbed a kitchen towel and tossed it at him. "Hold it on your wound to slow down the bleeding." I finished with a growl, "Not that you deserve it."

TJ caught my attention again. "Emma, phone. Call Craig."

"Yes…" I felt in my pocket and found my phone. I stabbed the recall button and somehow got the message out that we needed him. "It was Stanley. You were right. We need you. Come. Hurry!"

I think he said he was coming and calling 911, but I only truly heard TJ whisper my name. I went to my knees next to him. "I'm here."

"Do you think…" he glanced down at the ropes.

"OH! Of course…" Using the dagger, I released the coiled ropes. He rolled onto his hands and knees taking in deep breaths. Then he said something to make Ghost back away. Icarius's eyes narrowed to slits as he watched the dog. His hands curled into fists and…

TJ reared back and struck the kid in the jaw with his fist. His muscles quivered as he drew his fist back again, ready to deliver another blow. It wasn't necessary. The superstitious Greek boy was down for the count.

As TJ threw his arms around Ghost and buried his face in his fur, his voice cracked. "No one touches you!" Murmurs of *good boy* reached my ears. Then they crawled over to me, still kneeling by the chair, trying to get my heart to slow down.

"You, okay?" TJ asked, still fighting to catch his breath.

I answered with a big smile.

"And Mr. Big over there?"

Stanley groaned in response. I added, "He's not going anywhere."

TJ's expression changed as he looked at me. His hazel eyes, now deeply blue, sparkled. His face shown like a bright light of… what? Happiness.

He took my face in his hands, the hands that tended his crops, gently stroked his sidekick Ghost, who had comforted Rosie. He spoke words I shall never forget. "You are magnificent."

He pulled me close and kissed me.

CHAPTER FIFTY-EIGHT

"May you always have protection against a
curse and any bad things in life.
The greatest protection of all is love."
-- *Benjamin, Emma's Father*

We both jumped when Ghost barked and ran to the kitchen door. TJ barely had time to call out *Friend* before Craig burst into the kitchen, his gun drawn. He skidded to a stop and looked around at the mess in horror, then in admiration. His eyes went to the handsome boy curled in a corner sobbing and mumbling in his native tongue.

"Did you two do this?" he asked.

"We three," TJ clarified, putting his arm around Ghost's neck as he settled down beside his owner and best friend.

"Are you okay?" Craig asked, looking at me.

"No, I CERTAINLY AM NOT!" Stanley announced. "That woman, that fiend—"

"Yeah, yeah," nagged TJ. "You're just bitter because she stabbed you before you could kill her."

Craig exploded. "WHAT?!"

"It's a long story," A sigh escaped my lips. The adrenaline rush from everything—the threat, the terror, the fight, the kiss—was wearing off. Blue lights flashed on the kitchen walls. "Looks like the rest of the cavalry have arrived."

"You've got this?" Craig asked. When TJ nodded, he went to the door. "I can't wait to hear the blow-by-blow of this little party."

Uniformed officers took Icarius away. The EMTs declared it was safe for Stanley to go to the hospital for stitches. The old man wailed he was innocent, an innocent victim, as he was wheeled away. Nothing was his fault.

TJ couldn't resist. He called out, "It was all the Greek boy's idea to kill those people?"

"I just wanted him to scare them a little," Stanley assured him. "I can't be held responsible if things got out of hand. You know how hot-blooded Greeks are."

"Get him out of here," ordered Craig.

We sat down at the table together with a bottle of restorative. JTC would have approved. It was a nice bottle of brandy. TJ wanted to know if Craig would have trouble charging Stanley and getting a conviction.

"It's up to the prosecutor's office. I think I'll get enough for them to nail this guy. He's so entitled!" Craig shook his head and groaned. "I'm glad I don't have to deal with his defense attorneys." He pulled himself out of the chair, the long day and late-night excitement had taken a toll. "I'd better get going. Will you two come in tomorrow to give your statements?"

We both nodded. TJ added, "Not too early."

"Okay." Then he looked down at his hands. "I have to apologize to both of you. I shouldn't have left when I did. Being here probably gave them time to break in."

A sheepish look came over TJ face. "They didn't have to break in. I never lock my doors."

320

Craig closed his eyes in mock exasperation. "Bet you're going to change your mind now."

TJ shrugged. "Maybe."

Craig moved toward the door. "I need to get going. There is going to be a lot of paperwork on this one." Then he looked back at the pieces of the gentleman's walking stick spread over the island's countertop. "Bring it with you tomorrow, Emma."

After everything it meant to me, I didn't want to lose it to some police evidence locker. That was a fight best left until tomorrow. I agreed reluctantly.

Just as he was leaving, Craig turned to me. "Can I give you a ride back to the Cottage?"

"No," TJ answered quickly. "I've got her."

From the regret showing on his face, it was clear Craig had gotten the message. I felt sorry for Craig, but I was where I wanted to be.

CHAPTER FIFTY-NINE

"Happiness, not in another place but this place;
not for another hour, but this hour."
  –Walt Whitman

It was long past dawn when I sat down with TJ at my kitchen table, our hands wrapped around fresh mugs of coffee. Ghost sprawled in the corner, snoring. We stayed that way, in comfortable silence, words no longer needed to communicate how we felt.

"I never thought I'd be glad Uncle Jack is dead. I'm glad he died the way he did, quietly. At peace. Not at the violent hands of a maniac. He had found the walking stick, probably knew about the secret compartments. He must have suspected it belonged to a spy. Probably kept it close until he could prove it. Wendell knew he had a Civil War artifact in his possession and must have let Stanley know about it right away. I'm glad Uncle Jack died before they could do anything about it. If they had hurt him—" My words trailed away.

"They didn't. And thanks to you, we all survived the night."

I felt a shiver, remembering what happened, what could have happened. "I can't believe no one saw through that awful man. Wendell worshipped at the feet of Stanley Archibald Holt. It makes me sick."

TJ grunted. "It happens when people have direct contact with a very wealthy person. They worship the money, like it has some magical power, and kowtow to the people who have it."

"I hope Wendell won't be charged," I said softly.

"You can't charge someone for stupidity," TJ said halfheartedly. "I know I'm being harsh. Craig said Wendell was stunned when he was taken in. He felt sorry for the guy."

"It's hard to believe he didn't know about the violence, but then again, he is naïve in some ways. I hope he learned a lesson," I admitted.

TJ nodded. "Still, he comes in contact with rich people all the time. It's the core of his business... working with people who can afford to buy the fine things he has to sell."

"If he treated them like normal people, he might lose a client or two," I conceded.

"There is a difference between maintaining one's own values and becoming a pawn. I think he knows that now."

Several minutes passed as we sat lost in our own thoughts.

TJ glanced out the window. "It's a beautiful day. We should be outside."

I knew what he was really saying, but I shook my head. "I'm not ready to sit on the patio yet. When it gets warmer, Maria is going to help me plant lots of flowers around it, hang some baskets, and—"

"Change the look of the place?" TJ suggested. "Then..."

"Then I'll be ready. You could help..." I suggested playfully.

Laughing, he shook his head. "I do crops. Flowers aren't my thing."

I heard the unspoken comment that flowers were a girl-thing, which reminded me of one young woman in particular, Valerie. The daughter Dr. Kincaid never knew he had. Anger smoldered inside me. Stanley had denied her the chance to know her father. I remembered the fire I'd seen in her the night of the writer's meeting when she talked about going to college. I'd heard he'd left his legacy to the university. When they learned about his daughter and her dream of becoming a nurse, would they offer her an arrangement so she could earn a degree? It was a question for an attorney, a good one, with a heart and the gift of persuasion. I'd ask Maureen and Gertrude. If anyone could make it happen, it was those two ladies.

It was a relief I didn't have to get deeply involved. I wandered over to the kitchen window and the Lone Oak across the creek, standing there with all its secrets. If only it could talk. Then a question popped up only TJ might be able to answer.

"Where was Ghost last night when we were calling his name like idiots?" Hearing his name, the big white dog raised his head.

"Good boy!" TJ said. Ghost, hearing his master's voice, put his head down and went back to sleep "I think he'd gone out the doggie door I installed on the front side of the house. Since there are so many people coming and going around Waterwood now, I wanted to try and keep him away from the driveway as much as possible. It's a new area for him. The new smells and sniffs must have absorbed his attention."

"I'm glad he came back when he did. I didn't know you'd trained him to be an attack dog."

"I didn't," TJ said. "He was a trained police dog... trained when he was a puppy. Then a drug dealer shot him. The vets saved his life, but Ghost doesn't have the strength or endurance to chase bad guys anymore. He can handle a gentle game of ball and has the stamina to follow me everywhere. This arrangement works for both of us."

"I had no idea." I looked at Ghost with fresh eyes.

"Craig told me about the dog and helped me adopt him. I promised to pay for all his follow-up surgeries and rehab so they could put the money budgeted for him toward training another dog." TJ gave me a big smile. "You see, you're not my first patient in rehab."

I could feel my face getting warm. "I guess you're a good person to have around."

"To take care of you both."

I wasn't ready to delve into a discussion of our kiss the night before. Not yet. I still wanted to settle on what I wanted and where I wanted to be. "Did the police name him Ghost?

"No, I did. One night, soon after he came to Waterwood, we were out walking. There was a full moon. He was beginning to explore his new home and looked like a ghost moving between the trees. I thought it was better than Rex or Max, or whatever they named him."

Again, we shared a comfortable silence. When TJ got up to refill our mugs, he said, "I have a question for you. How did you know to talk about a ghost and in Greek no less?"

"I had a child in one of my classes who was part of a traditional Greek family. One day, during a tussle on the playground, a child grabbed her necklace, and it broke. When I got to the children, the Greek child had curled up in a fetal ball and was screaming for me to save her." I cringed at the memory. "It was very upsetting."

"Save her from what? Was it an expensive necklace? Why would—" He was as confused as I was at the time.

"It wasn't the cost of the necklace. It was what she believed the necklace could do. It had a small white bead with a little blue eye painted on it. We looked but couldn't find it anywhere."

TJ realized what the bead represented. "It was protection. It would ward off a curse."

"The Greeks are a wonderful people who have myths and superstitions as part of their culture. Many believe in ghosts. Since Icarius came here recently from the old country, I took a chance he did, too."

"That's why you launched into the story of the Ghost of Waterwood. Very clever Emma."

I shook my head. "I almost botched it."

"How?"

"I couldn't remember the Greek word for ghost. The family of the little girl used it several times when they came to the school and explained the importance of the necklace. I tried every word I could think of."

"No wonder you were talking like a thesaurus?" I nodded. "I'm glad you hit the jackpot. I don't think I'll ever forget the word *phantasma*. It saved our lives." He rubbed his chin. "Hey, if I ever get another white dog..."

"No," I said.

"I could name her—"

"No!"

"I could call her—"

I covered his lips with a kiss. I didn't even want to imagine what kind of a nickname he would concoct. And I didn't want to be constantly reminded of what had happened... and what could have happened last night.

"Coffee is getting cold," he mumbled against my lips. "And I have one more question for you."

Suddenly shy, we both sat down again.

"Have you given any more thought to Emma and her problem?" TJ asked. "Or have you given up on her search? I wouldn't blame you if—" He stopped when he saw the smile slowly growing on my lips. "Oh dear. You haven't forgotten."

"No, not at all." I moved my head with a little swagger. "In fact, I have a plan."

TJ's eyes grew wide in surprise. "You do? What is it, if I may ask?"

"As you can imagine, it is a challenge to find someone born 150 years ago."

"You could use Ancestry.com," he suggested. "It may help. Or one of the DNA matching services."

I gave him an impatient look. "Without a name, an address, even a city?"

"Then you've decided to drop it. —"

I interrupted him again. "I said I have a plan... and a suspicion. And we have your ancestor Joshua Thomas Collins to thank."

"How do you figure? He caused the problem."

I couldn't hold back any longer. "Joshua kept the letters addressed to Emma, written by Annabelle Jennings Miller."

TJ thought for a moment then shook his head. "Remember, I'm new to all this information. How do those letters play into this story?"

"I think she was the true Confederate spy in the North who was feeding Joshua the intelligence he sent down South. From the little bit of research I've done, she knew about the movement of weapons and where they were hidden in Baltimore. She could have sent all kinds of other information, like troop movements, supply routes, supply shortages, ammunition storage depots...information useful to the South."

"Whoa! Wait a minute." He put both hands in a defensive pose. "Now, don't get mad. Just hear me out." He took in a little breath to fortify himself. "Forgive me, but she was a woman."

"That's the point! She was a woman, probably lovely, dressed in fine gowns, entertaining important men in her fine home. She would have been a bauble to have around while the men discussed military topics. She could ask seemingly innocent questions the men would want to answer to show off their influence and position."

TJ stared at me with his mouth open a little in surprise. "You think…"

"I think Joshua sold Emma's baby to this Annabelle. I need to go to Philadelphia to track her down first. That will be a job all its own. It was the largest city in the country at the time."

"You do have a plan! Fantastic."

My shoulders sagged a little. This was the first time I'd voiced what I wanted to try. It sounded flimsy. "It's only an idea. I could be wrong."

"It's more than Emma had. It's more than we had last fall," TJ said. "The only thing I ask is you take me with you,"

"To keep me out of trouble?"

"There's no question you attract trouble, but you're smart. You deal with it pretty well."

I hoped he was right, that I was smart and on the right track to find the missing baby, wherever it took me… or us.

AUTHOR'S NOTE

Yes, I know: Little Women was first published in 1868. For the purposes of this story, I reset the publication date of this enormously popular book by Louisa May Alcott to early 1860. It was and continues to be a favorite.

Special thanks to Will Gorges of CivilWarShop.com for allowing me to use items and descriptions of items he offered online when I was drafting this story.

Lynn Gorges, also part of the Civil War Shop, is a nationally recognized expert of historical quilts. Her expertise added to the details in the auction scene.

Many thanks to Keith Shortall and his wife Beth of Shortall Farm on the Maryland Eastern Shore. Their continuing information and insights into farming and the life of a farmer bring TJ alive.

Christina Jones of Historic Houseparts, Rochester, New York continues to decorate and design Waterwood House and keeps it and other historical elements accurate.

As always, heartfelt thanks to the Talbot County Free Library, especially the staff at the St. Michaels Branch. They never roll their eyes at my sometimes off-the-wall questions... well, almost never. These librarians will search for good material to enrich the story.

Again, my writing buddies Donna and Jen were with me the whole way, always willing to read, evaluate, and offer suggestions. Thank you, ladies. You make me a better writer.

And, as always to my family with its newest addition. Delilah, I hope you'll like the story when you're old enough to read it.

St. Michaels
Silver Mysteries

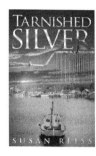  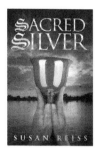

In Time
Series

 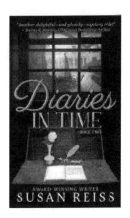

Made in the USA
Middletown, DE
17 November 2022

15357588R00203